THE NIGHTHAWK

Wings of the West Book 10

KRISTY MCCAFFREY

The Nighthawk

Cover: Earthly Charms

Editor: Grammar Chick

Proofreader: Diane Garland

Author Photo: Katy McCaffrey

E-book ISBN-13: 978-1-952801-41-9

Print ISBN-13: 978-1-952801–42-6

https://kmccaffrey.com/

kristy@kmccaffrey.com

BOOKS BY KRISTY MCCAFFREY

Wings of the West Series

The Wren

The Dove

The Sparrow

The Blackbird

The Bluebird

The Songbird (Novella)

Echo of the Plains (Short Story)

The Starling

The Canary

The Nighthawk

The Swan

The Falcon (Coming Soon)

Stand-Alone Novel

Into The Land Of Shadows

Short Story Collections

The Crow Brothers Collection

The West: A Romance Collection

Long Novellas

Alice: Bride of Rhode Island

Rosemary

Blue Sage

The Peppermint Tree

A Mirthful Wish

Contemporary Adventure Romances

Deep Blue

Cold Horizon

Ancient Winds

Sapphire Waves

Cobalt Sea (Coming Soon)

"I...commend McCaffrey for the historical accuracy of her stories...a phenomenal read that I'd recommend to anyone who enjoys historical romance, with a hint of the other." ~ Jonel Boyko, Reviewer

"Ancient Hopi and Havasupai legends have a new voice in McCaffrey. Her inspired writing made her main character's mystical journey into another realm entirely believable and kept the pages turning long into the night." ~ City Sun Times

The Blackbird

"With dastardly villains, plenty of action, a strong heroine, surprising twists and turns, and a sexy cowboy, all underlined by a sensual love story, this historical western romance has something for everyone." ~ Janna Shay, InD'tale Magazine

"A steamy, intelligent historical fiction set in the Arizona desert where the harsh environment matches the characters who populate it. Can two wounded souls find each other and flourish? Find out in Kristy McCaffrey's hard to put down, fourth book in the *Wings of the West* series, *The Blackbird*." ~ Chanticleer Book Reviews

The Bluebird

"The reader will find themselves often sitting on the edge of their seats...a quick and exciting read!" ~ Belinda Wilson, InD'tale Magazine

"...a fast paced read with a depth to the characters and the story that kept my interest from the first page to the last..." ~ Jo, Romance Junkies

"...packed with adventure and action that left me breathless...quite unable to put it down!" ~ Maia, The Silver Dagger Scriptorium

CHAPTER 1

Arizona Territory
Jerome
September 1899

Sophie Ryan stopped at the crest of the hill that buffered the town of Jerome and pulled a spyglass from her satchel. *Where could he be?*

Nothing stood out from the monotonous terrain. Vegetation was sparse, having been largely choked out from the smelter fumes courtesy of the extensive copper mining operations in the area.

She stowed the spyglass, tied her scarf more tightly beneath her chin to ward off the chill in the air, and continued her search. She didn't slow down when she slipped on loose scree, the urgency of finding the man pressing on her. She worried that he didn't have much time. She worried that the furious and panicked whispers of conversation she'd overheard between a woman and a man whose voices she hadn't recognized had been too late for Sophie to help the victim.

But one thing had stood out.

The woman had shot someone, and the frantic conclusion was to leave him in the hills to die.

It was midday in the Black Hills, but billowing clouds cast the day in somber expectation. A lightning bolt flashed in brilliance causing Sophie to jump, and the rolling thunder barreled through her chest. She held onto her hat as the wind blasted her and continued into the ravine. This area was known as the hogback, where a sharp turn in the road led into town, but she'd paid little attention to it when she'd arrived two weeks ago. It was also further from town than she'd remembered, and more rugged.

She hoped she'd overheard the woman correctly.

She should have asked for help except the conversation had filled Sophie with foreboding. The woman—and the man—were criminals. She was sure of it. There'd been mention of the town marshal along with his deputy, as if the perpetrators had known the law would be on their side, so she had to assume the lawmen were corrupt.

Still, she'd stopped at the doctor's office on her way, prepared to drag him with her, but to her dismay he'd gone north to Flagstaff and wouldn't return until the following day.

If she didn't act quickly a man could die.

She was on her own.

She rounded a rocky outcrop and barely caught herself from tumbling over a drop off, grabbing a handhold at the last second. There was no sign of town in the distance; she was well into the wilderness now. If she fell, she, along with the mysterious victim, would likely not be found for days or weeks.

Willing her racing heart to calm, she caught sight of a boot protruding from one of the few bushes present.

She'd found him.

Carefully, she shuffled to his location, not wanting to tumble into the ravine. Thankfully he'd come to rest on a flat spot.

He was unconscious, blood on his left shoulder seeping through his coat.

"Sir! Sir, are you all right?"

She cupped his face, trying to wake him, his dark hair coated with dust. His eyes fluttered open and she recognized him. He was the ornithologist who was in town to study the local birds. Or something like that. Sophie's boss at the Jerome Mining News, Olivia Bromley, had pointed him out from afar one afternoon, his deliberate demeanor as he walked his horse—the bay's coat shiny and her hind quarters sleek and strong—down the main street causing Sophie to stare a bit too long. Olivia had suggested perhaps a story on his work, and Sophie had tucked the idea away. But she hadn't seen him again after that.

Until today.

"You've been shot," she said. "You need to see a doctor, but we need to stanch the blood."

She removed the scarf from her neck, folded it several times, and tucked it beneath his coat and against the wound, pressing firmly.

He winced.

How would she get him to town? Her horse was about a mile up the hill since it had been too precarious to take the animal any further. She didn't think she could get the man up the incline. Should she leave him and take the risk of bringing her horse here?

"Can you stand?" she asked.

He groaned but said, "Yes."

She retrieved his hat from nearby and handed it to him before struggling to get him to his feet, her frame dwarfed by his. Thunder rolled across the sky, the ground trembling beneath her, and rain began to fall in sheets.

"My horse is some distance from here," she yelled above the din.

"Go down." He indicated the ravine.

"Is that wise? There could be runoff from the storm." Flash floods could strike without warning.

"There's shelter."

Sophie wanted to argue, but they both needed to conserve their energy, so she guided him downward.

Once they were off the slope, he weakly pointed forward as rain streamed from the brim of her hat. Water had already formed at the lowest depression of the land, and Sophie hesitated.

Then she saw it. A cave. He moved toward it and she had to pick up her step to keep pace. As they neared, wooden beams outlined the entrance. Not a cave, but a mine adit.

Once inside, it was a relief to be out of the relentless downpour. She was surprised to see a pallet, several books strewn about, and a crate with paraphernalia, some of it for cooking.

Was the ornithologist living here?

"These adits can flood," she said, not bothering to hide the alarm in her voice.

"I know," he answered. "But so far it's been dry."

How long has he been here?

She shed her water-logged hat and helped him remove his wet jacket. He grunted as she helped him to the pallet.

"Do you by chance have medical training?" he asked, grinding the words out.

"Some," she hedged, not feeling entirely confident about where this was headed. "My mother is a doctor. But I can't ...."

He sighed. "Excellent."

"Not excellent. You want me to ... extract the bullet? I haven't any instruments."

"I do. In the crate. Brown pouch."

Sophie's heart pounded. Was he insane? Frantic and shaking, and knowing time was of the essence, she went to the wooden box and found the pouch. She emptied the crate and turned it over, then laid the tools on top. Wanting more mobility, she removed her satchel and duster, then moved the oil lamp from the dirt floor and put it on the crate, lighting it with a lucifer. With the storm raging, visibility in the adit was poor. She would need every bit of help she could get.

"There's whiskey ...."

A quick scan and she found the bottle nearby.

"I think the bullet is below the clavicle and about two inches deep," he said.

"Are you a doctor?" She eyed the whiskey, willing her nerves to calm.

"My uncle was."

She popped the cork on the bottle and took a quick gulp.

"That wasn't for you," her patient quipped.

"Just for the jitters," she replied. "I need to remove your shirt."

"Cut it off."

Using shears from the pouch, she cut the shirt down the middle, then snipped further along the left sleeve until the affected area was clear. Blood continued to ooze. She applied pressure again with the now soaked scarf.

"Can you hold this?" she asked.

He brought his hand to hers and she guided it to where it was needed. With a deep breath, she examined the tools. Everything looked to be here. She placed her canteen of water nearby.

"Are you sure about this?" she asked.

His eyes met hers. "It'll be all right. Clean the wound with the whiskey."

She nodded as he removed the scarf. She poured the liquid, and he jerked and hissed, then closed his eyes.

She shut her eyes as well. He was going to hate the next step.

She removed the glass cover of the oil lamp, her hands still trembling, and ran the ends of the forceps through the flame. He turned away from her, the veins in his neck bulging, clearly girding himself for what was to come. She sopped away the blood to see the entry point as clearly as she could.

Just do it.

She dug the pincers into the wound and the guttural scream he released shook her clear to her toes, but she stayed the course, grunting as she pressed his opposite shoulder down to keep him still and holding his torso down with her knee. If she lollygagged, it would be only more painful if she had to do this again and again.

She moved the forceps in incremental motions and quickly located the bullet, but each time she tried to grasp it, the tips slipped.

Just do it.

She pushed deeper and clasped the bullet firmly. In one swift motion, she pulled it free of his flesh. His low scream drowned out the cacophony from the unrelenting rain, dampening her elation. She brought the scarf back to the wound to stanch the new blood spilling out.

With great focus, she threaded the needle and put the tip into the lamp flame, trying to ignore the man's rapid breathing, a clear indication of his pain.

She nudged him with the whiskey bottle. He opened his eyes, looking dazed.

"Drink," she said.

His right hand shook so she held the bottle steady as he took several gulps, her own trembling having lessened. He laid his head back, and she went to work stitching the wound. When it was done, she rinsed the area with whiskey again, and with a corner of the scarf that was less drenched she cleaned the blood and wetness away.

He stared upward, his gaze glassy and his bare chest heaving.

"Thank you," he said.

Sophie placed the needle on the crate. Her hands were covered in blood. His blood. Despite the chilly air, she was drenched in sweat and took a swipe at her forehead with the sleeve of her day dress, avoiding her reddened hands.

"You're welcome." Now that the panic in her bones was

receding, she felt weak and tired. She sat back on her rump, completely dazed by the day's events.

He held up his right hand, as bloodied as hers so she clasped it.

"I'm Ben."

"Sophie."

CHAPTER 2

Benton awoke, confused. But the searing pain in his shoulder brought everything back in a rush. The gunshot. Clearly a sharpshooter. Was his cover blown? He had to assume yes.

The woman. Sophie. She was still here, in the adit with him, sleeping on the dirt floor beside his pallet, her head nestled on a bent arm.

His assignment was the Weaver gang, more precisely Russell and Xander Weaver. It was unclear how many other possible members might be with them. The lead that had brought him here had only identified Xander on a stagecoach north of Phoenix.

Benton had been in town for a full week, and so far, had precious little to show for it. His boss, U.S. Marshal William Griffith, had forecast that Benton would have this wrapped up in a fortnight, but it was looking less likely as each day passed.

Except today.

Who had shot him?

He'd been in the wilderness, using his cover as an ornithologist to push further from town for clues to a possible hideout when he'd seen a woman in the distance.

The memory began to rebuild itself—her lifting the rifle, aiming at him. Him ducking at the last second but still getting clipped in the shoulder.

He'd been careless. If Sophie hadn't found him ....

But how had she found him? Her sudden appearance lent itself to suspicion.

He had to give the Weavers credit. If they were hiding behind women, it would explain Benton's lack of success so far in locating them. But it certainly would make his job harder. The young woman beside him was just that ... young.

There was no reason for her to be mixed up in this.

She was likely a wife, or a mistress. Or maybe a sister? But his intel hadn't indicated any Weaver women. She had helped him, however, so did that exonerate her?

Benton knew better than to trust a pretty face and a charitable personality, a woman who would help a stranger by operating on him.

She opened her eyes, pushing strands of dark hair from her face. "You're awake." She scooted over and laid the back of her hand on his forehead. "You're burning up."

"Who are you?" he asked, his throat parched.

"My name is Sophie Ryan." She retrieved her canteen and brought it to his lips.

"What are you doing out here?"

"Drink," she commanded.

He took several welcome gulps of water.

"I'm a reporter for the Jerome Mining News," she continued, capping off the canteen. "I overheard ... something I shouldn't have. And it led me here."

Benton sought to keep his response impassive, but he had no idea if it was working. He felt cold and shaky. "What did you hear?" he said.

"I live in town at Rose's Place. I overheard a man and a woman in the alley behind the house speaking in distressed whispers. She had shot someone—you—and she was afraid as to what to do. To my horror, the man told her to leave you be and she agreed, which ... well, that wasn't something I could live with. Somewhere during all that there was mention of the hogback, so I came in as much haste as I could muster. I did try to get the doctor to accompany me, but he's away. And I didn't feel you had much time."

"Who was it?"

"I don't know. I'm fairly new to town, and when I tried to catch a glimpse, they'd disappeared."

"Why didn't you go to the marshal?"

"There was an implication they could count on the man's silence in the matter."

Benton swore under his breath. He'd wondered if the local law could be trusted, and now he had his answer. He waited, since surely Miss Sophie Ryan was about to tell him his identity as a U.S. Deputy Marshal had been uncovered, and that his real name was Benton McKay.

"Why would that woman shoot you?" she asked. "You're an ornithologist, right? I've heard mention of you around town. Ben ...."

"Lewis," he offered, although why he was clinging to his alias, he wasn't sure. And then he added, somewhat reluctantly, "Why did the woman *say* she shot me?"

Miss Ryan paused, as if not sure she was remembering correctly, and then said, "She seemed to imply that you were following her, and that it was making her nervous. That she would take care of you once and for all. Should I be worried about you?"

But her tone didn't convey any fear of him. "No," he said.

"Was it someone you knew?"

Was she telling the truth? She seemed sincere enough. But he was shivering now and had to concede he wasn't at his best to correctly assess the situation. But maybe, just maybe, his cover hadn't been blown. Perhaps the woman who had shot him had simply been frightened by his presence, and if she were tied to the Weaver gang then that would explain her paranoia.

"No."

"I'm sure it was all a misunderstanding," she said. "Except it was unconscionable that she was unwilling to confess her mistake and help you. I couldn't very well leave you out here."

Either Sophie Ryan was naïve or had more backbone than was readily apparent in her pretty face.

"I'm indebted to you." He had no option but to rely on her good will. He hoped he didn't live to regret it.

He tried to sit upright but gasped when the pain kept him on his back.

"You need help, Mister Lewis. I think perhaps you're going to have to trust me."

Even in his state of pain delirium, he could see a sharp intelligence in Miss Ryan's gaze. Not naïve then. Was she even now gathering information to take back to the Weavers?

Time to use a story he'd been hoping he wouldn't have to employ.

"There've been accounts of bird killings and mutilations," he said, "and I've been looking for the culprits. You mentioned that the woman who shot me had some sort of inside connection with the marshal, so you can see why I don't want anyone to know about this yet."

"You believe that woman is some sort of bird killer?"

The skepticism in her voice wasn't hard to miss. Perhaps it was a bad cover story, which was why he hadn't used it as of yet. The gunshot wound had dulled his mind.

"I'm not certain," he replied. "It's just a theory."

She sighed. "Well, this is a bit of a mess, I'd say, but I suppose I agree with you, that maybe you should stay here for the time being. I don't think I can move you anyway. But surely you have a room in town? Someone is bound to miss you."

There was some truth to that perhaps. He had a room at the Connor Hotel, but he'd kept a low profile and didn't think anyone was watching him. Still, word had gotten around that he was the resident bird watcher. He supposed it was too odd of a profession to make him unassuming, but it also fed into the idea that he was a bit eccentric, which would explain any aberrant behavior others might notice.

"I just need a day or two to rest," he said. "Then I'll return to town."

She looked around. "And you'll stay here?"

"Yes."

"I assume you've been staying here for some time."

"Just a few days, here and there."

"To watch your birds." She said it as a statement. "What do you have for supplies? Any food? Water?"

"Some."

"May I look?" she asked.

Was there anything she shouldn't find? He did have firearms. Two were stored in town beneath his bed in the hotel room. He had two on his person, one in his coat and one strapped to his calf beneath his trousers. He'd made a point to remove his coat himself when they had arrived at the cave, and there had been no reason for Miss Ryan to remove his trousers, so the other weapon was still concealed.

"Yes," he replied.

She picked through the pile from the crate. "The bag of potatoes still seems edible, but I don't think you have enough water. And you need something for the pain."

"Not laudanum." He refused to be so drugged that he wasn't himself.

"It would help you sleep, but I can get you something else."

"Thank you," he said. "I appreciate your help."

"Should I be worried about this woman who shot you? What if she returns?"

It was a solid question. "I suppose it's possible. You don't have to stay here with me. You don't have to help me." *But would you keep my whereabouts and condition a secret?* He knew such a question would only raise her suspicion, so he didn't voice it aloud.

Miss Ryan arched a brow. "And just leave you out here?"

"That would be for the best."

She settled her gaze on him, her eyes indicating a perceptiveness that Benton wasn't sure he could evade, especially in his weakened state.

"I'll return," she said. "But I'll come under the cover of night."

Could he trust her? A part of him wanted to, and that unnerved him. But along with the tension in his gut was relief.

He needed her to return.

He needed her help.

CHAPTER 3

Sophie made it back to Jerome by late afternoon, promising to return to Mister Lewis after dark. The rain had returned during her trek, which washed the blood from her hands, but her clothing still bore bright red stains, although it was hidden beneath her duster for now. Her horse, Roger, a rental from the livery, was a bit feisty after she'd retrieved him, apparently annoyed at being left in the rain for several hours. She apologized profusely to him.

One bonus of the heavy rain was the lessening of the everpresent rotten egg sulphur smell from the nearby ore smelters. Sophie hadn't had to cover her nose with a scarf, which was just as well since Mister Lewis currently had it, now crusted with dried blood.

She'd been away from the newspaper for the better part of the day, so she would tell Olivia—Miss Bromley—that she had wanted to explore the terrain around town. While Charles Bromley, Olivia's father, owned the paper it quickly had become apparent that Olivia oversaw the day-to-day decisions of the business. In fact, Sophie had met with Mister Bromley only once since she'd arrived. She was beginning to suspect that her employment had been entirely at Olivia's discretion, and since the woman wasn't much older than Sophie they had agreed that a first name basis was acceptable.

Sophie slipped into Rose's Place and was glad to see the front parlor empty. She quietly went upstairs to her room and changed into a dry camisole and day dress. She tossed the wet garments into a corner, then thought better of it. Someone might see the blood-soaked items and start asking questions. As far as Sophie knew, Rose, the proprietress, an older woman in her sixties, didn't enter her room when she was gone—Sophie herself collected her water pitcher each evening as well as discarding the contents of her chamber pot each morning—but she couldn't be certain. Rose had offered to launder Sophie's clothing, but Sophie had yet to agree.

She stuffed her wet dress and under things into a valise. She would try one of the laundries several streets over that were run by the Chinese. With hope, they wouldn't question the blood. She would have to think of a cover story to explain it.

As she came downstairs, Rose appeared, her graying hair pinned neatly atop her head and an apron tied around her ample waist.

"Sophie, when did you come in?" She put a hand against Sophie's forehead much the way Sophie had done recently to Mister Lewis. "Are you ill?"

"No, I'm fine."

"Then why are you here in the middle of the day? Have you quit your job already?" Rose eyed the valise. "Are you leaving?"

"No. And I still have my job. I got ink on my clothing, so I came back to change. I'm going to take it over to Giroux Street for washing."

Rose gave a dismissive wave. "Don't be silly. I'll launder the items for you." She reached for the valise.

"No. I don't want to be a bother."

"You're no bother." Rose frowned when Sophie shifted the bag away from the woman. "You clean up after yourself, even after supper. You're the easiest tenant I've ever had."

"My mother taught me to be responsible for my own business."

Rose's warm reception to Sophie when she'd arrived and needed a place to live had filled Sophie with relief. Traveling from Texas to take her first newspaper position had been exciting and a bit overwhelming, although she never would have admitted it aloud to her cousin, Lucas, who had accompanied her before leaving for Tucson. She hadn't wanted him to relay back to her folks that she was indeed homesick, just as her younger sister, Ellie, had predicted she would be. Rose Palmer's affectionate welcome had made Sophie feel settled when everything was unsettled.

But now, Rose's nosiness regarding Sophie's business chafed, not to mention the woman's recent requests for "stories" Sophie should write, mostly about obscure prospectors around town. Sophie had politely declined since her focus was culture and humanitarian news, and mining news was handled by another reporter, Joe Atkins, but Rose had continued pushing ideas Sophie's way.

But more and more, Sophie was irritated with Rose prying into her business.

"All right." Rose threw up her hands in defeat and laughed. "You young women these days have a stubbornness to you that reminds me of myself."

"You're still stubborn, Rose," Sophie muttered.

"Oh, you cheeky girl. I'd like to think my daughter would've been just like you."

Sophie went still, sensing the undercurrent of anguish in the woman. "What happened to your daughter?" she asked quietly.

"She died. It was quite a long time ago. Very young, mind you. She was only three."

"I'm so sorry."

"Her name was Henrietta. You rather remind me of her."

Remorse filled Sophie. She shouldn't be so judgmental toward the woman. Rose was simply mothering her in lieu of the daughter she'd lost so long ago, and there was something bittersweet and tragic about it.

Rose collected herself. "Enough of that. Will you be here for supper?"

Sophie wanted to get back to Mister Lewis as soon as the sun set, but it was just as well if she adhered to a normal routine. She couldn't help the man if she didn't keep her own constitution strong.

"Yes, of course."

"Then I'll see you at six. It's fried chicken tonight."

As Sophie made her way to Giroux Street, she contemplated how to steal extra drumsticks for Mister Lewis. She soon had her laundry dropped off, telling the young Chinese woman that she'd assisted with the birth of a foal and hence all the blood. The woman had smiled and nodded, and Sophie wasn't sure she'd understood, but at least her favorite dress would be wearable again.

She made her way to the mercantile on Main Street before it closed for the day and collected dried fruit, cheese, a bag of pecans, and ground coffee beans, since she'd seen a coffee pot amongst Mister Lewis's things. She also decided to try a box of the new Nabisco graham crackers. If she wasn't successful with her fried chicken theft, Mister Lewis would need sustenance, and his potatoes would require too much preparation.

"Is Rose not keeping you fed over there?" Walt Jenkins asked as he tallied her goods on a ledger. The store owner had been the third townsperson Sophie had met, after Olivia and Rose, and she had warmed to him immediately with his bushy mustache and hearty laugh.

"She's an excellent cook and hostess, but I wanted a few things for when I'm out getting a story."

"Given any thought to my suggestion of writing about the purported Spanish gold in the area?"

Sophie smiled. "Yes, of course. I've added it to my list of ideas that I plan to present to Mister Bromley." *Whenever he might be in the office.* But she kept the acerbic response to herself.

"Oh, I wouldn't do that," Walt said as he wrapped her wares in brown paper.

"Why not?"

"Because Bromley has been searching for the gold longer than anyone, except maybe my brother, George, God rest his soul."

Bromley? That brought her up short. But first, she said, "I'm sorry about your brother."

Walt's normally cheerful demeanor became subdued. "He passed just a few months ago. Smallpox."

While the disease wasn't rampant in Jerome, Olivia had told her a few yellow flags had been raised in the area, indicating a quarantined home. While some survived the illness, sometimes left with blindness, many didn't.

"He was younger than me," Walt added. "It's not supposed to happen that way."

Sophie thought of her younger sister, Ellie, and possibly losing her, and she felt a sharp stab of sympathy for the man's pain. "No, it's not," she said quietly.

Walt added twine to her package. "I inherited his place north of town. It's called Nighthawk Ranch, but I'm hoping to sell it. I can't live out there and run the store. Anyway, George and Bromley were friends for a time, but when Bromley started hunting for Conquistador gold, they became estranged."

"Did George ever find anything?"

He shrugged. "Not near as I can tell. Maybe he hid it at his ranch all these years." That made him chuckle. "I guess I should dig up the place before I sell it." But his attitude indicated he had no such intention, which was odd considering he kept prompting her to do a story. Perhaps he was doing it in honor of George's memory.

But in truth, the proposed newspaper item was probably too fanciful to appear in a future edition. As near as Sophie could tell,

Olivia did all the typesetting herself, and with the pre-printed advertisements that came in batches from a press in Phoenix, space was limited. And even if Olivia's own father was bitten by the gold craze, the woman probably wouldn't want to run a story about it. Still, Sophie needed a gritty and unique piece to build her portfolio beyond the fluff pieces she'd been hired to do if she hoped to reapply to the Dallas Morning News, their recent rejection still stinging.

She filed away the idea just in case.

"Your total is one dollar and ten cents," he said. "Shall I add it to your line of credit?"

"Yes, thank you."

He pushed the bundle across the counter, then said, "Oh, I almost forgot." He reached into a bin. "This telegram came for you." Walt was also the postmaster.

"Thank you." She gathered her supplies and stepped outside, opening the letter. It was from her cousin, Lucas.

He was returning to Jerome and on an official assignment. Sophie was pleased. He had accompanied her from Texas as far as Phoenix but then had needed to go south to Tucson. As a newly appointed U.S. Deputy Marshal, he was to report to the Arizona Territory headquarters. She had been fine with it and had gone on to Jerome on her own but hadn't mentioned it to her folks in her letter home, since her pa and her uncle Nathan, Lucas's pa, had insisted Lucas accompany her until her very last step into Jerome.

Sophie wasn't so precious that she couldn't complete the remainder of her trip alone, but her pa would think differently.

But there was no denying Lucas's telegram filled her with happiness. Despite her stubborn resolve to make her way on her own, it would be nice to have a friendly face nearby. She could tell him about Ben Lewis and ask for counsel, except ... she scanned the last part of the telegram again. Lucas asked her not to say anything about his arrival. In fact, he would be undercover. No one should know that she was related to him.

Could Lucas's arrival have anything to do with why Mister Lewis had been shot? On the surface, nothing added up, but Sophie couldn't shake the coincidence of the two events. Perhaps she needed to keep her own counsel for now.

She tucked the letter into her satchel. Should she burn it? It could somehow be evidence. For what, she didn't know, but maybe she could get an exclusive scoop, and then write a story that might rival that of Nelly Bly, whose investigative journalism was something to which Sophie aspired. She had been thinking of her pseudonym for some time, leaning toward Molly Barnabas—Molly for her beloved aunt and Barnabas after an imaginary donkey Sophie had written about as a little girl. He had traveled the world having adventures, something Sophie would like to do. Her stop in Jerome hadn't been the route she'd wanted but she was trying to make the best of it.

She headed to the newspaper office, having dropped her rental horse at the livery. There had been no reason for her to bring an animal to Jerome, but as she would now need one more regularly she had tipped the livery boy, Trent, more than usual, asking him to keep her riding schedule to himself, alluding that it had something to do with her work as a reporter. She'd also requested he keep Roger available for her, as she was rather fond of the blue roan gelding.

"Miss Ryan?"

It was Marvin. No, Martin.

She smiled politely. "Mister Ennis, isn't it?"

"Yes." He grinned widely, revealing an array of crooked teeth. He seemed far too young for such bad dental issues. "But you can call me Marty."

She had met him at supper a few times at the boarding house, but she wasn't clear if he was living at Rose's Place, and she honestly didn't want to ask. His interest made her uncomfortable.

"Marty. I'm afraid I must get back to work."

"Oh sure. I just saw you and wanted to say hello. I'll walk with you."

Unable to think up a quick excuse, she fell into step beside him. "Thank you," she said. "That's very kind of you."

"That's a big package." He reached for it. "Let me carry it for you." He took it from her before she could stop him, and she picked up her pace to lessen the time they had to spend together.

"Whoa, slow down," he said, running to catch up. "There must be a breaking story."

"Something like that."

"So I think you've heard about the opera that's coming."

"Yes, I'm doing a story on it," she said, looking both ways before crossing the street to avoid a horse and buggy in the opposite direction.

"I wondered if I might accompany you to the performance. Rose got me two tickets."

She avoided eye contact by pretending to search the road for animal waste to avoid. "Oh, that's lovely of you to ask, but I'll be attending in a professional capacity, so I must decline. You understand."

"Sure. Sure." But his voice dripped with disappointment.

Sophie winced with a bit of remorse. Thankfully, they'd reached the newspaper, so she took her package. "Thank you for accompanying me, Mister Ennis."

"Marty."

She hesitated but then offered a placating smile. "Marty." She whirled around before he could continue the conversation.

As she entered the small building, she noted that Joe, the mine reporter, was absent—but he was frequently out-of-office, which had made Sophie conclude that maybe she could spend more time away without any repercussions as long as she completed her assignments. This might come in handy now that she had a secret in the hills—

Sophie stopped abruptly. A man sat opposite Olivia, conversing with her, his back to Sophie. He was familiar ....

"Sophie," Olivia said, her blonde hair pinned back and wearing a practical white blouse stiff with starch and a dark skirt. Sophie had appreciated the woman's practicality from the start. "I was getting worried," Olivia continued. "You've been gone all afternoon. I hope you didn't get caught in that dreadful storm."

"No," Sophie lied. "Just working." *Like Joe,* she wanted to add.

The gentleman in the chair swiveled slowly and met Sophie's gaze.

Lucas!

His telegram said he was coming, but was it today? He stood and took her hand.

"It's a pleasure to meet you." He was tall like his father, but his dark hair and eyes were all Aunt Emma. He gave her a hard glare that had her swallowing back the words on the tip of her tongue. Namely, *why are you here now?*

"Please forgive my manners," Olivia said and rounded her desk. "Mister Smith, this is our newest reporter, Sophie Ryan. Sophie, this is Nathan Smith. He's new to town and stopped to place an advertisement."

Sophie narrowed her eyes ever so slightly at her cousin.

Nathan Smith. *Very original, Lucas.* Nathan was the name of his father, her uncle. And one couldn't get more generic than "Smith."

"An advertisement for what?" Sophie asked, realizing too late that a frown had gripped her forehead.

"Shoes," Olivia replied. "Mister Smith is selling shoes."

Sophie choked on a laugh, then quickly composed herself. "What kind of shoes?"

A ghost of a smirk crossed Lucas's face. He didn't appreciate her questions.

"We hadn't gotten to that part," Oliva said, all pleasantness and professionalism. Sophie liked that about her as well.

"For the miners, and everyday wear for men and women," Lucas said.

"That seems like a pressing need for certain," Sophie replied slowly. "I wish you the best of luck, *Mister Smith.* How long will you be in town?"

"For the foreseeable future."

"And how are your accommodations?" Sophie asked. She needed to know where he was staying so she could find him later and riddle him with questions.

"Oh yes, where are you staying, Mister Smith?" Olivia added. "Can we recommend an establishment to you?"

"I'm at the Connor Hotel," he replied.

"It's a fine place," Olivia said. "You'll be very comfortable."

"That's good to hear."

"I need to finish up some work, so I'll let you two get back to business," Sophie said.

"Pleasure to meet you, miss." Lucas's gaze flashed with amusement which disappeared as he and Olivia quietly went back to their discussion.

Sophie took a seat at her desk, donning her eyeglasses, and went to work finishing her article about the local Catholic church. Last year it had burned down, but a pastor from nearby Prescott had helped launch a new brick building and Sophie was to report on the progress. Olivia had confided that the piece was meant as a rebuttal to a recent newspaper story out of Phoenix that had called Jerome "the Sodom and Gomorrah of the West." Jerome had not one but two churches, and Sophie was to work in a mention of the Baptist one as well.

Although she had scrubbed her hands, there was a bit of blood still rimming one of her fingernails, reminding her that she'd had quite the day already. And now Lucas had arrived, and they would have to pretend to be strangers.

She would need to speak with him before she rode back into the hills this evening. The last thing she needed was Lucas stopping by her room at Rose's Place and discovering she was gone.

Once Lucas had completed his meeting with Olivia, he left without much fanfare, donning his hat and not giving Sophie more than a cursory glance.

She suppressed her annoyance.

Olivia sat back in her chair and blew a strand of hair from her forehead, smiling. The gesture, and the misplaced hair, completely out-of-character.

"Am I missing something?" Sophie asked.

"No, I just ... do you think he's handsome?"

"Who?"

"Mister Smith."

Sophie made every effort to school her features. "Oh. Yes. I suppose."

"I don't think he's married," Olivia continued.

No, he's not.

"Well, perhaps I should have supper at the restaurant beside the Connor Hotel," Olivia suggested. "Maybe I'll run into him again. Would you like to join me?"

A vision of the ornithologist lying unconscious in a possibly unstable mine adit filled Sophie's head. "I'm afraid I can't tonight. I have ... plans. Why don't you take your father?"

A shadow briefly crossed Olivia's face, then was gone. "That's an excellent suggestion. My father could stand to get some fresh air and a change of scenery."

Sophie put the finishing touch on her article and brought the parchment to Olivia.

"Thank you," Olivia said. "On time, as usual."

"I like staying busy. Can I ask you something?"

"Of course."

"Is your father not involved in the paper any longer?"

Olivia's face pinched in consternation then she forced a smile. "He decided to step back earlier this year, and I was more than happy to take the reins. Is that a problem for you?"

"No, certainly not." Sophie considered broaching the subject of the Spanish gold, but then thought better of it. If Sophie was to eventually reapply to the Dallas Morning News, she would need a recommendation from Charles Bromley and not his daughter, but it would likely be Olivia who would have to intercede with her father on Sophie's behalf.

Sophie grabbed her coat and satchel. "I'll see you in the morning."

Olivia nodded. "Have a good evening."

CHAPTER 4

A soft knock at Sophie's door startled her.

"Yes?" she asked.

Lucas's voice came from the other side. "It's me."

He's *here?*

She quickly stuffed her valise into the wooden chest at the foot of the bed since the bag was filled with food supplies and other items for Mister Lewis, then she opened the door. She grabbed Lucas's arm and pulled him inside.

"How did you get past the parlor without being seen?" she whispered, scanning the hallway for a sign of anyone.

"I was careful. I figured you wouldn't be."

She scowled at him and shut the door.

He glanced around. "Why does it smell like fried chicken in here?"

She'd snatched several half-eaten pieces earlier and had wrapped them in cheese cloth. They were currently stuffed in her valise to be delivered to her patient.

"Mrs. Palmer made it for supper," she said hoping he wouldn't pursue it. "I just got your telegram today, by the way. And you're lucky I did, otherwise I might've blown your cover." She crossed her arms. "A shoe salesman," she added with a snicker.

He ignored her jab. "I was able to come sooner."

"So, are you gonna tell me?"

"Tell you what?"

"What you're working on."

"I can't say."

"You mean you won't say."

"This is my job now. And I'm trying to keep you safe, Sophie. I'm just here to see how you're doing, and to remind you that your folks are expecting a letter."

"I've written them. Once. I have another almost done." Not entirely true. She'd started another correspondence, but her homesickness had been bleeding through, and she hadn't wanted to worry them. Surely her feelings of melancholy would pass soon. And then she'd write an accounting of her first days in Jerome with much more enthusiasm.

"Have you mailed it?"

She grumbled under her breath. "I will."

He nodded. "How's your new position going?"

"Very well, thank you."

"Does Miss Bromley usually handle newspaper business?"

"So far, yes."

"I thought her father, Charles Bromley, was the owner."

Sophie nodded. "He is, but in truth I've only met him once. He's never in the office, but thankfully Olivia is quite capable."

"Are there any other reporters?" he asked.

"Yes. An older man named Joe Atkins handles all the mining news and because of it spends much of his time on site and isn't at his desk much. Wait! Is the newspaper somehow involved in your case?"

Lucas didn't answer, and her mind raced with possibilities. "I can help you," she said in a rush. "I can gather intelligence. You just have to tell me what you need."

With obvious reluctance, he said, "How much do you know about Mister Bromley?"

His question surprised her, but she quickly collected herself. While she was loath to accuse the man she worked for of something ... criminal? ... she wanted to keep Lucas talking.

"As I said, I've only met him once. And the meeting was very underwhelming."

"How so?"

"He was very dismissive of me. I'm guessing that it was Olivia who hired me and not him."

"And what's your assessment of her?"

She couldn't help but think there was something more than investigative curiosity in his question. As the eldest Blackmore boy, Lucas had always been somewhat reserved, keeping his four younger brothers in line. And ever since he'd become a Deputy Marshal, he was even harder to read, if that were possible. But earlier he'd had an easy rapport with Olivia that had been hard to miss.

"She's been welcoming to me," Sophie said. "She's competent in juggling the duties of the newspaper as well as her writing and editing skills. To be honest, I would find it hard to believe if she were involved in anything underhanded. She simply wouldn't have the time."

Lucas responded with a nod.

"But I can keep my eyes and ears open for you, Lucas," she added.

"All right, but please don't take any unnecessary chances."

Guilt squeezed her chest. Should she tell him about Ben Lewis? But then what? Lucas would insist she stay away from the man.

"I should go," he said, "but I'll be in touch."

"Can you give me any direction as to what I'm looking for in regard to Mister Bromley?"

"Not really. Just let me know if something seems odd."

She frowned. "What does that mean?"

"Exactly what I said."

She suppressed a grumble. He was being vague on purpose.

"Fine," she said with a sigh. She didn't point out the obvious— that she was so new to Jerome that she'd interacted with few people and if this was the barometer then dozens of people *didn't fit*. Including Ben Lewis.

But as Lucas started to leave, Sophie hugged him.

"What's this?" he asked, his tone softening.

"It's just good to see a familiar face," she replied into his coat, her emotions threatening to spill forth in an embarrassing display of waterworks. She stepped back, willing herself to be an adult. Because she was, at long last, on her own. And she was determined to make a go of this. How would she ever be an investigative journalist if she wept every day from homesickness?

"If you need anything, you let me know." He gently squeezed her shoulder.

"And how would I do that, Mister Undercover Agent?"

He thought for a moment, then said, "Smoke signals?"

She lightly punched his arm. "You're a scoundrel."

He was referring to a time when she was eight years old and her sister, Sarah, had been ten and they'd decided to communicate from one side of Dove Crossing—her folks' ranch—to the other using a fire, a blanket, and interim smoky puffs. It had been a disaster with Sophie burning the hem of her dress and Sarah unable to light her fire because of damp wood. The Blackmore cousins had given them plenty of grief over their poor outdoor skills, and she and Sarah had mucked the stalls for a week once her pa learned of it.

"Leave a note at my hotel that you need to discuss advertising with the newspaper and put a time," he said. "I'll meet you at the livery."

She silently agreed. "Let me clear the way out for you." She slipped from her room, then waved him on to make a safe exit.

She waited thirty minutes before heading to the livery that he'd spoken of and retrieved Roger, then she took the darker alleyways to get out of town and back to Ben Lewis.

CHAPTER 5

McKay struggled to open his eyes, his entire body aching. Darkness greeted him. He was in the adit. Alone. The pain in his shoulder reminded him of the past twenty-four hours.

Thirst clawed at him. He fumbled around and found a canteen tucked against him. With effort he opened it and with a shaky hand took a drink, gulping hungrily, spilling a good portion onto his face and neck. Shirtless except for the bandage, he shivered from the chilly air meeting the sweat on his body. He felt around for a blanket and pulled it over him, then slid back into unconsciousness.

He awoke again to a cool hand on his forehead.

"You're burning up, Mister Lewis," a familiar voice said, the soft feminine tone soothing.

You came back.

He was happier than he should be. "Thank you," he said, his voice rough.

"For what?"

"For returning."

"I've got medicine for you," she said. "It will help with the fever. Not laudanum. Willow bark tea. I'll make you a cup, but it would help if you chewed on the bark directly."

He nodded and she handed him a piece. He put it in his mouth and grimaced.

"It's very bitter," she added. "Have some water with it."

She built a small fire at the adit entrance and brewed tea for him. He didn't have the energy for conversation, and she seemed content to let silence fill the space between them. He drank the tea and before long he became drowsy. Just as he was falling asleep, she pulled the bark from his mouth.

"Wouldn't want you to choke on it," she said, her face near his. She smiled at him, and he couldn't help but stare at the vision before him.

Had he died and was now being tended by the most angelic woman he'd ever seen?

When he next opened his eyes, it was still pitch dark. He thought he was alone but then she stirred from beside him. He wasn't a man prone to being afraid, but the relief that she had remained flooded him with a surge of gratitude to which he wasn't accustomed. He relied on others as little as possible.

"Water," he croaked, his mouth devoid of moisture.

She brought the canteen to his mouth, and he quenched his thirst. The fog had cleared from his brain, and he felt more alert.

"How long did I sleep?" he asked. "A few hours?"

She lit the wick of the oil lamp, illuminating the space. A horse stood at the entrance.

"You've been asleep an entire day," she said. "It's Saturday evening."

McKay was stunned. But the pressing needs of his body didn't allow him to wallow in it.

He cleared his throat. "I need to ...."

"Use the outhouse?" she supplied with a bit of humor in her voice.

"Yes."

"Let me help you up." She held his arm with a strength the surprised him given her slight frame, and she helped him upright.

He was weak, and he hated it. He waited until the dizziness receded.

"The smell .... Why is there a horse with us?"

"Oh, well you seemed adamant about keeping this place a secret. It was too far for me to keep coming on foot, so hence the horse. His name is Roger. I brought him inside to hide him, but don't worry. I've only come at night both last night and tonight. I'm afraid you were alone today, but since you can't seem to recollect anything, you must've slept the entire time."

She helped him stand. When he seemed able to continue on his own, she went to the horse and guided him out of the cave to give Benton room to pass.

"I didn't notice the smell," she said. "I was raised on a ranch. But I'll clean up the mess."

McKay would've done it himself, but he really didn't have the capacity. "I'm obliged."

He went into the dark and found a private spot, then he returned.

Sophie had a small shovel and had disposed of the horse's droppings, and Benton laid a hand on the animal's neck as he passed by, murmuring to him.

"I'm afraid the chicken I brought you last night is spoilt but I've brought more food," she said as he went back to his pallet and sat. "Do you think you can eat?"

His stomach was a bit sour, but he knew that without sustenance he would get only weaker by the day. "I'll try."

She unwrapped a cloth, producing bread, cheese, and salted pork. "I told my landlady that I was going on a picnic, and she gave me these. There are also some dry goods that I'll leave with you."

She used a knife to slice off pieces of pork, making him feel like a child. But still, he was grateful. The food was welcome, and he ate his fill.

Then Miss Ryan said, "You should let me look at your shoulder."

He agreed, and she untied the bandage, pulling it carefully from the sticky wound. It was sore, and he flinched.

"It's inflamed," she said, her forehead pinched with worry, her breath igniting gooseflesh along his collarbone. She had a straight nose that was in perfect proportion with high cheekbones and the most beguiling eyes he'd ever seen. They'd filled his dreams.

A heaviness in the air settled between them entirely caused by her proximity. He shifted away slightly.

"Will you let me put a poultice on it?" she added, also moving to offer more space between them.

"Yes."

She was too beautiful for her own good. For his own good. He had no business finding this woman compelling.

She retrieved a pouch and went to work mixing the ingredients in a pan with water, then invaded his personal boundaries once again as she smeared it onto his shoulder. With fresh linen from her bag, she wrapped his shoulder.

She had a deft touch, soothing and confident, and it should have relaxed him but instead had the opposite effect.

"You should come back to town and see the doctor," she said.

"I like the doctor I have." The words were out before he could stop them.

He caught her gaze and her cheeks glowed red in the muted light of the oil lamp. Awareness flashed in her eyes of this sudden attraction between them, but then her brows crashed together, and her wariness returned. She moved away, stashing the poultice pouch in her satchel.

She propped herself on a rock shelf. "I'm a reporter, Mister Lewis," she said. "So maybe in exchange for my help, you would let me write about you. Perhaps even about the woman who shot you. Much later, of course," she added in a rush. "Once this situation is figured out. But I could do my own investigating in town."

Her offer set off alarm bells in McKay's head. She wanted to stay close to him, which again made him wonder if she was somehow tied to the Weaver gang. He most definitely didn't need her hovering over his investigation, and yet ... If she *were* involved, wouldn't it make sense to keep her near? She would be sure to slip up at some point. It had nothing to do with the fact that he found her ... interesting.

"I'm not sure there's a story here," he said. "And now that I'm feeling better, I can manage on my own."

"I suppose," she said. "But I went to a lot of effort to save your life, so I'd rather not come back in a fortnight to find you expired. And aren't you curious why that woman shot you?"

"Like you said before, it was probably just a misunderstanding."

"She's not a bird killer anymore?" she countered.

"I wasn't myself," he said. "I was probably being too paranoid."

"Then why am I here under the cover of night?"

Instead of answering, he asked, "Have you told anyone about me?"

"No. Should I?"

"I can't tell you what to do, Miss Ryan."

"Then how about you let me interview you about ornithology? As a thank you for my help. You know, in saving your life, hiding your whereabouts, and bringing you medicine and food."

The edge in her voice matched the sharpness in her gaze.

McKay laughed. "You're stubborn, I'll give you that." And she *had* helped him, more than he could repay at the moment. "Fine. Ask your questions."

"Now?" But she recovered quickly from her surprise and pulled a notebook and pencil from her gear.

Sophie gathered her thoughts and eased into the interview with a general question. "Tell me about the study of ornithology."

"I've always been fascinated by birds."

"My sister has been pursuing a controversial theory about them."

"Controversial how?"

"She's a student of paleontology, almost a paleontologist herself, and she believes she's close to finding proof that birds descended not only from dinosaurs, but from theropods."

"Truly? That's a bold idea."

"As she explained it to me, birds have a unique feature—a wishbone. And so do theropods."

"Interesting."

"Do you have a favorite bird species?" she asked.

"The nighthawk."

Hadn't Walt called his brother's homestead Nighthawk Ranch? "Are they popular birds around here?" she asked.

"Yes."

She jotted down a few notes. "Tell me about them."

"They're birds of mystery. A mottled hide gives them excellent camouflage, so much so that they oftentimes nest on the ground in the open."

"They hide in plain sight," she said.

He nodded. "They're difficult to see as they only come out at dawn and dusk. They have very small beaks but large mouths that help them ingest insects whole."

"They sound formidable," she said. "Are they hawks?"

"No. They're related to the nightjar, found in Britain. The ones around here are the Lesser Nighthawks. They're quiet and fly low to the ground, their presence almost ghostlike and you might mistake them for a bat. You can identify them by a white stripe on the bottom of their wings."

"So you're saying they're unassuming, almost sweet in appearance, but actually quite lethal."

"I've found that to be true of some people as well," he said.

"You seem too young to be so cynical."

"The world doesn't care how old you are when it's dealing cards of fate. How old are you, Miss Ryan?"

"I'm almost nineteen."

He shifted to lean back against the adit wall. "Where are you from?" he asked.

"Texas."

A shadow crossed his gaze, and she couldn't help but feel he didn't like her answer.

"Why would you come all this way? What could possibly bring you out here?" he pressed.

She thought of all the things she could say—that she'd overheard her pa speaking to her ma a few years ago about how Sophie would never leave home, that she was too reluctant to venture from her comfort zone—and how it had made her feel as if she somehow had already failed, unable to pursue her dreams.

But she stuck to a truth that was easy enough to share. "Professional growth."

He gave her a questioning look.

"I want to work at a big newspaper, but I don't have enough experience," she continued. "So I'm here—"

"To get experience," he finished for her.

She nodded.

"There wasn't anything closer to home?" he asked.

"Well, if you must know, I was looking for an adventure." *And to prove to my family that I'm capable of being on my own, as well as to the Dallas Morning News that I can hack it in a remote and rugged environment and write serious content.* "You seem to be implying that a woman might not want to pursue a professional occupation," she added.

"That's not what I'm saying. But don't most young women anticipate marriage and children? I'd think you'd want to be closer to your family for that."

"Am I to assume that your job as an ornithologist has placed you close to *your* family in anticipation of marriage and children?" She didn't bother to hide the sarcasm in her voice.

He smiled, thankfully looking away or else he would have seen her briefly spellbound. She jerked her gaze from him.

"My ma died many years ago," he said, his tone softening and a bit somber, "and my pa ... he was never a part of my life."

Sophie immediately felt contrite. "That must've been hard. Have you been on your own all this time?"

"My aunt and uncle raised me in California." He was silent for a long moment, then said, "I first heard of nighthawks from my mother. It's one of a handful of memories I have of her. If you'll hand me my coat, I'll show you a memento."

She did as he asked, and he pulled an ivory kerchief from the pocket. He handed it to her. A faded embroidery of a bird graced the cloth. "A nighthawk?" she asked.

"Yes. My mother made it shortly before she died. She often would tell me about the bird. The one I recall the most was how the nighthawk was sometimes called the 'corpse bird' or a 'goat-chaffer.'"

Sophie frowned. "What does that mean?"

"In the old stories, it was said the birds lived on the milk of goats, that their large mouths and small beaks allowed them to latch on to the teat."

She laughed. "We had goats at Dove Crossing, and I hardly think that's true."

Ben's eyes glinted with amusement. "It does seem farfetched, but it was an intriguing story. It made the birds seem otherworldly.

We had goats as well, and I would spend hours watching for the birds."

"Did they ever come?"

"No. But you could always hear them. They were associated with death."

She had resumed her notetaking to avoid staring at the man across from her, but glanced up and said, "Why?"

"Fear of the unknown, I suppose. Animals like bats and owls and nighthawks are active at night and that makes them seem elusive. When you can hear something but not see it, your mind will come up with all sorts of stories about it."

"That's true." Why did it feel like Ben was quizzing her? Or maybe 'testing' was a better word. Was he trying to tell her something?

"But I like to think there's more to nighthawks than fearing them," he said. "I've been trying to understand their nocturnal activities—how they vocalize, what they eat, how they hunt. And how they conduct their courtships."

Sophie stared at what she'd written, only raising her eyes when she felt in control of her intense curiosity about the man.

Mister Lewis leaned forward, bringing his face near to hers and his presence seemed to engulf the narrow space of the adit. The gunshot wound only served to make him appear dangerous and a bit wild. She remained perfectly still, meeting his gaze, determined not to cower. To stand her ground.

"Are you going to write about me?" he asked.

"I may pen a tale about the nighthawks."

"It might ruin your reputation, Sophie."

A shiver went through her at the sound of her given name on his lips.

She cleared her throat. "Let me worry about that."

CHAPTER 6

S ophie awoke with a start, Roger nudging her feet. A quick
check showed Mister Lewis to be slumbering calmly, a good
sign.

Roger was stomping a foot, so she quickly ushered him outside.
It was just before dawn. She offered him water and oats, and then
stretched her back. She wasn't accustomed to sleeping on hard-
packed dirt and rock.

It was Sunday, and while she didn't have work today, she would
need to return to town soon. Rose would have too many questions if
Sophie missed breakfast, her stomach growling as she envisioned the
hot coffee, scrambled eggs, and potatoes the woman would be
serving.

Sophie had filled four pages in her notebook with Mister Lewis's
answers to her questions about his profession before he'd fallen
asleep, and in her exhaustion, she'd lain down for a brief rest that
had turned into several hours.

Should she wake him before leaving? It would be easier if she
didn't. He was innocuous while asleep but awake there was an
energy to him that filled her with anticipation along with a good
dose of hesitancy.

Was there something more to his shooting? Was there something more to him?

But her interview during the night had revealed nothing amiss. He had been knowledgeable about birding, and in addition to the nighthawk he'd discussed various other species in the area. Never mind that her nerve endings had tingled when he'd looked at her a tad longer than was proper, and more than once. And how he'd gone still when she'd applied the poultice to his shoulder, as if he liked her and didn't like her at the same time.

Sophie didn't have a vast amount of experience with men, but there was no missing a thread of something between them. Something delicious and exciting.

But she wouldn't let whatever this was deter her from her objective, which was to save the damned man's life. And continue to pursue a story that would elevate her work beyond the gossip and cultural angles she'd been hired to report on.

She would let him sleep, and then return in the evening. She went back inside the adit and left cheese and bread for him along with a note to soak the bread in water to soften it before eating. With one last look, she checked him for any sign of distress, but his breathing was quiet and steady. Still shirtless, he exuded a coiled strength. She turned away before she gave in to the urge to touch him one last time.

SOPHIE RETURNED to the boarding house in time for breakfast with the other boarders. Rose was chatty and didn't seem to suspect that she'd spent the night in the wilderness with Ben Lewis. After the meal, Sophie went to her room and meant to rest for only a brief respite, but instead napped well into the afternoon, having been more tired than she'd realized.

Once she'd awakened, she had gone to the parlor and Rose had brought her tea. She worked for a bit on her notes from her interview with Ben, trying to decide what kind of story she could write about him. She didn't want to present the idea to Olivia until she had something worked out.

When Rose needed a package picked up at the mercantile, Sophie offered to retrieve it for her, needing to stretch her legs. And since it was Sunday, the sulphur fumes would be less intense than usual, and she could pretend that she was getting some fresh air at the same time.

"Hello, Walt," Sophie said as she came to the counter. "I've come to get a package for Rose."

"Just give me a minute," he said and walked into the back room.

Sophie set her satchel on the floor and perused the bolts of cloth nearby. She wasn't much of a seamstress, but maybe she could have something made. As she considered whether a pale yellow or a dark brown would suit her figure better, Ben Lewis crossed her mind. What did he find attractive on a female?

"Son! Watch yourself!"

The commotion drew Sophie's attention. A young boy had bumped into an older woman and was quickly escaping out the store as she yelled at him.

"Where is his mother?" the woman muttered under her breath.

Sophie smiled politely and returned to the counter so as not to lose her place in line, then noticed her satchel was crumpled on the floor and pushed aside. She knelt and scanned the contents, noting what was missing.

The boy!

With her bag in hand, she ran out of the store, rushing past the annoyed customer. "Does no one practice manners any longer?" the woman exclaimed. "And on a Sunday, no less!"

Once on the boardwalk, Sophie glanced up and down the street.

There he was!

She hustled to follow, slipping her satchel crosswise across her body to move faster. He went into a saloon.

Sophie didn't hesitate and pushed through the batwing doors. Despite it being Sunday, most drinking establishments were open all day, every day.

The interior was dark, and she had to pause to let her eyes adjust. A few patrons glanced at her, but she squared her shoulders and went to the barman.

"That boy who just ran in here," she said. "I need to speak to him. Do you know where he went?"

"You mean Ned?" He wiped a glass with a rag.

"Yes."

"He's a troublemaker. Probably out back looking through the trash."

She inclined her head. "May I go out there?"

"Suit yourself."

Ned was picking through detritus behind several empty barrels. Sophie grabbed his arm before he could bolt.

"Let go of me!" he yelled, struggling against her hold.

"Not until you return what you took from my bag. I have three sisters who frequently pilfered from me so I can hold on for a long time."

The boy, scrappy with a mop of dark hair, stopped resisting, his body going limp. He produced the spyglass in his opposite hand. "I just wanted to look at it. I was gonna return it."

She took the stolen loot from him and released him. "When? Do you even know who I am?"

"You're Rose's new boarder. The lady reporter."

Sophie put the spyglass in her bag. "Yes. I'm Sophie Ryan."

She extended a hand. The boy stared at it, so she reached down to clasp his and gave it a gentle shake.

"I'm pleased to meet you," she said. "And you are?"

"Ned."

"Ned what?"

He licked his lips and shifted from foot to foot. "Why? Are you gonna call a lawdog?"

"No. But stealing is a sin."

"I was gonna give it back," he insisted, his tone verging on exasperation. "And God don't care about me."

"I don't believe that's true. Do you go to school?"

"Yes, ma'am. I just started at the elementary school."

"That's wonderful. An education can help you make something of yourself. How old are you?"

"Almost ten."

She began rummaging around in her satchel. "Well, since you're determined to take something from me, I'll give you this." She handed him a tattered copy of *The Adventures of Oliver Twist*. "It's about an orphan boy struggling to survive in London. That's in England."

Ned took it with all the enthusiasm of a plate of greens. "I'm no orphan. And why do you carry books in your bag?"

"You didn't notice it when you were groping through my personal belongings?" She arched a brow, mimicking her mama when she was cross with Sophie or one of her sisters.

"What am I supposed to do with it?"

"Can you read?"

He nodded, but Sophie wasn't sure if he was telling the truth.

"If you're looking for something to occupy your time," she said, "then instead of stealing, maybe you could read this book. It's a far better use of your smarts, I can assure you."

The boy accepted the gift, a skeptical look on his face. "You think I'm smart?"

"A thief would have to be," she said. "And this is a loan. I expect you to return it when you're finished."

He nodded.

"And in exchange," she continued, "I won't tell the lawdogs what you did."

"Oh, I get it now. This is my punishment."

"Reading shouldn't be a punishment. It's more like a reward."

She walked him to Main Street and as he ran off it was clear he was relieved to be free of her. It was likely she'd never see that book again. She'd have to ask Rose if she knew him. Which reminded her ... Rose's package. She headed back to the mercantile but stopped short when she saw none other than Mister Lewis enter.

He's left the adit? Why hadn't he told her he was planning to come back to town? And by all appearances, he didn't look injured, his coat covering any bulge from the bandage on his shoulder and his hat shading a face that had been a bit pale after his ordeal.

It was a different coat. This one was clean with no blood or bullet hole. Not only had he returned to town, but he'd already gone to his place of residence, wherever that might be, and changed his clothes.

She peeked through the window. Walt handed him a letter. As he exited, she stepped into the café next door so he wouldn't see her. Once she was certain he was gone, she went into the mercantile.

"There you are," Walt said. "What happened to you?"

"My apologies. I saw someone I needed to speak to. Was that the ornithologist who just came in?" she asked as nonchalantly as she could.

"Mister Lewis? Yes, that was him. Just picking up some mail."

"Bird mail, I suppose," she joked.

"It did look official." He handed her Rose's parcel.

"Oh?" She struggled under the weight of whatever was inside the rectangular package wrapped in brown paper. What on earth had the woman ordered?

"Government official. He must be more important than he's let on."

That was curious. "You know what?" she said, pushing the

bundle across the counter. "Can you keep this a bit longer? It's much too heavy for me to carry."

"Of course. In fact, I'll get that boy at the livery to deliver it to Rose."

"That would be Trent. And thank you."

She left the store as quickly as she could without being rude. Once again, she searched the street as she had for Ned earlier.

Taking a guess, she turned left and headed the same way the boy had gone. She didn't know exactly where Ben was staying, otherwise she wouldn't have to revert to following him. Or so she kept telling herself. She caught sight of his silhouette up ahead, pulling her toward him much the way Ned had been drawn to her spyglass. She couldn't blame the boy, really. Curiosity was a powerful motivator.

Ben entered the Connor Hotel. It had recently opened and was the nicest establishment in town—it was fully wired for electricity and each room had a call bell for service. Bird watching must pay well.

And Lucas was staying here too.

She debated whether to march inside and confront Mister Lewis, but then decided her best course of action was to wait and see what he did next. Would he head back to the adit in anticipation of her returning to check on him? She had even planned to get extra meat loaf from supper tonight and bring it to him. And here he was, living in luxury. Why on earth was he staying in that musty and cramped adit at all?

The laundry where she'd dropped her dress was nearby, and she went to pick up the item and pay for it, then she asked if she might sit on the bench in front of the store and read her book. It was surely an odd request, but it would give her a good view of the hotel entrance while also being out of sight, and luckily the Chinese proprietors, who spoke broken English, agreed.

Suppertime came and went, and Sophie's stomach grumbled in

protest. She hoped that Walt had had Rose's package delivered by now because the woman would be twice irritated with her, first missing supper and second not returning from the errand to the mercantile.

And then Mister Lewis exited the hotel, his hat on despite the sun having set. He headed north and Sophie followed at a discreet distance. He went to the livery, gave Trent a coin, and went into the stables.

Sophie hesitated. Was he renting a horse to return to the hills and await her arrival?

After twenty minutes, impatience pressed on her. He'd never come out. She was about to cross the street and investigate when movement in the shadows shifted her attention. Another man had appeared and was speaking with Trent.

Lucas!

He disappeared into the stalls as well.

CHAPTER 7

McKay waited with his horse in the furthest stall at the back of the livery. When he'd arrived a week ago, he'd told the boy who managed the animals that his horse had anxiety if near other animals, allowing privacy when needed.

It was late, and guilt pricked McKay's conscience. Sophie would presumably be returning to the adit. He'd planned to be there, but then circumstances had changed, not the least of which was that he was feeling better. He didn't like idleness, despite the pain in his shoulder. And he hadn't checked his mail in three days. Or was it four? The gunshot had derailed his schedule.

Impatience pushed him back to town.

According to protocol, he was to check with the postmaster each day if his superiors needed to communicate with him. And sure enough, there had been a message. A backup agent was being sent and McKay was to make contact with the man tonight. The agent had been briefed to come to the livery.

But after, McKay would try to find Sophie. She had said she was staying at Rose's Place. With hope he could intercept her before she rode out of town alone to help him. It wasn't safe, and now that he felt better, he didn't want her taking such chances on his behalf.

Perhaps she wasn't who she said she was, but without her help, he might very well have died, so he owed her for that. She might be young and with a beauty that evoked a certain innocence in her, but she also exhibited a bit of grit and determination.

The fact that she'd come here to be a reporter was ... impressive. If that was truly what she was.

McKay soothed his horse as a young man with a height matching his quietly joined them.

"Who sent you?" McKay asked.

"Griffith."

It was easy enough to learn the name of the District of Arizona's appointed U.S. Marshal—and McKay's boss—William M. Griffith.

"Your horse's name is The Belgian," the man added.

"You could've easily bribed the livery boy for that information. Try again."

He produced a letter from his coat pocket. It was from Griffith, vouching for the agent. McKay recognized the handwriting.

"I'm Lucas Blackmore."

"Benton McKay."

They shook hands.

"Any progress?" Blackmore asked, his demeanor serious despite his young age, which McKay guessed was early twenties.

"Very little. Why did Griffith send you? It's a small town. I've got it covered."

"He was concerned about the mines."

"Why?"

"He wanted an agent to focus fully on that. You have your hands full searching outlying areas."

McKay bristled, mostly because he hadn't found any other leads. "The Weavers won't be working in the mines. They don't need to. They're simply in hiding."

"Nevertheless, I've been assigned to watch the miners, and the general activity in and out of the United Verde."

"And how are you going to do that? What's your cover?"

"Shoe salesman. Nathan Smith. I'm peddling my wares to the men in town."

"Anything?"

"Not yet. And I'm also looking into Mister Bromley."

Benton frowned. "The owner of the newspaper?" The same paper where Sophie worked.

Blackmore nodded.

"Why?" McKay asked.

"He's made some odd purchases out of Phoenix."

"Such as?"

"Sheet metal and rubber hoses."

"While I agree that's strange, it doesn't necessarily make him suspicious."

"True," Blackmore said. "But Griffith wants us to watch him."

"Fine. I'll take care of it." Since it might well involve Sophie Ryan.

"I've already made friendly contact with his daughter," Blackmore said. "I can handle it."

McKay decided not to belabor the point with Agent Blackmore. With some irritation, he slipped out of the livery using a back entrance.

***

As Lucas left the livery, Sophie was about to intercept and interrogate him, but at the last second, she remained in the shadows. She knew he'd refuse to answer her questions.

And she had to admit she was far more curious to ask Mister Lewis what was going on.

Was he an informant for Lucas? Did this have something to do with Mister Lewis getting shot? Had he sent for Lucas somehow?

Or maybe ... Ben Lewis was also a Deputy Marshal.

The idea began to take root, gaining ground the more she entertained the idea. But why were he and Lucas in Jerome? As far as Sophie knew, there weren't any large criminal enterprises in the area; most scuffles with the law were drunk and disorderly charges that resulted from inebriated miners causing trouble in one of the many saloons in town. But there was the implication from the woman she'd overheard—the one who purportedly had shot Mister Lewis—that the local law was, for want of a better word, corrupt. Perhaps that was it. It would explain why Mister Lewis wanted to keep his shooting from getting out.

But Lucas was also interested in Bromley, her boss. Was Sophie closer to this—whatever *this* was—than she knew?

She waited but Ben never exited the livery. Had he left a different way? Should she try to find him at his hotel? She stepped away from the protection of the laundry porch and ducked around the back of the building, but in the dark she didn't see the clothesline until too late, landing on her rump in a pile of something soft and squishy.

Manure.

The smell was unmistakable.

It only got worse as she tried to stand and got it all over her hands.

SOPHIE TRUDGED BACK to the boarding house, forced to abandon her plans since she now smelled like a horse's stall. On the porch, she removed her coat and left it draped over the railing. Not wanting to soil Rose's carpets she also removed her shoes, which would also need a good cleaning. Holding her satchel away from her with her left hand, she entered the parlor, and was startled to see Rose sitting with Ben Lewis.

He stood, hat in hand, his gaze focused on her.

"What happened, Sophie?" Rose exclaimed, taking her satchel from her and setting it off to the side.

"I fell in horse excrement."

Rose waved a hand in front of her nose. "I can tell. Let me get a rag and a basin of water." As she left, she added in a conspiratorial whisper, "Mister Lewis is here to see you."

Sophie faced Ben, his expression difficult to read.

"It's nice to see you, Mister Lewis," Sophie said. "You look well."

"I am."

"I thought you were out of town these past few days."

"I was but now I'm back. I wanted to stop and give my regards. And to give you this." He reached for a parcel he'd set on the floor and held it out to her.

She couldn't tell if the ridges in his forehead were from him trying to impart some secret message to her about the fact that he was no longer in the adit, or if she simply smelled bad. Probably a bit of both.

With a slight shake of her head, she indicated that she was unable to take the package without soiling it.

He opened it and produced a scarf. "I thought you could use a new one."

The soft fabric was a deep blue, and she couldn't stop the tug of a smile on her lips. "It's beautiful."

"I'll leave it here." He set it on the chair he'd just occupied. "How did you fall in horse droppings?"

Trying to follow you. "It was dark, and I wasn't paying attention."

Rose reappeared, setting a pan of water on a nearby table along with a bar of soap. Sophie washed and dried her hands on the accompanying towel while Rose inspected the hem of Sophie's dress.

"We'll need to get you out of these, and then I'll launder them. No visit to the Chinese this time. I can take care of this. How embarrassing, Sophie," she muttered under her breath. "Mister Lewis, I'm afraid your visit with Miss Ryan will have to happen at another time."

"Of course," he said. "Miss Ryan." He gave a nod and put his hat on, then said to Rose, "Ma'am." Then he left.

Rose came eye level again and said, "Sophie, what in the name of all things holy is going on?"

"I'm not sure what you mean."

"You have a suitor, and you didn't tell me?"

"I don't."

"Then why is Mister Lewis sniffing around trying to see you? Isn't he that bird man?"

"He is, and I can't say," Sophie stammered out. "Although I may do a story on him." She shrugged. "I suppose it was the sniffing that sent him away."

Rose burst out laughing, and Sophie couldn't help but join in.

"Child, you do stink," Rose exclaimed. "Go on upstairs and get changed."

Sophie did and only when she was in her nightgown and tucked into bed did she finally relax. She wouldn't have to ride in the dark to the adit tonight, so that was something.

She rubbed the soft fabric of the scarf Ben had given her, enjoying the feel of it as well as the warmth in her belly over the gift.

He was trying to smooth things over, and despite the obvious secrets he was keeping from her, she appreciated the gesture.

CHAPTER 8

McKay guided his horse toward the homestead of Charles Bromley. A discreet inquiry via the sole male reporter at the newspaper had revealed the elder man was rarely in the office of late. McKay could simply have asked Miss Ryan, but the wrath in her gaze from the previous evening had been hard to miss, her incident with the horse dung notwithstanding. Although, she had seemed pleased by his gift, a last-minute purchase when he'd been at the mercantile picking up his correspondence. The memory brought a smile to his lips.

At least she'd gotten the message that she didn't need to return to the wilderness and care for him. He had hoped to have a private conversation with her, but Rose Palmer had been too nosy for that. It was just as well. He needed to get back to work, and Sophie Ryan was an unnecessary distraction.

While he couldn't begrudge the presence of Agent Blackmore, it was imperative that McKay find the Weavers first, in particular Russell Weaver. So here he was, pursuing the lead that Lucas had shared with him last night, determined to ferret out any connection Bromley might have with the gang.

Charles Bromley's homestead was located northwest of town

along a road that led to the Haynes Camp, recently created after gold was discovered in a deep mine shaft in the area. It seemed an odd place for the man and his unmarried daughter to live, especially when they ran a newspaper in town. Wouldn't they want to be closer to the townsfolk and the news they were reporting on?

But as McKay came to the location—described to him by Walt Jenkins at the mercantile—one thing stood out. A large barn was located behind the house.

McKay dismounted, tied The Belgian to the hitching post, and knocked on the door. No answer. He stepped off the porch and scanned the surroundings. Tucked slightly behind the house was a small corral and lean-to with a horse munching hay near a water trough. A buggy that had seen better days was parked nearby.

Someone was home.

The low din of voices drew his attention to the barn. The door was partially closed, allowing a narrow view to the interior. It was cluttered with equipment. An older man was talking—presumable Bromley—but when McKay shifted slightly, he was surprised to see Sophie along with another woman who wore a straw hat perched atop her dark hair. Familiarity tugged at him, but he couldn't place her.

The gathering seemed very ... private.

Their discussion wasn't loud enough for him to hear, so he stepped away before they noticed his presence. While the meeting was likely benign in its intent—Sophie worked for the man, after all —McKay couldn't help but feel it might be something more. He tried to ignore the slowly rising disappointment in his chest. After Miss Ryan had aided him, most likely saving his life, he had decided at some point that her appearance hadn't been suspicious but rather lucky instead. He'd been damned fortunate that she'd come into the hills to search for him.

But was she involved in whatever Bromley was?

With reluctance, McKay added her once again to his list of possible accomplices to the Weaver gang.

He returned to his horse and was mounted and headed back to town before any of them were the wiser. He would need to regroup with Blackmore.

SOPHIE TRIED to keep her composure as she spoke with Mister Bromley, certain the woman with him had been the one Sophie had overheard admitting to having shot Ben Lewis. The voice was too distinctive.

A good night's sleep had given Sophie a chance to consider Mister Lewis's situation, and her anger toward him had faded to mere irritation. In truth, it had wounded her pride that he hadn't confided in her more, but that was a silly notion. If he *was* a federal marshal, he probably had the same stalwart principles and adherence to rules as her cousin Lucas. Irritating but admirable at the same time.

Obviously, she would abandon her idea of writing about Ben Lewis, ornithologist, since that was likely a lie. She was busy enough with pieces on the upcoming opera in Jerome as well as the charity work of the Catholic church. But she couldn't pass up the chance to visit Mister Bromley, to possibly help Lucas, and maybe help Mister Lewis.

She had ruminated over what reason she could have to speak with Bromley and finally came up with bringing a cake to thank him for hiring her. Rose had made it at Sophie's request—she'd led Rose to believe that it was for the staff at the newspaper, so it wasn't entirely a lie. But Olivia had been out of the office this morning along with Joe, so it had been easy for Sophie slip away under the pretense that she needed to deliver the sweet dessert before it spoiled.

A part of her had hoped that Bromley couldn't possibly be caught up in something criminal. Not that she knew him well, but it didn't bode well for her employment if he were to be hauled away by a U.S. Deputy Marshal. Not to mention that she liked Olivia, and she felt a bit heartsick that the woman's father might be duplicitous.

But here she was with the mystery of Ben's shooting front and center, and perhaps Bromley somehow being involved. Sophie waffled between cordiality to her boss and maybe just spitting in the woman's face.

Bromley accepted the box that held the cake and said, "Thank you, Miss Ryan. You've come a long way for such a flimsy reason."

Sophie's face heated with embarrassment. "I just wanted to express my gratitude for the job, sir. Perhaps we could have a slice of cake and a cup of tea?" She smiled and shifted her gaze from him to the woman standing beside him. He still hadn't introduced them. With great effort, Sophie extended her hand and plastered a fake smile on her face. "I don't believe we've met. I'm Sophie Ryan. I work for Mister Bromley's newspaper."

"I think I've figured that out." The woman didn't even try to temper her derision, but she did clasp Sophie's hand. "Deborah Gibbons." She wrapped her other hand around Bromley's upper arm, the implication clear—she was staking a romantic claim.

They were an unconventional pair, except for maybe their mutual rudeness. He towered over her, his thin frame in contrast to her rounded proportions, his gray hair opposite her chestnut locks wrapped in a thick bun atop her head. The age difference was ... decades? Mister Bromley must be twice her age. Maybe thrice. Did Olivia know?

Sophie shifted attention back to her boss. "Are you an inventor, Mister Bromley?" The barn was filled with metal parts, wooden structures, and rubber hoses.

"He certainly is," Miss Gibbons replied, gushing like a besotted fool.

"Let's go to the house. To have that cake and tea," he added with a grumble.

He plopped the cake box into Sophie's hands and ushered her out so quickly it was obvious he didn't want her prying into his business, which piqued her interest. She glanced over her shoulder one last time, but she had no idea what she was looking at, and then he was shutting the doors and affixing a padlock.

Sophie soon had a cup of tea in hand courtesy of Miss Gibbons. They were in Bromley's parlor, the messiest room Sophie had ever seen. Beside her on the sofa was a pile of books that seemed to be mechanical in subject matter, and she feared the tall stack might spill onto her if she leaned the wrong way, which was why she had yet to reach for her slice of almond cake on the table.

Crates lined the walls with various types of gadgets. A bookshelf was packed to the brim with more books. A desk was covered in piles of papers, with similar piles on the floor nearby. Dust motes hung in the air from the three of them simply entering the room. Either Olivia was a terrible house cleaner, or she had given up on this area altogether.

"I take it this is your room, sir?" Sophie asked.

"I work better with it like this," he replied. "Olivia leaves me to it."

Sophie admired Olivia's restraint. Perhaps this was why they lived so far out of town. It was too embarrassing to have houseguests drop by.

Sophie lifted the teacup to her lips, and before taking a sip she asked, "And how do you two know one another?"

She didn't miss the glare Miss Gibbons cast her way, but Bromley answered, "She recently moved to town. Olivia hired her to cook and clean."

Sophie almost spit out her tea, and instead coughed to cover it.

If this room were any indication, then Miss Gibbons was terrible at her job. Bromley was apparently using the guise of domestic help to cover his romantic trysting with this woman.

But Sophie couldn't help but feel that Miss Gibbons' interest in Bromley wasn't genuine. The woman had tried to kill a possible U.S. Deputy Marshal, and Bromley's involvement with her was a moral quagmire, since he ran a newspaper that should report impartial news. Not to mention the personal risk to which he was exposing himself.

Would Deborah try to harm him?

Sophie reached for her cake by stretching her arm as far as it would go without moving her upper torso. She managed to grab the edge of the plate with her fingertips and hold it in hand without being buried by the book pile. She released the breath she'd been holding, flush with pride at her success. She supposed it gave her the gumption for her next statement.

"I heard there was a shooting in the hills recently," she said, and looked directly at Miss Gibbons. "Would you know something about that?" She took a bite of the cake, marveling at the rich texture. Rose was an excellent cook.

Miss Gibbons's gaze darkened. "And why would I know about that?"

"What shooting?" Bromley said, setting his empty plate on the table. "I've seen no report about it."

"I've heard talk about town, but perhaps that's all it was," Sophie said.

"You should take care with gossip," Bromley chided her. "It's not how Olivia conducts the paper. Get the facts. Have her send Joe Atkins to the marshal to get the story, if there is one."

Sophie nodded. "I'll tell her."

Did this command exonerate him? Sophie had no idea.

Bromley stood. "I need to be getting back to work."

Sophie gazed at her uneaten cake, wondering how fast she could stuff it down. It was too delicious not to finish.

"It was nice to see you, Miss Ryan." He left the room before Sophie could respond, the front door opening and shutting.

Miss Gibbons hopped to her feet. "I'll be right back." She followed him outside.

Sophie jammed a large bite of the confection into her mouth, glancing at a pile of papers on the floor off to her right. She forgot to swallow as she realized what she was looking at.

SOPHIE HADN'T TAKEN a horse to the Bromley homestead. Instead, she had walked, not realizing how far out of town it was until it had been too late to turn around. When she was finally in her room at the boarding house, she was covered in a layer of perspiration and panting for breath after nearly running for most of the return distance, shifting to a brisk walk once she'd been on Main Street.

Now, however, she could relax at last, and her shoulders sagged in relief.

She pushed aside the guilt gnawing at her. It was just a piece of paper she'd taken, stuffing it into her satchel before Miss Gibbons had returned. The woman had quickly made it clear that their social time was at an end, and Sophie hadn't even had time to finish her cake before being pushed out the door.

The woman's brusqueness had only strengthened Sophie's resolve that something was amiss. Deborah Gibbons had tried to kill Ben Lewis, and now she was possibly in collusion with Bromley. Lucas had told Sophie he was interested in Bromley, presumably for his case, and now Ben was tied up in it as well.

The end justified the means.

She pulled the paper—the map—from her satchel.

Would Bromley notice it missing? It seemed a stretch,

considering the disarray of his parlor, but Sophie would copy and return it before he was likely to know.

She went to the narrow desk in the corner of her room, which she'd had to request from Mrs. Palmer since she had planned to do work during her off hours. The woman had grumbled but had managed to locate one. It had wobbled until Sophie had stuffed a bit of cloth beneath one leg.

She went to work transferring the map to a blank page at the back of her notebook. As she sketched, examining the details more closely, it became clear it was a map of the hills surrounding Jerome. The locations were written in Spanish, but she had an adequate working knowledge of the language. And if she wasn't mistaken, it was a map to the location of Conquistador gold.

Walt had been right.

Bromley was a treasure hunter.

———

McKay paid the livery boy, Trent, to deliver a note to Blackmore. It was an innocuous message should it be intercepted but it would convey McKay's desire to speak with the other agent. And then he found himself walking straight to Jerome Mining News.

Why? Miss Ryan was probably still with Charles Bromley, but McKay's aggravation over this turn of events was palpable. He was determined to learn more. That was all.

He entered the office. Only Joe Atkins was present, no sign of Miss Bromley or Sophie.

"Do you have another question, Mister Lewis?" Joe asked.

"I came to see Miss Ryan this time."

"She should be back any time. You can wait at her desk, if you like."

McKay nodded, following Joe's silent direction, and sat in a chair near her workspace. He casually inspected her desk. For clues of course. He was simply doing his job.

There was a book about birds sitting off to one side. Was she trying to catch him in a lie about his cover? The story about the nighthawk had been true, and it was a good enough backstory to survive a little digging by a reporter, or at least he'd thought so. Or was she simply wanting to add to her knowledge to impress him?

He grimaced. He was a fool. She was up to something. He'd do well to stop being so distracted by her captivating smile and forthright manner. It was all a ruse. It had to be.

Blackmore entered the office with Miss Bromley. The blush on the woman's face told McKay everything he needed to know—Blackmore was laying on the charm, and she was falling for it.

McKay stood and said, "Mister Smith."

"Nice to see you again," Blackmore replied.

"Are you here to see Sophie?" Miss Bromley asked McKay.

"I am."

As Sophie transcribed the map, trying to match the details carefully, the scope of it astounded her. Was it true? Had the Conquistadors left gold in the area? She didn't know much about them, except that the Spaniards had come through this area over two hundred years ago. The land was dry, harsh and at times unrelenting. Why would they haul gold only to leave it here?

Who had made this map? Mister Bromley? Perhaps he had knowledge that he'd learned in his time as a newspaperman. Or from the storekeeper Walt Jenkins' brother, George? And what of Deborah Gibbons? How was she connected?

And she had shot Ben Lewis ....

Sophie paused, her pencil poised above the page of her notebook. What if Ben were involved? Was he looking for the gold as well? Maybe she had been too quick to assume he was a lawman. Perhaps he was the opposite.

He was too solemn, too careful, with a shrewdness in his gaze. And there was an aura of danger about him, something she'd told herself she was imagining. But maybe her instincts were right.

Was that why he was out in the hills so much? Not looking for birds, but in a race for the gold that Bromley and perhaps Deborah Gibbons were looking for?

The implication made her feel disheartened. She'd fallen for his story, lock, stock, and barrel. And then she'd fallen for a fanciful daydream that he was a U.S. Marshal. And maybe *she'd fallen for him*. Just a little.

Foolish.

She squared her shoulders. A hunt was possibly afoot, and none other than her boss was involved, which meant the newspaper was compromised. Was Olivia also embroiled in it all? Was this why Lucas was here? Did he know about the gold? Would he answer her truthfully if she asked?

No, she was on her own. She would need to launch her own investigation, and her best source was Ben Lewis. She would need to remain close to him.

With her new resolve, she completed copying the map and then tucked her notebook into the waist of her skirt behind her back. She then slipped the stolen map into her boot and fluffed her skirt over it. She checked her hair and straightened her bodice.

First, she needed to check in to work.

And then she would need to return to Bromley's home and replace the stolen map.

CHAPTER 9

Sophie entered the office and said, "Good morning." It was almost noon, but she didn't want to emphasize her tardiness.

Olivia looked up from her typesetting. "You're late."

So were you, but Sophie didn't say it aloud. "I was here earlier."

As usual, Joe was gone. Olivia's ability to keep tabs on her staff was an obvious challenge. Sophie decided to tell the truth about where she'd been, since Bromley was sure to inform his daughter of the visit. But first she settled at her desk, her back stiff from the notebook in her waistband. She would need it for the article she was working on about the opera but hadn't thought it through when she had decided to hide it on her person. And now the map tucked into her shoe was poking her ankle in a most bothersome way.

"My apologies for not leaving a note," she added. "I took a cake to your father."

Olivia stopped her work. "You went to my home? And saw my father?"

Sophie tried to get comfortable in her chair, but it was exceedingly difficult. "Yes. I wanted to thank him for the opportunity to work here. And I had the pleasure of meeting Miss Gibbons."

Olivia frowned. "Was he ... friendly?"

"Yes, of course." It was certainly a day for bending the truth. "His barn is impressive. Is he some kind of inventor?"

"Something like that."

"What does he build?"

"To be honest, I'm not certain. He likes to tinker, and it keeps him busy. It was why I hired Miss Gibbons. I thought it best he wasn't alone all day. He can be forgetful at times. It's why he doesn't work here full-time any longer."

Olivia's countenance seemed so sincere, tinged with sadness, that Sophie believed her. But Bromley had seemed perfectly lucid to Sophie. Was he lying to his daughter about his mental faculties?

"How did you find Miss Gibbons?" Sophie asked. "She's so new to town."

"Rose Palmer suggested it, and it's worked well. My father seems to like Miss Gibbons."

I'll say.

Then Olivia said, "Mister Lewis was here."

The change of subject left Sophie a bit unbalanced. "This morning?"

"He was looking for you."

Ignoring the nervous tumble in her stomach, Sophie asked, "Did he leave a message?"

"No. I suppose he'll find you later. Are you two ...?"

"Oh no." Sophie shook her head and reached for her pen and ink. She liked to give Olivia a finished product written in ink and not her usual pencil scratches.

Olivia's expression softened. "He's very interesting. And he seems attentive to you."

Sophie focused on her paper. "Well, I don't know about that. I don't really have time for such nonsense."

Olivia nodded and asked, "Are you going to wear your coat all day?"

Sophie had left her duster on to hide the notebook. She laughed and said, "I've been chilled all morning."

McKay had spent the day scouting Cottonwood six miles to the east but had turned up nothing. In the late afternoon, on his way back to Jerome he stopped at the cemetery just outside of town.

It had been on his mind since he'd arrived in Jerome, but he'd convinced himself he was too busy to visit until now. The last time he'd been here, he'd been four years old, and it turned out his childhood memory had been faulty since it took some time to find the gravesite.

But when he finally came to it, unexpected emotion filled him. The simple headstone read:

Moira McKay
Born 1855
Died 1877
Gone too soon

His memories of his mother were fleeting unformed images. In the years that had passed, his mind had filled in the gaps with more tangible imaginings. Creations of his own mind. And it filled him with grief because he knew many of them weren't real. Perhaps not even the stories she would tell him of the nighthawks.

He'd had so little time with her. Not enough to even remember her properly.

He knelt beside the headstone and touched it, bowing his head. He'd come here to find his father. To bring him to justice. But he'd also come to see her.

"I'm sorry it's taken so long," he whispered.

He vowed to get a better headstone, one befitting a woman who had died at the tragic age of twenty-two.

According to his uncle Albert, who had raised him along with his wife, Orla, and was actually a second cousin to Moira, Benton had lived in Jerome from the age of two until he was four years old. Upon his mother's death, he'd come to live with them at the request of a man named George Jenkins. Benton and his mother had stayed with George at his Nighthawk Ranch, which had supposedly been named by her.

Had she been in love with George? It had never been clear to Benton, and he'd hoped to speak to the man, but to his disappointment George had died recently. He'd yet to discuss any of this with Walt, George's brother, mostly because Benton was undercover and couldn't admit to being a McKay.

As he guided The Belgian back to town, he found himself heading to the newspaper office, the urge to see Sophie strong. But as he approached, Charles Bromley arrived in a buggy and promptly went inside, so McKay hung back.

When Sophie exited, walking hurriedly toward Main Street, he followed. She went to the livery and got the same horse she'd used to see him at the hogback, then she headed out of town toward the Bromley place.

Luckily there was traffic on the road, since it went past the Jerome Blast Furnace and the main entrance to the United Verde Copper Company, and it helped to hide his presence, although Sophie was at least a half mile ahead. He assumed she was going to the Bromleys' and the fact that Charles and Olivia weren't at home made her actions highly suspicious.

The sun had set, and dark clouds had collected, casting the land in deep shadows. She hobbled Roger some distance from the homestead and continued on foot. He did the same with The Belgian in a depression out of sight of her animal. By the time

McKay reached the house, the wind was gusting, and Sophie was nowhere to be seen.

Maybe she hadn't come here. Maybe she was following some newspaper lead, and his suspicions of her were unwarranted. It surprised him how much he wanted that to be the case.

The air smelled of rain and the angry sky foretold an impending deluge. He was about to turn back when the front door opened and out came Sophie. She then spent several minutes fiddling with the locking mechanism.

She was picking locks and trespassing, but why?

A clanking noise caused Sophie to freeze. Someone else was here. She disappeared around the corner of the house as a man emerged from the opposite side, somewhat nondescript but with a confident gait.

McKay didn't recognize him, although his features weren't clear with the distance and the lack of light. That Sophie had hidden herself meant she'd had no intention of meeting this man.

McKay quietly pulled his gun.

The man knocked on the front door, waiting with hands on hips for an answer that never came, then he stepped off the porch and went around the house from where he'd come.

McKay left his hiding spot. The man veered toward the corral and the dash of a shadow to McKay's left showed Sophie slipping into the rather large barn. McKay did the same.

The interior was cluttered with all sorts of apparatus and debris. McKay ducked to the right, searching for her. There was barely enough room to move, and he was forced to creep along one of the walls.

The rustle of clothing, barely more than a whisper, alerted him to her whereabouts. As the barn door opened and lamplight chased away the darkness, McKay holstered his weapon and clamped a hand over her mouth before she gave them both away. He pulled her against him, her back against his chest, and ignored the stab of pain from his shoulder wound. With a side-eye glare, she stared at him. He gave a slight shake of his head to reassure her, then he eased his hand from her mouth.

She smelled of the Sophie he'd come to know—subtle, flowery, and something so familiar that it triggered an ache in his chest. She also carried a sour aroma of panic, a smell he was also familiar with.

Sophie was nervous.

He put his finger to his lips, indicating for her to be quiet. She set her jaw, but she gave the barest hint of agreement. They both turned to watch the man doing an inspection of the various ... equipment was the only way McKay could describe it.

The door opened wide, and Bromley entered. "You're not supposed to be in here," he said.

"I went to the house," the man replied. "I thought maybe you were deep in work and had forgotten the rest of the world."

"Next time, wait on the porch."

The man shrugged. "Maybe leave your door open so I could wait in your parlor."

Bromley moved past him to a table. "Can't figure out my lock, can you?" He grinned over his shoulder.

"I didn't feel like it." The man sighed. "We're not paying you for lessons on lock picking."

"It might come in handy." Bromley unrolled a large piece of paper, securing the corners with several heavy tools.

"Is this it?" The man scanned the layout.

Bromley nodded, his face aglow. "I think it's just what you and your brother are looking for."

The man pointed at a drawing. "You think this will help us find the gold?"

"I do."

"How long to make it?"

"Maybe three days. I've already tried to build something similar.

I think I can use that framework again. It'll make the design go faster."

"But what about the other problem?" the man asked.

Bromley straightened and grinned. "Let me show you."

Bromley moved so quickly that McKay had to tighten his hold on Sophie, pressing them both behind two large wooden planks leaning against the barn wall. He was barely able to get them out of Bromley's line of sight, as he rushed past them holding the lantern high.

The other man followed. McKay's position with Sophie impeded his view, but he didn't dare move. Sophie's breathing was rapid, her chest heaving in short breaths.

Keep it under control, Sophie.

"Damn, Bromley," the man said. "Will this work? Is this safe?"

"It'll work."

"Have you tested it?"

"Not exactly. Not much water around here."

"How're we gonna get it there?" the man asked.

"Xander, you have so little faith in the process," Bromley said. "I'll get it to you."

"No. We'll take it from here."

"That wasn't the deal," Bromley said. "I told you that you could trust me."

"If it was up to me, then I'd be fine with it. Russell is saying no."

Russell? It had to be Russell Weaver. McKay's father. And this man was Russell's brother. Uncle Xander.

McKay dipped his head, allowing his nose to rest against Sophie's hair, her scent both beguiling and comforting, his body hungry for the touch. That she hadn't twisted out of his arms and proclaimed their presence spoke volumes. She wasn't involved with the Weavers. Relief rushed through him.

"Tell Russell to come here, and we'll go together," Bromley said.

"Maybe."

"You'll need me on site. I may need to fine tune as the excavation progresses."

"All right," he conceded. "In the meantime, you'll get the other device made."

"I will," Bromley said.

"I'll be back in three days."

Xander left and McKay wondered how fast he could get out of here to trail him. Rain pelted the roof, and any tracks would be obliterated in minutes.

Sophie shifted and McKay tightened his embrace, his mouth hovering near her ear. A barely perceptible shudder rippled through her body.

Bromley moved back to the table and set the lantern down. Then he cursed beneath his breath, took the light, and left the barn.

Sophie pulled free. "What are you doing here?" she whispered.

"I could ask you the same, but I don't have time."

He went to the barn door as Bromley's light disappeared around the house. McKay stepped into the storm, searching the ground for Xander's path. It became futile quickly, the ground a muddy slop. And he couldn't keep lurking around the Bromley house. The man might see him.

When he stopped abruptly, Sophie slammed into his backside. He grabbed her shoulders before she fell, her duster slick with rain. "We need to go," he said.

Grabbing her hand, he dragged her behind him, not stopping until they got to her horse.

"Were you following me?" she demanded.

He ignored her, grabbing her waist and hoisting her onto Roger. He took the horse's reins from her.

"I can ride on my own," Sophie said loudly above the din of rain.

McKay walked Roger to his own horse. Once mounted, he continued to hold Roger's reins, not wanting to lose Sophie in the storm. It was slow going, but he finally got them to the livery where they left the animals for the night. Then McKay took her hand again and led her to his hotel.

"Where are we going?" Her voice was exasperated.

"We need privacy," he said, taking a back way, entering the Connor Hotel through a rear entrance.

When the way was clear of employees, they went through the kitchen and took the stairs. He unlocked his door but when he stepped inside, Sophie refused.

"I'm not going into your room," she whispered. She was dripping water all over the carpeted floor.

"Now's not the time to play hard to get, Sophie."

He pulled her inside and shut the door.

CHAPTER 10

S ophie stared at Ben Lewis, unsure what to do. His appearance
in the Bromley barn had been surprising. Alarming, even. But
during their ride back to town as sheets of rain had blanketed them,
she'd come to realize that it wasn't surprising. Or alarming.

Ben Lewis wasn't who he had said he was.

And tonight had proved it.

Her instincts were validated.

Ben had shed his hat and jacket, and he was now unbuttoning
her coat. Then he pulled it from each arm. She frowned as he
handled her like a child. He put her wet garments on a hook on the
back of the door, then reached for a towel, wiping his face and wet
hair, then handed it to her. She didn't move. Her instincts may have
been validated, but she was apparently in a state of shock.

"You're cold," he said. He gently wiped her face, then grabbed a
blanket from his bed and wrapped it around her, then he guided her
to a chair in the corner of the room, rubbing her arms a few times.

He sat on the edge of the bed across from her, running a hand
through his wet hair. "Why did you break into the Bromley house?"

She was beginning to shiver and pulled the blanket tighter.

"Why?" he asked again.

"I didn't." Her brain was beginning to function again, and she sought to organize her thoughts. "You were in the barn with me. Technically, we both broke in. Except the door was open, so I must point out that we didn't really break in."

"I'm talking about his house."

Oh. He saw that.

"Am I in trouble?" she said. "Are you going to arrest me?"

"Why would I do that?"

"Because you're not an ornithologist, are you?"

He considered her question. "It's complicated, Sophie," he finally said.

"Right."

Was he a good guy or a bad guy? And why did she wish so fervently that he was a good guy?

Self-preservation demanded that she lie. "I wasn't breaking into the Bromley house. He'd asked me to return something."

Ben's expression was edged with skepticism. He didn't believe her.

"Then why did you hide in his barn?" he asked.

"That other man, Xander, scared me, that was all."

"Then why didn't you speak to Bromley once he arrived?"

"Because you had me confined."

That, at least, produced a momentary look of chagrin on Ben's face.

"Why were *you* there?" she asked. "Does it have something to do with that man, Xander? Do you think he was behind your shooting?"

That seemed to surprise him. "Why? Did you recognize him?"

"I believe he was the one I overheard talking to the woman who did it. And I know who she is now."

"Who?"

"Her name is Deborah Gibbons. She's Mister Bromley's

housekeeper, according to Olivia, but I believe she's something more."

"Something more?"

"His ... paramour."

"She's the one who shot me?" he asked.

"Do you know her?"

"No."

"But you know why she tried to kill you?"

"No, I don't."

Sophie narrowed her eyes. "Who are you? Why are you really in Jerome?"

Ben released a heavy breath. "The less you know, the better."

"Says who?"

He met her gaze, the conflict in his own readily apparent.

"You can trust me, Ben," she said, warming to this game they were playing. The chill in her limbs was slowly being replaced with a delicious warmth and not just from the blanket. The man across from her was better than a crackling fire.

A smile tugged at his mouth. "Can I?"

The silent standoff stretched between them, the question dripping with more than just Deborah Gibbons and Charles Bromley and whomever Ben was—lawman or criminal.

"I *did* take something from the Bromley house," she said, conceding a bit of the truth to win him over. "And then I needed to return it. Unseen."

"Did you pick the lock?"

He *had* been spying on her.

"I did."

"How did you learn to do that?"

"One of my cousins was rather keen on locks. He collected them and was always pulling them apart and tinkering with them. I watched, and I learned." Travis wasn't always happy to have her lurking about, but Lucas's brother had always been a bit of a loner, and the truth was, so was Sophie.

"And that was in Texas?" He drew the words out, as if he were doubtful of her claim.

She frowned. "Yes." Did he think she had lied about that? But in the beginning, she hadn't felt the need to keep the truth from him. That had been a recent development.

"What was this cousin's name?" he asked.

"Travis Blackmore."

"Blackmore?" he asked, clearly startled.

"Do you know him?"

He seemed to recover himself and answered, "No. What did you take from Bromley?"

She considered another half-truth, but all this subterfuge was making her head hurt, so she retrieved her notebook from her satchel, flipped to the page of the map she'd copied, and handed it to him.

"I suppose I shouldn't have ... borrowed it," she said. "But I'm a reporter. It's my job to investigate a good story."

"But this is your employer," he said, his focus on the map.

"A small and somewhat uncomfortable detail," she murmured.

He met her gaze. "Spanish gold?" His bewilderment seemed genuine.

"Intriguing, right? After what we saw in the Bromley barn ...."

"And what was that?"

"Oh, that's right. You ran out so quickly. I took a glance at the drawing that was on the table. It was dark but I think it was a schematic of an underwater diving suit."

"To use around here? There's no water."

"Well, maybe there is," she said. "There was another drawing of two wooden platforms with wires running between, and some other device connected to it. I think it was some kind of metal detector. Mister Bromley is an inventor."

"You think he's planning to dive for gold?"

"I know it sounds outrageous, but the mines in this area do have issues with groundwater. And look." She leaned close and pointed to a spot on the map. "It seems the place they're interested in is near the Verde River. Perhaps this location is flooded. Perhaps Bromley has built an apparatus to help this Xander person find the gold. And you ...."

He raised his eyes to hers.

She was too close to him. Much too close, but she held his gaze, instinctively not wanting him to know he unnerved her. "Are you here for the gold, Ben?"

His eyes flashed with surprise. "No."

"Are you a Pinkerton?" Her cousin, Kate, was a Pinkerton.

"No."

"But you're ... something."

His gaze dropped to her mouth then back to her eyes. "I'm something," he agreed.

"But you're not going to tell me."

"I'm not at liberty, Sophie."

The sound of her name sent a shiver through her, and it had nothing to do with being cold. Then she saw the blood staining his shirt.

"Your wound," she said. "You've reopened it."

He followed her gaze. "It looks that way."

"Let me have a look."

"I'm fine."

"I didn't stitch you back together to have you undo it all."

She reached for the collar of his shirt, but he caught her wrists before she could touch him. His hands were warm and larger than she'd realized, his gaze hard and filled with wanting. For her.

It had always been there, some part of her having sensed it, but now she knew for certain.

"You probably shouldn't keep touching me," he said.

"*You're* touching *me*."

She was close enough to see the slight flare of his nostrils and the rapid pace of his breath. He gave a slight nod and released her. She leaned away, putting distance between them.

"Will you at least rebandage it?" she said.

"I'll look at it."

"Then it's time I left." She picked up her notebook that he'd placed on the bed beside him.

"Will you promise me something?" he asked.

She waited for him to continue.

"That you won't follow that map by yourself."

"Are you offering to accompany me?"

"Sophie, this is dangerous. You should give that evidence to me and let me handle it."

The rush of euphoria from a moment ago slid away. Was Ben Lewis playing on her obvious weakness for him to manipulate her? Her cheeks heated with embarrassment, and she hid the response by standing and reaching for her satchel.

"After I went to all the effort to get it?" she said, placing the notebook in her bag, the blanket dropping from her shoulders and falling to the floor. "If it's all the same to you, I'll hang on to it."

She put on her coat, still soaked, but she didn't care, and grabbed her drenched hat. "I'll be seeing you, Ben."

"It's late. At least let me walk you back to Rose's."

"No thanks." And then she slipped from his room before he could argue with her.

CHAPTER 11

F atigue pressed on McKay and his shoulder ached as he waited in the livery stall just after dawn. Changing his bandage himself had proved more difficult than he'd thought. But that was just part of his restless night, his sleep disrupted again and again by her. By Sophie. Her presence in this case—in his life—had become a distraction he didn't need.

His need ....

Last night in his room, the pull between them had escalated, and he'd barely had the presence of mind to stop her before she started running her hands over him. He had been tired and annoyed and surprised to find her poking around the Bromley home, breaking the law in the process. And then there was that map, a new lead, as was Bromley's firm connection to the Weavers. Xander's presence confirmed, finally, that he and Russell were in the vicinity.

It was still unclear how Sophie was involved, but the fact that he wanted her compromised his position. And he'd been very careful to avoid being compromised.

He hadn't hidden his connection to the Weavers from his boss. Griffith knew that Russell Weaver was McKay's father, and McKay had assured him that nothing would distract from pursuing the gang, that it would be justice not only for the train conductor the Weavers had recently killed but also for McKay's mother, who had fled the Weavers when Benton was two.

So much for carefully laid plans. A young female reporter had upended McKay's world, and now a new wrinkle—was she somehow connected to his recently arrived partner?

Lucas entered the stall, looking disheveled as if he'd just rolled out of bed, which he probably had.

"Thanks for coming," McKay said.

"You're lucky I saw the message. Has something happened?"

"I need to ask you something. Do you know Sophie Ryan?"

To Lucas's credit, he didn't give any outward indication that he was being cornered. "The woman who works with Olivia at the paper?"

"She claims to have a cousin named Travis Blackmore, and I thought it too much of a coincidence that you should also have the same last name."

Lucas's shoulders sagged. "My apologies, sir. I never meant to lie to you. Yes, she's my cousin."

"Does she know about me?"

"No. Of course not. I've said nothing. But she knows that I'm a U.S. Deputy Marshal and that I'm obviously here on a case. And ...."

"What did you tell her?"

"She's very persistent, and she's smart too. I emphasized how important keeping my alias intact was, and she assured me she would, which is why we've been pretending not to know each other." He paused before adding, "I told her Charles Bromley was under suspicion."

So that explained why she was poking around the man's house and stealing secret maps.

"You could've requested to be reassigned," McKay said.

"True, but this offered the opportunity to check in on her. She can be a bit obstinate and her father—my uncle Logan—wasn't thrilled with her coming all the way here, but she insisted."

The confession seemed genuine, so McKay relaxed. A little.

Lucas continued, "I decided to tell her about Bromley because I was worried about her. She works for him, and we have him under surveillance, and I wanted her to be careful. I know I shouldn't have done that. I'm sorry."

McKay held up his hand. "It's fine. But I will need to ask you not to mention me. Am I clear?"

"You mean ...."

"Don't tell her that I'm a marshal, and don't tell her you and I are partners."

"Of course."

Since Sophie could very well tell Lucas about their previous night's escapades, he reluctantly said, "Xander Weaver is in town. I saw him last night."

"Was it a positive ID?"

"Yes." *For the most part.*

"Did you trail him?"

McKay shook his head. "I lost him in the rain."

"Where was this?"

McKay hesitated. "The Bromley barn. Bromley and Xander were discussing an apparatus Bromley was building. I believe it involved some of those rubber hoses you mentioned."

"So the connection has panned out," Lucas said, a hint of disappointment in his voice.

"It would seem so. Anything on your end?"

"Just something odd that I picked up while trying to sell shoes to the men over at the United Verde. There's talk about a man named Marty Ennis. He likes to hire mine workers to transport crates down to Pecks Lake and dump them. He tells them it's bad batches of whiskey from a still he has."

"Why dispose of them that way?"

"It doesn't make much sense, but it gets better. One of the men claimed it wasn't whiskey but gold in the crates."

"From the mines?" McKay asked.

"Maybe. There's no proof, just talk."

"And this is relevant because …?"

"The Weavers have stolen a lot of gold over the years. Maybe they're using Marty to hide it."

"Why would they trust this Marty?"

Lucas shook his head. "I'm not sure. But Marty has a connection I don't really like."

"What's that?"

"He's some sort of second cousin nephew to Rose Palmer."

ROSE POURED tea for Sophie as they sat in the sitting room of the boarding house. Sophie had overslept this morning, and when Rose had come knocking on her door, the woman had decided that Sophie was under the weather and should take the day to rest. She had sent word to Olivia at the paper and had brought Sophie breakfast in her room.

But Sophie wasn't sick, she was simply tired after her long night at the Bromley place and with Ben after. And she had tossed and turned much of the night, so it was hardly surprising she had overslept. She felt a bit guilty for missing work, but she hadn't had the energy to argue with Rose.

But now it was midday, and they had the parlor to themselves, and Sophie decided to make use of the opportunity to get more information out of the woman.

"How long have you lived in Jerome, Rose?"

Rose sat across from her and took up her embroidery. "Several years now. I moved here from Phoenix after my husband died. It was rather a mess, his estate and all, but he left me some land in Jerome."

"And you built your boarding house on it?"

"No." She laughed. "It's out of town. Believe it or not, I made whiskey when I first came. There was good money in it, and I used it to buy this place. You must make your own opportunities in this world, Sophie. I made the mistake with Carl of believing he would take care of me. I'm here to tell you, trust no man."

"It must've been hard to lose your daughter and then her father," Sophie said, trying to step gingerly around such a painful subject.

Rose's expression sobered. "Carl wasn't Henrietta's father. He was my third husband."

"Oh," Sophie said surprised.

"I guess I'm a hopeless romantic," Rose said, contradicting her previous statement. "I was very young when I met my first husband, Oscar. I thought he would save me. I had always planned to be an actress, to be somebody, but life had other ideas, and I ended up working in a saloon when I met him. He wasn't a very nice man, but he did teach me about distilling whiskey. But it was a relief when he died, and I was able to move on. Then I met Lawrence. He was a real looker, if you know what I mean. He was Henrietta's father."

"What happened?"

"He went to Alaska. I was in Oklahoma City with our daughter, so I stayed behind. But then she ... well, she was only three years old. The pox took her. Near broke me in two. I wrote to Lawrence, but he never responded, so I picked myself up and went looking for him."

"In Alaska?"

Rose nodded.

"Did you find him?"

She shook her head. "I never did. I stayed there for almost four years. Maybe it was five. That's when I met Carl. He helped me legally declare Lawrence deceased so that he and I could marry. I didn't really want to leave Alaska, and I hope one day to return, but love led me astray once again."

Sophie wasn't sure what to say. She was nearly nineteen years old and clearly didn't have the life experience that Rose had. But still, there was something rather chronic about the way the woman seemed to go through husbands.

"But then that damned man left me with debt," Rose continued. "Hence the need for the whiskey production. I needed to do something, and I didn't want to run an establishment like Jennie's Place." A brothel on Main Street. "Her place has burned down twice now. Hellfire has rained down on her. She deserved it, I suppose."

Sophie was taken aback by Rose's sudden religious fervor. The frequent blazes in town had suffered from a lack of water. Earlier this year, the town was finally incorporated, allowing for the formation of a fire department.

But rather than point out that technicality, Sophie said, "You don't like prostitution." Sophie didn't necessarily like it either, but it was pervasive in towns like Jerome.

"I don't. And my place has never burned. The Almighty rewards those with pure hearts."

And that's when Sophie knew, though she couldn't say exactly how, that Rose's time with Oscar had been as a scarlet lady. The righteous gleam in Rose's eyes was simply a façade to mask the very real pain underneath. And once again, Sophie's emotions toward the woman took an ambivalent turn.

"Perhaps you should write about it," Rose said.

"Prostitution?"

"Well, if you pursued the prospectors I've told you about, they surely frequent those places."

Most of "those places" were in the red-light district down on Hull Avenue. Along with the accompanying ladies' jail, Sophie found it all somewhat distressing and was glad her newspaper assignments had so far avoided the place. Olivia seemed to handle the hard news when it involved something other than mine business.

"I suppose," Sophie hedged. "Remind me again why I should be reporting on general prospecting in the area?"

"Well, it's so fascinating. You should accompany those men into the wilderness and tell us what they're up to."

To be honest, it sounded a bit dull. Small-time prospectors were likely finding nothing of merit. The United Verde had bought up most of the serious claims in the area dating back to the 1870's. And besides, those men would never allow a young woman reporter to interrogate them. That much was obvious to Sophie, making Rose's request even more peculiar.

"I'll pitch it to Olivia again," Sophie murmured, wanting to get the woman off her back. "Speaking of which, I met a woman yesterday at Mister Bromley's home. I believe you know her. Deborah Gibbons?"

Rose frowned then her expression brightened with recognition that Sophie was certain she was faking. "Yes, Miss Gibbons," Rose said. "She came to town last month, and being new and all, I wanted to help her out. I'm glad she was able to find employment with the Bromleys." She leaned forward, her blouse straining against her bosom, and lowered her voice, "I'm sure you've noticed, but Charles Bromley can't run that paper any longer. Thank goodness for Olivia. She's turned out to be quite competent. But Deborah has been a boon for them. That man shouldn't be alone all day while Olivia is working."

"No, he shouldn't." But Sophie's brief experience with Mister Bromley had shown him to be sound in body and mind. Why were all the women around him trying to say otherwise? "Walt Jenkins told me about the lure of Spanish gold in the area."

Rose returned her attention to her needlework. "It's a popular story in these parts."

"He said that Bromley has been looking for it. Do you think there's any merit to it?"

Rose shrugged. "Perhaps. Wouldn't it be something if it were found?"

"Walt told me his brother was also obsessed with looking for it."

Rose waved a dismissive hand. "George Jenkins was full of hot air. I didn't believe a word he said when he was alive, and I wouldn't believe any words that seem to be coming from the beyond through Walt. He's just trying to create an aura around George's property so he can sell it for above market value."

The confidence with which Rose spoke of the place caught Sophie's attention. "Are you thinking of buying it?"

"What?" Rose laughed. "No! It's too far from town and a bit worthless, if you ask me."

Sophie couldn't help but feel that Rose was lying. But the question was why.

SOPHIE LEFT the boarding house with the excuse that she needed a walk. She covered her face with the new scarf Ben had given her since the sulphur fumes were especially strong today. Her destination was the mercantile. She needed to learn the location of George Jenkins' ranch and Walt seemed the best source. She thought to pitch the idea that she could write about the property for the paper, and thereby help Walt sell it. The Jerome Mining News was distributed to many surrounding communities, and editions even made it to Phoenix occasionally if a local story was big enough.

It would give her an excuse to visit the ranch.

As Sophie entered the mercantile, she bumped into Deborah.

"Miss Gibbons. It's nice to see you again."

Deborah flicked a glance her way. "I suppose." She resumed her shopping.

"I'm thinking of doing an article on Mister Bromley's inventions. Perhaps I could interview you."

Deborah's brows furrowed into a deep frown. "Why?"

"You're quite close to him. I'm sure you have insights that would be revealing as to his process."

"Is Olivia all right with this?"

"Why wouldn't she be?"

Ned suddenly appeared and ran up to Deborah. "Can I get a peppermint stick?"

"No," she replied.

"But why?"

"Because I said so."

"Are you two related?" Sophie asked, thinking she saw a resemblance.

Deborah looked at Sophie as if she'd forgotten she was there, then cleared her throat. "He's my son."

That was a revelation Sophie hadn't expected.

"Now I know your name," Sophie said to Ned.

"You've met?" Deborah asked.

Sophie decided not to share his thievery. "I've seen him around town. I loaned him my copy of *Oliver Twist*."

Suspicion filled the woman's gaze. "Why would you do that?"

"To broaden his horizons. It's a book about poverty and social classes."

Deborah scoffed. "How does knowing about that broaden his horizons?"

"It helps to understand how other people live. It breeds compassion."

"But it's a make-believe book."

"That doesn't mean it can't have merit." Sophie looked at Ned. "Have you started reading it?"

The boy gave a slight and almost imperceptible nod. Sophie wasn't certain if it was because he'd started reading and didn't want his mother to know, or if he hadn't and he didn't want Sophie to know.

"I live at Rose's Place," Sophie added. "If you have any questions, I'd be happy to discuss the book with you. With permission from your father, of course."

Another silent assent from the boy.

Deborah placed a proprietary arm around Ned. "You're a very nosy woman. If you must know, his father is gone. Now, I'm very busy so good day to you." With Ned still in her clutches, she spun away.

Was Miss Gibbons "sweet" on Mister Bromley to secure a father for her son? Did Olivia know about the boy?

Sophie purchased a tin of tea and Walt was happy to give her directions to Nighthawk Ranch. He offered to take her himself, but it would have to be early morning or late evening. Sophie insisted she would have a walk around, so there was no need for him to accompany her.

Since she was out and about, she walked to the newspaper office to work for a bit, feeling guilty about playing hooky all morning. Also, the opera was tonight, and she wanted to assure Olivia that she would still attend on behalf of the newspaper.

She considered Miss Gibbons. Was she really Ben's shooter? Why would a young, single mother feel the need to gun down a man from such a great distance? From what Sophie had learned from not only Miss Gibbons but also Ben, the shooter had been more than two hundred yards away. How could Deborah Gibbons possibly be such an excellent marksman? And in truth, despite the woman's frostiness the two times Sophie had interacted with her, she had a hard time believing that a mother could be that cold-hearted.

So perhaps Sophie was amiss in thinking the woman was a suspect in the shooting. But if she wasn't wrong, that meant Deborah was afraid.

But afraid of what?

CHAPTER 12

Sophie's first glimpse of Nighthawk Ranch was underwhelming. Her childhood had been spent at Dove Crossing, a large spread belonging to her family and adjacent to her uncles' ranches: the Rocking Wren, Sparrow Station, and Blackbird Mountain Ranch. They ran thousands of heads of cattle and the homesteads had grown to be sprawling over the years.

In contrast, George Jenkins' property was surrounded by rocky, undulating land, and the homestead was small, with an equally modest barn and corral, and no bunkhouse. Perhaps there was a line shack or two in the hills where ranch hands could reside?

It was late afternoon, and she let Roger pick his way along the path to the main house. Gusts of wind pushed at her and while fluffy white clouds filled the sky, it didn't look like rain, which would be a pleasant reprieve from the constant showers of the past several days.

Sophie dismounted and tied Roger to the hitching post. She stepped onto the porch, a wooden plaque with an etching of a bird hanging at the entrance. She admired it while trying the front door, but it was locked. While she could certainly bypass it, she did have some scruples and wouldn't willfully trespass without a good reason.

Circling the house, she made her way to the barn, but froze at the sight of a horse in one of the stalls. She spun around, searching for the owner, but there was no one. Had the poor thing been here since George Jenkins had died? How long ago was that? Six weeks, she thought Walt had said.

She went to the animal, sick with worry, but he greeted her with a friendly nuzzle. He wasn't underfed and appeared healthy. She let out a sigh of relief.

But that meant someone was here.

With a gentle pat on the horse's neck, she left him and slipped out of the barn. As she rounded the building, she caught sight of the backside of a man standing inside a coop with several chickens moving about.

Should she announce her presence? Walt hadn't said anyone would be here, so perhaps she'd do well to leave and return with someone. Like Lucas.

She took a step back when the man turned and met her gaze, his frame tense and his gaunt face sporting a serious expression.

Kicking herself for not acting more quickly, she said, "Hello."

"Who're you?"

"Walt Jenkins said I could look at the property. He owns this ranch."

His expression remained wary, but he acknowledged her answer with a nod.

"Does he know you're here?" she asked.

"The land agent hired me to look after the place. To keep the riffraff away." It was obvious he considered her riffraff from the way he scrutinized her.

"Forgive my manners," she said, trying to quell her nerves. "I'm Sophie Ryan."

He wiped his hands on a rag. "You can call me Buzz."

"I'm a reporter with the Jerome Mining News. Walt asked me to come so I can write about the property and maybe help the place to sell."

Buzz made a noncommittal sound, then said, "Can I offer you some coffee?"

Sophie glanced around, aware of the isolation of her situation, and the fact that Walt had never mentioned Buzz, which led her to believe the storekeeper didn't know of him.

"No, thank you," she said. "It's getting late. Might I ask who the land agent is? In case I need to contact him for the story."

"His name is Artie Sewell."

She retrieved her notebook and jotted down the name, then she asked, "Did you know George Jenkins?"

"Yes."

"Then would you know about the bird carving beside the front door?"

"It's a nighthawk," he said. "George called this place Nighthawk Ranch."

Walt had said as much.

"It's beautiful," she said. "Did he carve it?"

"No, a woman named Moira did."

"George's wife?" Walt hadn't mentioned that his brother had been married.

"No." Buzz's response was swift and definitive. "George had no kin besides his older brother."

She was probably pushing her luck questioning this man, but she asked, "And how did you know George?"

"We'd been friends a long time. Georgie was a dreamer. He tried to make a go of the ranch, but he struggled. He debated whether he should move to town and go into business with his brother, but it didn't appeal to him." Buzz looked around. "It's a shame he's gone. Someone should take over this place who'd do right by it."

"Are you planning to buy the property?"

"Now that would be a twist of fate," he murmured.

"Since you knew George, can I ask about his search for Spanish gold?"

"Walt told you about that?"

She nodded. "It seems to be a popular pastime for some townsfolk in these parts."

"George was a bit obsessed, yes."

"Did he ever find anything?" she asked, knowing it was a rhetorical question.

"Not that I know of."

She sensed she was overstaying her welcome. "Well, I best be going," she said. "Thanks for chatting with me."

She hustled back to Roger and kicked him into a gallop. She had the distinct impression that Buzz watched her until she was out of sight.

THE TOWNSFOLK WERE abuzz about the opera being in town, so McKay had secured a seat. Would Russell or Xander make an appearance? While unlikely, he couldn't discount it. He'd had no luck today tracing leads to Xander's presence in the area. Both he and Russell were proving to be ghosts. Or nighthawks? Only appearing for a short time at dusk with their mouths wide open, consuming prey that had no clue they were even being hunted.

Confronting Bromley was an option, but McKay didn't want to do that just yet. It might cause everyone involved to scatter, including Marty Ennis, who was now a suspect.

And then there was Sophie. He'd entertained the idea of asking her to be his date for the evening, but he hadn't been able to find her. He'd stopped twice at the newspaper office—the first time Miss Bromley had said Sophie was under the weather, the second time she had left on an errand. He couldn't help but feel she was avoiding him. While it stung his pride a bit, he also worried she might've gone into the wilderness with her stolen map in search of the gold.

After having a bath, McKay put on his nicest jacket and tie, and made his way to the Masonic Hall well before the audience was due to arrive. Located on the third floor, the Jerome Opera House was still undergoing construction, but a traveling show on its way north had agreed to stop and perform.

He took up residence nearby in a shadowed corner of an alley to watch the comings and goings. People began arriving with much chatter and a general air of excitement, the ladies in fine gowns and the gentlemen in black and gray wool suits. Everyone was clearly excited to have something to do other than their usual day-to-day routine.

He scanned the many faces but none of the men stood out. Rose Palmer appeared with the woman McKay had seen at the Bromley barn when he'd been shocked to find Sophie there as well. Was that Miss Gibbons? Sophie was certain the woman had been the one who had shot him. He honestly couldn't say for certain, the distance had been great, and he was skeptical that this short and somewhat unassuming female could have made the shot. It had been the work of an experienced sharpshooter, and she didn't appear to have the fortitude for such a skill.

But if he couldn't identify her then she probably couldn't identify him. Still, he would steer clear of her, filing away her association with Rose, who was connected to Marty. And according to Sophie, Miss Gibbons was also connected to Bromley, romantically so.

And Bromley was connected to Xander.

McKay swore. Where *was* Bromley?

As if on cue, Lucas Blackmore arrived with Olivia Bromley on his arm, and behind them was her father, appearing as if he'd rather be anywhere else. Miss Gibbons sidled up to him and pulled him away, her presence bringing a smile to the dour man's face. McKay didn't miss the look of annoyance Olivia cast their way, but she did nothing.

Lucas briefly met McKay's eyes, conveying he had the situation in hand. Then Sophie arrived and in the warmth of the lamps at the building entrance she all but glowed in a cream gown.

She was stunning, and McKay caught himself staring.

Had she arrived with Lucas? Did Olivia know the two were cousins? But the couple continued forward while a man detained Sophie, and she stopped to speak with him. Her countenance immediately became stiff, almost wary, and McKay left the shadows to intercept her.

"Sophie, darling," he said, inserting himself between her and the man. "I've been looking for you. The show is about to start. We should be heading in."

Wide-eyed, Sophie looked at him, her face taut, her cheeks rosy, and she gave a rapid nod. McKay took her gloved hand and tucked it inside his elbow.

"I thought you said you were working," the younger man said to her.

"I am," she replied. "I'm sorry, Marty. I was trying to let you down gently, but Mister Lewis had already asked me to attend with him. I was trying to spare your feelings."

Marty Ennis? The man had a wild look in his eye, the air surrounding him awkward and thick.

McKay gave the man a stern look. "You can stop bothering Miss Ryan."

Marty squared his shoulders. "Fine."

McKay guided Sophie away, falling into the throng of people moving forward.

"Thank you," she said quietly.

"What was the problem?"

"He invited me to the performance, but I declined." Her subtle perfume, like a bouquet of roses, teased his senses. "And Olivia had wanted me to attend on behalf of the paper, although she's here as well. She's a bit taken with Luc—" she caught herself "—Mister Smith. I get the feeling she doesn't socialize much, but she couldn't resist the invitation to accompany him." She offered him a quick smile. "I thought I could slip in, and no one would notice me."

"That's not possible. Who was he?" he asked, to confirm his suspicions.

She glanced over her shoulder. "Marty Ennis. He stays at Rose's boarding house."

If the man was harassing her in public, what might he do in private?

She started tugging her hand from his hold and said, "I think it's fine now."

But McKay held tight. "If it's all the same, we should stay together."

They entered the first floor and began moving toward the stairs when Rose Palmer pushed her way through the throng of people and greeted them.

"You do have a beau, Sophie," she said, flicking her eyes to McKay, a gaudy necklace catching the light.

"I ...." Sophie was uncharacteristically speechless.

"I guess the incident with the horse manure wasn't a deterrent after all," Rose said. "Well, Marty won't like this, but that's all right. You were out of his league anyway, and I told him that. But I suppose you shouldn't have turned him down and then showed up after all." The censure in Rose's eyes was razor sharp, and McKay didn't care for it.

"I'm afraid it's my fault," McKay said. "Sophie and I haven't made our courtship official yet, although she wanted to. We had a bit of a fight yesterday, but it's all been ironed out. Unfortunately, Mister Ennis may have had his feelings hurt in the process, and for that I'm sorry."

Rose smiled, her countenance placating. "Of course. I just wish you had told me, Sophie dear. I could've handled the Marty situation for you. I'm glad you two are working things out. You make such a handsome couple. Tell me, how did you meet?"

Sophie frowned, so McKay interjected. "She approached me about a story regarding my work. I found her delightful, and here we are. And Marty is your nephew?"

In surprise, Sophie slid a glance at him, but McKay kept his attention on Rose, who assessed him with a calculated look.

"He's family, yes," Rose said. "Distant, I'll add, but I do look out for the boy."

"I'm sure he appreciates that."

Rose waved at someone in the crowd. "Olivia."

Olivia and Lucas came beside them.

Rose pinned Olivia with a glare. "You didn't tell me my tenant has herself a suitor."

Olivia glanced at all of them. "I'm not sure what you're talking about."

"Sophie and Mister Lewis."

Olivia's look of surprise seemed genuine, while McKay didn't miss the hard edge of Lucas's gaze.

Rose glanced at Lucas. "I'm afraid I haven't had the pleasure of *your* acquaintance."

"Nathan Smith, ma'am." Lucas gave a nod.

"Are you new in town as well?"

"I am."

"He's a shoe salesman," Olivia added, smiling a bit nervously at Lucas. "I do think we should all take our seats. The show will be starting soon."

Rose offered a serene smile as McKay ushered Sophie up the two flights of stairs, avoiding Lucas's gaze, and they took seats near the back, the only ones left.

"This is getting out of hand," Sophie said in a low voice, leaning close. "You don't need to pretend to be my beau."

"Is there another man I should be concerned about?"

"No. Of course not. I didn't come to Jerome looking for a husband."

"Duly noted. However, a young woman alone can present an easy target for the unscrupulous."

"And you're scrupulous?"

He was saved from answering when the curtains parted, and a robust woman began the performance. For the next forty-five minutes he found himself relaxing for the first time since this job had begun, enjoying an evening out with a compelling woman.

When the intermission came, he anticipated conversation with Sophie, but she excused herself, saying she needed a bit of fresh air.

"I'll come with you," he said.

"No. I'd like to speak with Olivia."

She departed in a flurry before he could argue. He thought to follow, scanning for Marty Ennis, but then Sophie found Olivia and the two made their way to the stairs.

Lucas materialized and took Sophie's seat. "Is there some reason you're romancing my cousin?" he asked, keeping his focus forward.

"It wasn't planned." McKay kept his voice low. "She needed an escort. It's a ruse."

Lucas cast an irritated look at McKay. "I told you she wouldn't be a problem, but she's resourceful. Be careful."

"I appreciate the observation." But Lucas wasn't telling McKay something he didn't already know.

McKay glanced around. No one seemed to be paying them any mind. "I need you to do something," he said. "Sophie has a map in her notebook. I need you to get it for me."

Lucas grimaced, his jaw set hard. "How am I supposed to do that? And a map of what?"

"It belongs to Charles Bromley, and she's made a copy. It may tie into what you told me about Ennis, who, by the way, has been pursuing Sophie himself."

Lucas went silent, then said, "Maybe she knows more than she's saying. Maybe she's pursuing Ennis for a story."

Except she wasn't pursuing the man if this evening was any indication. She'd had every opportunity to accompany Ennis to the show, and she hadn't taken it.

McKay's happiness over that fact wasn't lost on him. But perhaps Lucas was right.

"How am I supposed to convince her to give the map to me without telling her why?" Lucas added.

He had a point.

"Maybe romance it out of Miss Bromley," McKay said. "It seems you cousins enjoy using your charm to gain confidences. Although if I had to say, I'm not sure she knows about it."

From the corner of McKay's gaze, Lucas's face went a shade of red. Dammit. The man may have been using Olivia to get close to her father but he was also falling for her.

And McKay was falling for Sophie.

Weren't they a pair.

"How did Sophie find it?" Lucas murmured.

"How do you think?"

Lucas swore under his breath. "Is she gonna end up in jail over this?"

"Not if I can help it." And that was the truth.

But Lucas didn't appear satisfied with the answer and said somewhat belligerently, "Since you're romancing my cousin, and I don't believe it's a ruse—I can see the way she looks at you—then why don't *you* get the map?"

McKay let Lucas's insolence pass, as well as the reference to Sophie's true feelings for him. He wasn't sure he believed it. "She doesn't trust me."

Lucas gave a quiet laugh, still looking straight ahead. "All right," he said. "I'll get it. Can you give me more details?"

"It's a map for Spanish gold. I only got a quick look, but I think it's in the same area as the whiskey and gold shipments that Ennis is rumored to be involved with."

Without further conversation, Lucas stood and walked away.

So Sophie hadn't told Lucas about the map, unless Blackmore was lying about his knowledge of it, but McKay didn't think so. She was playing her own angle. For the sake of journalism? Possibly.

McKay recognized the ambition in her eyes. It mirrored his own.

CHAPTER 13

S ophie stood in the small lobby, fanning herself. Sitting beside Ben Lewis for the last hour had left her a tad overheated.

"This building was built by the United Verde Mining Company," Olivia was saying. "There are stores located on the first two floors and the fourth is used by the Masons as well as the Knights of Pythias, Woodmen of the World, and the Rathbone Sisters." Olivia paused. "Do you want to write this down?"

"Oh, yes, of course." Sophie didn't have her notebook with her since it had been too big to stash in her reticule looped at her wrist, but she dug out a piece of paper and a pencil she'd stuffed inside. As she wrote down what Olivia had told her, she said, "So you're here with Mister Smith?"

Olivia's cheeks flushed pink, a perfect match to her dress. "I'll admit I had no intention of coming, as my father wasn't going to attend. But then he changed his mind, and Mister Smith extended the invitation to me, and it seemed like it would be a nice evening, and Nathan is very ...."

Sophie didn't want to utter the word, but felt she had no other option. "Handsome?" she squeaked, because when she imagined "handsome" it was Ben who flashed in her mind and not Lucas.

Olivia didn't answer but her face said it all. She was starry-eyed. Over-the-moon. Swept away by love's passionate embrace.

Sophie's heart stuttered. Olivia's attachment to Lucas was under a pretense fabricated by Lucas. Should she tell her?

"He's a salesman, Olivia," Sophie blurted. "He probably won't stay in town long. It would be wise not to get too attached."

Olivia's face fell a bit. "You're right, of course. It's not as if it's headed to matrimony. It's just a pleasant evening out. And what about you and Mister Lewis?" Olivia's question was earnest, and Sophie felt a bit guilty for trying to warn her away from Lucas.

"The same," Sophie answered with matter-of-factness. "Just a pleasant evening with a handsome gentleman."

"I suppose we both must take care with our hearts."

A ruckus across the room interrupted their discussion. Marty was arguing with an older gentleman who looked ridiculous in a top hat. It was far too fancy for the likes of Jerome.

Sophie leaned close to Olivia. "Who's that with Marty Ennis?" she asked.

"Arthur Sewell."

The land agent.

The two men seemed to realize they had attention on them, and the conversation became more subdued. Mister Sewell did most of the talking and then he left Marty where he stood, looking a bit peaked.

"Do you think Marty's buying land?" she asked Olivia. And how had Sophie missed the fact that Rose and Marty were related?

"No. My feeling is Marty does dirty work for the man, but it's nothing I can prove."

What dirty work did a land agent engage in? Was poor Walt in jeopardy of losing his brother's ranch? On impulse she excused herself from Olivia and went in search of Walt, certain she had seen him earlier but too distracted by Ben's presence at the time. She found him just as the second act was about to begin so she didn't have much time.

"Walt!"

He turned and offered a wide smile. "Sophie, you look beautiful."

"Thank you."

"Did you make it to the ranch today?"

"Yes. In fact, I met a man named Buzz who said he was caretaking the place for the land agent."

Walt's face went from confusion to understanding. "Oh yes, now I remember Sewell saying something about that."

"You're all right with it?"

Walt nodded. "Why? Is this Buzz up to no good?"

Sophie thought it might be the case, but she had nothing but a bad feeling to go on. Not definitive proof. "No, not that I could see. I just wanted to make sure you knew."

"I appreciate it, dear," he said. "We best be getting inside, or we'll miss the start of Act Two."

She made her way to her seat beside Ben, thankful they had no chance to talk since she was sure he was itching to ask why she'd been delayed.

When the show ended and the audience dispersed, Ben tucked her hand into his elbow once again.

"You don't have to walk with me," she said, as he led her out of the building and onto the street.

"We wouldn't want your harasser to return, but I'm concerned that he lives in the same establishment as you."

Yes, that was going to be a problem. "I keep to myself," she said, and it was largely true. "I'll be fine."

"You should consider moving."

"Perhaps." But funds had been tight, and Rose had given her a reduced rate on her room. However, these weren't concerns Sophie would put on Ben Lewis, who wasn't someone she entirely trusted no matter how fascinating she found him, or how chivalrous he'd acted, as he had tonight.

"What do you think of Mister Smith and Miss Bromley?" he asked, making an abrupt change of subject.

"I'm not sure what you mean," she hedged.

"Do you think they make a good couple?"

She shrugged. "I suppose. It's none of my business really."

"I heard you were ill today, but you were nowhere to be found."

He'd been checking up on her. While Olivia might have swooned over the romance of it all, Sophie cast a skeptical eye at him.

"Doing a bit of investigating?" he asked.

"I'm a reporter. I'm always open to a new story."

"I know."

As she walked beside him, her shoulder gently bumped against his. The contact sent tendrils of electricity through her, annoying her. Why did she have to like him so much?

"I suppose you have plans to leave Jerome and move on to bigger and better things," he said.

"Why do you say that?"

"You're smart and ambitious, and driven. It's only a matter of time."

The compliment took her aback, but she soaked up the praise. "And what about you? Will you be moving on to bigger and better things when you're finished here?" And then added, "Studying those elusive nighthawks, that is?"

He grinned at her. "Maybe our story won't end here." Her heart leapt at the thought.

They came to Rose's porch, aglow from light through the window.

She faced him. "Thank you for your help this evening."

"I'm always available."

He held her gaze, the longing impossible to misinterpret.

"Why are you doing this, Ben?" she whispered.

"Damned if I know."

He kissed her, his lips warm against hers, holding the contact longer than he should but far less than she wanted. And then it was over.

"Good night, Sophie." He tipped his hat and left her.

In shock, she watched him go. *What just happened?* She wanted to call him back, to ask for a real kiss instead of that poor attempt he'd bestowed on her. Because in her heart she knew that a true kiss, one that was long and deep, from Ben Lewis or whoever the hell he was, would be something to behold. Just thinking about it made her heart race and heat slide up her spine.

Gathering her composure, she spun on her heel and went inside. What a foolish road this was. She cursed the man under her breath with every step she took up the stairs. Hadn't she warned Olivia of this very thing tonight? Of losing her heart to a man who had no permanence to him?

She entered her room, stunned to see Lucas kneeling on the floor, rummaging through her satchel.

She shut the door before anyone else knew he was here. "What are you doing?" she demanded in an angry whisper.

He at least had the decency to look remorseful as he pushed to his feet.

"My door was locked," she said. "How did you get in here?"

"You're not the only one who can pick locks. Travis taught us all."

"Are you stealing from me?" The implication filled her with disappointment. Ben Lewis might use her, but not Lucas.

And then it hit her. Ben had kissed her to delay her, not because he'd wanted to. He'd somehow known that Lucas was here.

"Are you and Ben Lewis partners?" she demanded.

Lucas sat on the edge of her bed and sighed. "Why would you say that?"

She shook her head and suppressed an eye roll. *Never mind.* "What are you looking for, Lucas?"

"Did you copy a map that was in Charles Bromley's possession?"

"Aha!" She pointed at him. "You and Ben *are* partners. He's the only one I told about that. Is he a U.S. Marshal?"

"Soph." The warning in Lucas's voice was clear.

She relented. "Okay, fine, so you came here to steal the map from me."

"It's safer if you hand it over. By the way, did you steal it from Bromley?"

"I *borrowed* it, and then I returned it."

"He doesn't know you have it?" Lucas asked.

"No."

"Well, that's something, at least."

She leaned down and pulled her notebook from a hiding place she'd made beneath her bed, then she pulled a loose paper from the back and handed it to him. It wasn't the original she'd made but a copy, but she didn't tell Lucas that. It was a failsafe, in case something happened to the original, like her cousin deciding to rob her.

He inspected it, then said, "Promise me, Soph, that you won't go following this trail alone."

She planted her hands on her hips. "Like you promised never to lie and steal from your cousin?"

"I never promised that," he said with a slight smirk.

She sat beside him. "Like you, I'm just doing my job," she said.

"Spanish gold will only attract people who are crazed."

"Perhaps."

"You wanna tell me what's going on with you and Ben?" he asked.

"Nothing." And that was the truth. She needed to keep her

heart in line from now on. "But how about you and Olivia? Are you using her as well?"

He frowned. "Ben is using you?"

"I didn't say that, but I must remind you that you're misrepresenting yourself to Miss Bromley."

"Tell me something I don't know." The anguish in his voice brought her up short.

"Just be careful with her heart," she said a bit more gently, echoing her own fears. "And yours."

CHAPTER 14

The following morning, Sophie got into the office early and finished her article about the opera, wanting to make up for her previous day off. When Olivia didn't show, Sophie left it on her desk with a note that she would be out interviewing townsfolk about the new Catholic church. She left as Joe was arriving.

"There's coffee on the stove," she said, pointing at the pot-bellied stove used both for heating and cooking purposes.

He nodded. "How was the opera?"

"Wonderful. I left my article on Olivia's desk. I'll be back later."

In fact, Sophie had already interviewed several folks for her next piece, so instead she took up a post outside the Connor Hotel and waited for Lucas. Perhaps following him was underhanded, but he'd tried to rob her, so her conscience was clear on this one.

When he departed and rode toward the smelter, she retrieved Roger and followed, although Lucas had enough of a head start that she lost sight of him. She loitered in the area as men came and went from town, and wagons stirred up dust clouds. She pulled her scarf over her mouth as the fumes were stronger here, but she became weary waiting and after a time she returned to town.

What had she expected? She was sure Lucas would follow her map and explore the trail laid out. But why was she waiting for him?

Because he'd asked her not to go on her own, and she was abiding by his request.

Enough, she decided.

She collected extra food, filled her canteen, and got oats and a water pouch from Trent so she could feed and water Roger, then she set out to the east intent on following the map she had taken from Bromley.

And where was Ben Lewis? She had no idea. Maybe he already had the map from Lucas and was ahead of her.

As she headed out, veering past the hogback where she first had found Ben, she took in the expansive view of the Verde Valley spread out before her, rimmed in the distance by the red rock of the Mogollon Rim, and her mood became lighter. She inhaled deeply since the headwind left the smelter fumes behind her, and the weight of the stress of the past several days slid away.

She needed this and hadn't realized how much until this moment.

So much worry had been sitting on her, not only about her job but also hiding her connection to Lucas, dealing with Marty, worrying about Charles Bromley and whatever he was mixed up in, the overbearingness of Rose, and Deborah's supposed wickedness. But more than any of that was Ben. And that kiss.

Why couldn't she get it out of her mind? She doubted he was dwelling on it.

It was a blessed relief to be alone, with only the sun and the sky and the wide-open land her companions. And her horse. "You've been a true friend, Roger," she said, with a pat to his neck. "Probably the only one I have here."

The distance to Pecks Lake wasn't far, maybe six or seven miles but the terrain was rugged and uneven, and she soon had to give her full attention to it, conferring with the map periodically.

At last, she came to a bluff that overlooked a broad depression, the Verde River meandering in a u-shape in the distance, a silvery snake slithering across the landscape. There was a large body of water that had collected along the river's path. This must be the lake.

The sun had set, and she was glad she had brought supplies and gear since she might need to bed down for the night. She'd done it enough times growing up that it didn't concern her. She would make a quick inspection of the area at first light tomorrow and then return to town to be in the office on time. She feared she was starting to stretch her work relationship with Olivia too much, which had started only with the appearance of Lucas. And Ben.

She studied the map once more. The gold was located near the lake. Or in it? With more scrutiny, the gaps and imprecise distances were becoming readily apparent, and she was beginning to doubt she would learn anything useful from this excursion. That would make Lucas happy, she supposed.

Without warning, a searing pain split the back of her scalp and she fell from Roger, hitting the ground with a bone-jarring thud. She wheezed for breath, and then her vision went dark.

SOPHIE AWOKE, her cheek pressed into the ground and dust in her mouth. The ache in her skull was sharp, and she moaned as she tried to swallow against her parched throat. Gritting her teeth, she pushed upright. It was night and everything around her was pitched in black, but the inky outline of rock walls was visible, along with a small, starry patch of sky.

She was in a hole, and there appeared no way out.

Her fingers fumbled in her braided hair and located a large lump above her neck. She grimaced from the touch, which ignited a new wave of pain. Something had struck her. No, *someone* had struck her, and then they'd dumped her here if the stiffness in her right shoulder and hip was any indication. Looking upward, she was unnerved by how far she must've fallen.

She could've been killed. A shiver rippled through her that she had managed to make it through such a heinous act.

She hadn't seen it coming.

Roger!

Had he been taken by whomever had done this? Or worse, had they hurt him? Panic gripped her, and she gasped for breath.

Please be okay.

She steadied herself. She needed to think rationally about this. She could yell for help, but what if the perpetrator, or perpetrators, came instead? There were prospectors in the wilderness, the very men Rose had been pushing her to write about. Had one of them done this? For her horse and gear?

She decided that Rose was officially insane.

Her satchel was still crosswise across her torso. As she rummaged through it, a growing unease began to build. She dumped the contents to be sure.

Her notebook was gone.

Whomever had attacked her had taken it. For the map? She at least had another copy, or rather Lucas did. She would have to get it back. And if by some chance Roger had escaped, then maybe he would make his way back to town and to the livery. And then maybe someone would come looking for her.

She quickly dismissed the hopeful theory, slumping in defeat. It was no plan to hang her future upon. She'd told no one where she was going, and Trent would hardly think to say something unless she was there to prompt him with a bit of coin.

For a long moment, she considered what it would be like to die a slow death with no food or water. Then anger pulsed through her. How dare she even consider surrendering to this?

No. Not today.

With renewed resolve, she stood and inspected the rock walls again. Maybe she had missed something. Maybe there was a crevice through which she could escape.

A rope slapped against the rock, startling her. Craning her neck, she winced as a new wave of pain blasted through her head.

Olivia?

Unbelievably, the woman was leaning over the edge.

SOPHIE COLLAPSED on the ground beside Olivia. The woman had worked hard to pull her free, anchoring a rope around a knotty bush that had thankfully proved up to the task.

"How in the world did you find me?" Sophie asked between gasps, her heart bursting with immense gratitude.

"I saw it." Olivia wiped her sleeve across her forehead, her hair coming free of the pins. She shoved a clump aside, leaving a smear of dirt on her cheek. "A man used a slingshot and knocked you from your horse. I tried to get to you before he threw you over the side of this ledge, but I didn't have a weapon. I had no way to protect you, so I had to wait until he was gone."

"Who was it?"

"I didn't recognize him."

"Where are we?" Sophie asked.

Olivia rubbed her hands on her skirt. "Not far from Pecks Lake."

"What are you doing out here?"

"What are *you* doing?" Olivia countered. "Clearly you weren't at work again."

"Neither were you!"

They went silent and then Olivia laughed, filled less with humor and more with relief. Sophie joined her until tears threatened.

"Have you seen my horse?" Sophie asked, emotion thick in her throat.

"No, but mine is nearby." Olivia paused, then said, "I was following my father."

"Why?"

"He said he was going to test one of his inventions, and he offered vague answers to my questions. I told him he couldn't go alone, and he insisted he wasn't, that Miss Gibbons was meeting him in town and would accompany him."

"And you let him go?" Sophie asked.

"I couldn't exactly stop him, but I did follow."

"That was dangerous."

"I'd say it was more dangerous for you. Why are you here?"

"Exploring." It was the truth, at least. "What was this invention your father had with him?"

Olivia looked flummoxed. "It was some kind of rubber suit that a man would wear."

"Underwater apparatus," Sophie confirmed.

"Yes, I think so, though I can't fathom what he's doing with it."

"Where is he now?"

Olivia sighed. "I'm not certain. I lost him as I neared the river. I was certain this was where he was headed since it's the only body of water out here, but now I'm not so sure. What do you know of all this?"

"I think it may be tied to the gold."

Olivia groaned. "Not you, too."

"I can assure you I've not lost my mind over it. I thought it might be worthwhile to pursue for a story. Walt Jenkins told me about his brother's interest in it, and your father's." She didn't mention the map in Mister Bromley's possession since Olivia might not take kindly to Sophie having "borrowed" it.

"Why didn't you ask me about this sooner?"

"Because I figured you'd say no," Sophie answered quietly.

"You'd be right about that. So you think my father is trying to find the gold in the lake?"

"I do."

The sound of an approaching horse reached them, and they both went still.

"We need to hide," Sophie whispered.

"Follow me." Olivia scrambled away from the edge of the hole, staying low.

As Sophie passed a shrub, she wrangled a branch free, scratching her hands.

"What are you doing?" Olivia demanded, having reversed course when Sophie had stopped.

"We need to cover our trail." Sophie backtracked several yards and brushed the dirt with the bushy end, although it was more skeletal than lush.

"Here, come up onto these rocks." Olivia waved her on. With hope, this would be enough to confuse whoever was behind them, probably checking the hole.

"We should hide," Olivia said. "There's a place over here."

"No," Sophie argued, believing they should head away from the lake. She grabbed Olivia's arm and dragged her onward through the uneven desert landscape. They ran as fast as Sophie could muster without tripping, trying to navigate the terrain in the dark.

Then something hard and big slammed into her.

CHAPTER 15

McKay immediately realized his mistake when he landed on the soft body beneath him.

Sophie!

Not a Weaver.

Lucas had subdued the other runner. Even in the darkness, McKay knew it was another woman.

Olivia.

Dammit.

Sophie twisted beneath him and shoved hard against his chest. Then she saw him.

"Ben?"

He stood and pulled her to her feet. "I'm sorry."

"Why did you attack me?"

"I thought you were someone else."

Lucas had Olivia upright as well, who was pushing against him.

"What are you doing here?" Olivia asked at the same time McKay and Lucas questioned them.

"We're exposed," Lucas added.

"Agreed." McKay grabbed Sophie's elbow and ushered her to the west.

"There's someone behind us," she said.

"Noted."

She was out of breath as she said, "They attacked me, knocked me out, then threw me into a hole."

He stopped abruptly. "Are you hurt?"

"No."

He willed his racing heart to slow, but it was on a trajectory never traveled, because Sophie was a path that would never come his way again. That was blindingly obvious.

Ignoring the rush of feelings for this woman, he guided her to where he and Lucas had hidden their horses.

Once they were concealed, he faced her, Sophie's gaze flicking between him and Lucas.

Hell.

She would want to know why he and Lucas were together. Lying to her was getting more untenable by the minute.

"I don't understand what's going on," Olivia said. "Why are all of you out here?"

Lucas cast a hard look at McKay. The jig was up, and McKay couldn't do it anymore. Kissing Sophie the night before had been the beginning of the end.

"You can tell them," he said to Lucas.

"We're U.S. Deputy Marshals. Undercover."

Sophie narrowed her gaze at McKay. "I knew it."

"How did you know?" Olivia asked.

"Lucas is my cousin."

"Who is Lucas?"

Sophie pointed in her cousin's direction. "Nathan Smith, shoe salesman." Then she turned her attention to McKay. "And you're not Ben Lewis, ornithologist."

"Benton McKay."

She nodded slowly, a glint in her gaze, a challenge, and he held it longer than he should have.

"Are you Sophie Ryan?" Olivia asked. "Or are you some kind of undercover agent as well?"

"No, no. I'm Sophie. Reporter and curious bystander, just trying to crack this case."

"What case?" Olivia asked.

Sophie returned her attention to him and Lucas. "Yes, what case?"

"Our assignment is to locate and apprehend the Weaver gang," Lucas said.

"The train robbers?" Olivia exclaimed. "They're here?"

"We believe so," McKay said.

Lucas stepped closer to Olivia and took her hand. "We believe your father might be involved with them."

She yanked free of him. "Are you delirious?"

"Why are *you* out here, Olivia?" he demanded.

She gaped at him, her body stiff with anger. "You think I'm involved too? Is that why you've been flirting with me? Am I part of your assignment?"

Lucas put his hand over her mouth and pulled her against him. "You need to be quiet," he said in a low voice.

Olivia stopped fighting against him. She nodded, and he released her. Then he said, "What do you know about the map?"

"What map?"

"The one possessed by your father."

She huffed in frustration. "My father has lots of maps. I have no idea where he gets them, but I'm guessing your referring to a treasure map for Conquistador gold?"

Everyone was silent.

"Look," she whispered. "I'll admit my father is obsessed, but that doesn't make him a criminal. And I can assure you that no one from the Weaver gang has been to our home."

"That's not true," McKay said. "He met with Alexander Weaver two nights ago."

"How do you know?" she demanded.

"I was there."

"So was I," Sophie added quietly. "In your barn."

Olivia rubbed her temple. "My father is a good man."

Lucas reached for her again and this time she let him keep her hand in his. "Then maybe we can talk to him and get him to lead us to the Weavers' hideout."

Lucas met McKay's gaze, obviously looking for approval, and McKay gave a slight nod. He didn't believe that Bromley was as innocent as they would all like to believe, but for now he was their best connection to the Weavers.

"Why did you come out here, Miss Bromley?" McKay asked.

"I was following my father. He was insisting that he needed to leave town to test his latest invention. When I told him he couldn't go alone, he said it was fine, that Deborah Gibbons was accompanying him. It didn't feel right, so I followed them."

"Where is he now?" McKay pressed.

"I don't know. I lost him several hours ago. And then I saw a man attack Sophie and drag her to a drop off that had no escape route, so I waited until I could get her out."

"And I'm forever indebted that you did," Sophie answered.

"You both shouldn't be here," Lucas said, his voice punched with emotion.

"I was following the map, same as you," Sophie replied. "I knew you had given it to Ben." Her scowl was subdued as she turned to him. "What should I call you? Benton? Mister McKay? Marshal sir?"

Her anger flashed to the surface, and he wished they were alone so he could address it properly.

"Ben is fine," he murmured. "You said the man had returned?"

Sophie nodded. "Maybe. We heard a horse."

He said to Lucas, "We need to investigate."

"Agreed."

"You two stay here," McKay said. "Stay hidden. Do you know how to shoot?" he asked Sophie.

She nodded.

"Lucas, does she know how to use a gun?" he asked, not taking his eyes from Sophie. He didn't miss the irritation that crossed her face from not believing her answer. But he needed to be sure.

"She does."

McKay had a gun holstered to his hip, but he also had one in a shoulder strap hidden beneath his jacket. He pulled that one, flipped it around, and handed the butt to her. She took it and checked it, assuring McKay that she understood how to use it.

"Try not to shoot us," he said.

"Try not to sneak up on us, then," she countered.

He smiled, then with a flick of his head he indicated for Lucas to follow him.

———

Sophie's heart pounded as U.S. Deputy Marshal McKay disappeared into the night with Lucas, her suspicions confirmed. He was the good guy. She crouched beside Olivia.

"Nathan is your cousin?" Olivia asked.

Sophie felt a bit sheepish. "Yes. I'm sorry I couldn't tell you. He was undercover, but I didn't know much more than that. I'm in the same situation as you. I didn't know about Ben Lewis."

"Some reporters we are, huh? I didn't even realize what my own father was involved in."

"Don't be hard on yourself. But now that we know, maybe we can help each other."

"Sophie, I have to find my father. I have to convince him to stop whatever it is he's doing."

"I understand," Sophie said. "But maybe he can help locate the Weavers."

"It's risky. Look at what happened to you!"

The sharp pain had subsided, but Sophie was still nursing a dull headache.

Olivia craned her neck to look beyond although there was nothing to see in the shadows. "I can't stay here. Not after what you've all told me."

"No, Olivia!"

"What if something's happened to him? I have to go look."

Before Sophie could protest further, Olivia sprang up and was gone. Sophie groaned with frustration. She couldn't leave the other woman out there alone, especially after all the effort she'd exerted to save Sophie. Had Olivia not found her, Sophie might not ever have been found.

Reluctantly she followed. With hope, they'd regroup with Lucas and McKay later.

CHAPTER 16

McKay searched the surrounding area with Lucas but found no sign of anyone, although tracks were in abundance. There had been multiple individuals coming and going, and he and Lucas came to what he believed to be the hole where Sophie had been dumped. Olivia had the foresight to retrieve the rope she'd used, so the perpetrator likely had concluded that Sophie climbed out on her own. But a quick inspection, even in the darkness, showed it to be near impossible.

"Do you think you could tell your cousin to mind her own business and stay out of ours?" McKay said to Lucas as they both leaned over the edge.

The resignation in Lucas's voice was hard to miss. "I can try."

Neither of them acknowledged the truth of the situation. They weren't close to solving this case, and Sophie and Olivia were now involved, putting their safety at risk.

McKay pushed back to his feet and dusted off his hands. "Could we send them both to Phoenix for a holiday?"

"Until this is over that would be a solid plan."

But it was wishful thinking.

"I'm staying out here," McKay said. "At daybreak, I want to search the area further."

"Good idea," Lucas said. "What about the women?"

"You should take them back to town."

But they soon discovered the ladies were gone.

McKay's irritation that they couldn't follow one simple instruction was outweighed by a new rush of concern.

Lucas scouted the perimeter. "I've got their trail," he said, his displeasure obvious. "They left on their own."

"Why doesn't that surprise me." But the anxiety in McKay's chest eased.

He and Lucas mounted their horses and followed the tracks. They found the women a quarter of a mile away, riding together on one horse and heading back to town.

Lucas cut them off. "Why did you leave?" he demanded.

"Olivia wanted to find her father," Sophie said.

"And did you?" Lucas said to Olivia, anger in his voice. His careful demeanor around Miss Bromley was cracking.

Olivia lifted her chin. "No. And you don't need to use that tone with me. Whatever we were, Lucas, it's over. You lied to me. It's clear to me you never cared."

"You have no idea how I feel. And you're not traipsing out here at night any longer. I'm taking you home. McKay will stay, and he'll look for your father." Lucas shifted his attention to Sophie. "You're coming too."

Sophie swung down from Olivia's horse. "No, I'm staying. I was only going with Olivia so she wouldn't be alone."

"Sophie, for once in your life will you listen to me?" Lucas said. "It's not safe. You've already been attacked. You need to get your nose out of this."

"I appreciate your concern, but you're not my father. And you *should* return with Olivia. You don't know who might be at her home with her father."

"I don't need you chaperoning me," Olivia said to Lucas. "Despite everything, I don't believe my father would harm me."

That remained to be seen, but McKay didn't say it aloud. Instead, he said, "Sophie, ride with Lucas. I'll find your horse."

She crossed her arms. "I said no. And I'll find my horse myself. I was planning to come back for him anyway, if he's still out here. If you want me to help you search for tracks, *Marshal McKay*, I will, otherwise I'll do my own reconnoitering. Don't worry, I still have your gun."

It was clear to McKay they were getting nowhere. "All right, you can stay," he said. "But you're not to leave my side. Lucas, take Miss Bromley home."

"I'm trusting you with her safety," Lucas said to him. "Please don't take it lightly." Then he added with emphasis, "Sir."

"I won't."

Olivia kicked her horse into a gallop and Lucas quickly followed.

Alone in the hills with nothing but the stillness of the night around them, McKay extended a hand. "Unless you wanna walk," he said to her.

The starch in her spine was the only indication of her mutiny. The chill in the air matched the coldness of her fingers as he closed his palm around them, and she swung behind him with a surprising agility, tucking herself against his backside.

"Are you cold?" he asked.

"No, I'll manage."

He knew better than to argue with her.

"There's no reason for you to be here," he said.

"So you'll share what you learn with me?"

No.

"It's personal now," she added.

"In what way?"

"Someone tried to take me out. He must know who I am. He must be worried about my journalistic skills."

The thread of sarcasm and humor in her tone was subtle but it was there, and the smile sprang to McKay's lips of its own accord.

"I promise I'm not trying to be an impediment to your job," she continued. "But I feel I must point out that if not for me, you'd still be lying out on the hogback, crow bait by now. Or maybe nighthawks? Do they eat meat?"

"The meat isn't of the human variety. Beetles, moths, grasshoppers, that kind of thing." He guided his horse to the south, letting The Belgian find her footing while he scanned the surroundings.

"You took your cover seriously."

"I wanted to be an ornithologist when I was young," he admitted.

"The boy who liked birds."

And then she went silent, which was just as well since they were entering the area where she'd been captured. McKay suspected the man who had attacked her was gone, but perhaps in the light of day he'd find a clue. Was Charles Bromley diving in Pecks Lake for Spanish gold? Had Xander and Russell been here as well? And most importantly, had it been one of them who had hurt Sophie?

Sophie was cold and sank deeper into her duster, flipping the collar up to protect her neck, regretting that she'd left the scarf he'd given her in her room. McKay sat a few feet from her, appearing unaffected by the chill. After retrieving Roger, McKay hunkered down to await first light. She'd decided to keep his gun.

She'd been beyond happy to find her horse, and Roger had been unharmed. He'd wandered from where she'd been attacked by some distance with her gear intact; the only thing taken was her notebook. She'd lost not only the map but all her notes for potential stories she had been working on. Thinking about it only made her head hurt more, the aftereffects of her attack catching up to her. There was so much to discuss between her and Benton McKay, but fatigue pressed on her, and instead she dozed off only to awaken with a start. The eerie silence of the night had been almost soothing, but her ears rang as if something loud had accosted them.

McKay was beside her, a blanket draping her.

"Thunder," he said quietly. "It's not close. With hope, it won't reach us."

"I dreamt of a hole filled with water. Thank you for the blanket," she added, pulling it to her chin.

"You were coiled like a turtle trying to hide in its shell. I couldn't let you suffer."

"Such a gentleman, McKay." With his shoulder a hair's breadth from hers, she gave up her annoyance and rested her head against him, closing her eyes again, but sleep eluded her.

"How long have you been a deputy marshal?" she murmured.

"Two years." His deep voice filled the space between them, causing her to shiver. "I was working for the sheriff in Albuquerque, and he recommended me to the position, encouraging me to go after it."

"Because you're good at lying to people."

"Are you really angry about that?"

She harbored a secret yearning that he might've told her because he'd wanted to, but she knew it to be foolish and would never admit to it. "No," she replied. "And I'm sorry that I compromised Lucas."

"You've both been a complication I hadn't anticipated."

"Your secret is safe even if they try to torture it out of me."

"They? Did that man hurt you?"

"Except for the bump at the back of my head, no. But he did take my notebook which included my copy of Bromley's map. I'm guessing you have the one I gave to Lucas."

"You had two copies," McKay said. "Smart. So whoever attacked you is also a treasure hunter."

He reached around, not disturbing her resting place on his shoulder, and gently felt the back of her skull. His hand was warm, and his arm shielded her face from the cold, but she hissed when his fingers found the large welt.

"It's the size of an egg," he said. "This was more than a knock on the head. Why didn't you say anything?"

"It's fine, really." She reached her hand back, grazing his, and felt the wound crusted with blood. "I didn't realize it had bled. I'll clean it up at the boarding house."

"No, we'll deal with it now. You took care of me when I was shot. Let me take care of you."

"I'd say you're getting the better deal."

He offered a brief smile, then retrieved a kerchief and his canteen and set to work gently cleaning away the blood.

"What did he hit you with?" he asked.

"I don't know. Olivia said it was a slingshot, so a rock, maybe?"

"The wound doesn't look deep, thankfully."

When he was finished, he gently moved her braided hair back into place.

"Thank you," she said. "And I'm stronger than I look." She faced him, determined to present an unyielding front.

"I can see that." He cupped her cheek, his palm warm.

She leaned away. "I'm not falling for that again."

He dropped his hand. "What are you talking about?"

"That kiss last night. You were just trying to distract me so Lucas could sneak into my room and steal my notebook."

"That's not true. I didn't even know he was there."

"But you told him to get the map from me."

"Yes, because I didn't want you doing this." He indicated their surroundings. "Coming out here, alone. You could've been seriously hurt tonight, Sophie. This is *my* assignment. Not yours."

"You have no authority over me," she countered.

He sighed. "No. I don't. I've tried my damnedest to conduct myself with discretion and care for your safety, but you've managed to upend it at every turn. And I'll have you know that I kissed you because I wanted to. I want to now." He ran a hand down his face. "But I apologize if I've offended you. That's the last thing I'd ever want to do."

The carefully laid barrier around her heart began to dissolve. "You didn't offend me. I was embarrassed because I seem to have an … affection for you."

"Do you like me, Sophie Ryan?" he teased, bumping her shoulder with his.

"Just enough to be a nuisance."

He watched her, holding her gaze, then he slowly leaned over. Her pulse hammered in her veins as a shiver of anticipation rippled through her. She didn't withdraw this time and he brought his lips to hers.

His face was rough with whiskers, his lips soft and hungrier than the previous kiss. Every nerve in her body was on fire, chasing away the cold and replacing it with heat and need and desire.

She had wondered what kind of woman he liked, what kind of woman left him distracted and frustrated and alive with excitement. She very much wanted to be that woman.

He deepened the kiss and she shifted to meet him more fully, clasping the back of his neck to keep him with her, her hands and face and body eager to touch him, relieved that she finally could.

As he explored her mouth, she was emboldened to show him she knew what she was doing, despite her limited experience with the opposite sex. She shifted to face him more fully and slid onto his lap, startled by his reaction to her between her legs, hard and firm.

He stopped abruptly. "This is a bad idea," he said, panting for breath.

She nodded, trying to collect her thoughts. This was perhaps a tad faster than she'd anticipated. "You're right. You're a lawman and I'm a reporter, and we'll surely have a conflict of interest as this case unfolds."

But it was a smokescreen, and he chuckled his understanding.

"And you're afraid that I'll demand marriage," she continued, teasing him in return. "I assure you I won't."

"You won't?" he said, lines marring his forehead.

"I don't want to get married."

"What if I did?" he countered.

"Do you?"

"Doesn't everyone?"

The lightheartedness she was going for faded away. She shook her head. "No. There was a time when my sisters and I agreed that getting married was so very confining, narrowing a woman's choices in life. We all concluded we wouldn't pursue it."

"And they haven't?"

"Well, my sister, Sarah, is married, but it was an accident really."

"She was with child."

"No. Well, yes, she is expecting, but that's not why. Jack married her so she could join his expedition in the Painted Desert. She's the one I told you about who studies paleontology. That's the study of dinosaurs."

"I know what it is," he said with amusement.

"But it turned out Jack was really in love with her, and she with him. My pa was very unhappy—he thought that Jack took advantage of her when he was simply being a gentleman—but my mama brought him around eventually."

McKay put more distance between them, and she shifted off his lap, missing his warmth immediately.

"What's wrong?" she asked.

"I don't want your pa to think I'm taking advantage of *you*."

"Because you are?"

McKay took her hand in his. "No, of course not."

"Maybe I'm taking advantage of you."

"Sophie, this is complicated."

She smiled. "I know. You need to find the Weavers, and I need to find the Spanish gold."

"Why the gold?"

"That story is going to be my ticket to a job in Dallas. If it overlaps with the Weavers, then we should work together."

He went silent.

"Oh," she said. "You're one of those."

"And that is?"

"You like to work alone. It must be an inconvenience having Lucas around."

"It's not. It's just that ... I had this case under control."

"Did you?" she asked. "You were shot, Ben. If I hadn't have found you, what would've happened?"

"And I'm grateful that you did find me," he replied, frustration tinging his words. "But I can't do my job while looking out for you all the time."

"Wait, so now I'm simply in the way?"

"No, of course not. In the beginning, I thought you might be tied to the Weavers."

That brought her up short. "You thought I was a train robber?"

"You did steal that map from the Bromley house."

"I *borrowed* it, and if you must know, it's all been in service to *you*."

"Me?" He frowned. "I thought this was for your epic news story that would get you out of this dusty little nowhere town and onto bigger and better things."

She grumbled under her breath. Was he romancing her because he thought she would lead him to the Weavers? Damn. Had she fallen for his charm again?

But wouldn't she do the same in pursuit of a story? She wanted to believe the answer was no, but was he right? Was she as opportunistic as he was?

"You're correct," she said. "I can't wait to get out of Jerome."

CHAPTER 17

As the stars faded against a gray canvas, McKay considered the woman sleeping beside him. He'd kissed her twice now, and it was probably a mistake but that didn't seem to quell the desire any less.

After their brief argument, she'd tucked herself back into her turtle position and fallen asleep, except this time she'd made a point not to touch him.

It was fine. Really it was. It was better this way. And if he kept telling himself this, he was sure to believe it. Eventually.

He left her and tended the horses hobbled nearby. He and Lucas had come here based on her map. If Bromley had been at the lake testing his underwater equipment, they had managed to miss him. And who had attacked Sophie? The man had taken her notebook, so it had to be related to the gold. The Weavers were tied up in this as well since Xander was working with Bromley on the inventions, but McKay couldn't fathom why. They had plenty of gold. Why would they pursue a treasure hunt that was based mostly on hearsay and myth?

Sophie was awake when he returned, grimacing as she probed

her wound at the back of her head. Purple bruising was forming at the base of her neck.

He knelt beside her. "It's looking nasty."

"Have I grown a second head?"

He gently probed the welt, ignoring his disappointment that she startled when he touched her. "I probably shouldn't have let you sleep. You could be concussed."

"I have been known to cuss."

A smile tugged at his mouth, accompanied by relief that her sense of humor was intact.

"Are you always this happy in the morning?" he asked.

"I know you're being facetious, but I'll answer you anyway. I shared a room with Sarah and my usually good disposition annoyed her, so I made it a point to be extra cheerful most mornings."

"This is you being cheerful?"

"At least you won't have to drag my unconscious body back to town." She pulled away from his touch and stood, as did he.

"I never made you drag me to town," he said.

"But it was a distinct possibility in the beginning in the adit. Which, by the way, was more dangerous than me being concussed."

He cleared his throat. "All right, I confess the adit seemed like a good idea when I couldn't find the Weavers in town. It gave me the ability to watch the coming and goings on the hogback road." He paused, then said, "You've had a long night, and for that I'm sorry. I'm taking you back to town before I scout around. I'm worried about your head. And you shouldn't be alone."

"I must point out that I'm not alone since I'm with you. And don't be ridiculous. We can scout now before any evidence might disappear." She held up a hand. "I no longer have a headache."

"When you return, you shouldn't be left unattended." Was he offering to stay with her? Impossible of course. "You should tell Rose that you fell," he added quickly to cover the tracks of his heart.

"Let me just answer that with a no up front."

"What's wrong with Rose?"

"She's nosy," she said. "And there's her association with Deborah Gibbons."

And Marty Ennis. "Maybe you could stay with Lucas," he suggested.

"I'm not supposed to know him."

"What about Olivia?"

She frowned. "What about her?"

"Why don't you stay with her, and then you could keep an eye on her and her father."

Sophie narrowed her eyes. "Are you asking me to spy for you, McKay?"

"I've a feeling you're going to keep poking around whether I tell you to stop or not." But was she safer at the Bromleys'? He wanted to believe Olivia's assertion that her father wouldn't willingly put his daughter in danger. And moving Sophie out of Rose's Place would get her away from Ennis's attention.

"Are we partners now?" she asked, her eyes lighting with hope.

"No."

Her face pinched in frustration, but the spark remained in her eyes. And that spark was going to be the end of him if he wasn't careful.

"You could ask Lucas to ask Olivia on your behalf," he said. "I bet she'd do it then."

She scoffed. "After last night? Did you not witness the fireworks flying between them?"

"I did." He leveled his gaze at her until a flash of understanding registered.

"You're implying they have some kind of love match," she said.

"You said it. I didn't."

Sophie mulled over this information, then said, "You and Lucas will leave when this case is over. You'll move on, and Olivia's heart will be broken."

Tightening the cinch strap on The Belgian, he said quietly, "I'm not in love with Olivia."

He glanced up in time to see the raw vulnerability in her eyes. "I'm glad to hear it," she said, then squared her shoulders. "Perhaps I should advise Olivia to guard her heart, and to pursue her own ambitions of running the newspaper."

"That's probably wise. It doesn't help to let emotions guide your path." But as hard as he'd tried to keep his own under wraps, they were tripping him up more and more of late.

"You're not very trusting, are you?" she asked.

And just like that his feelings for her burst past the barriers he'd carefully constructed. "You're young, you're beautiful, and you're smart, Sophie." The truth spilled from him like floodwater. "You're going to do great things."

The vulnerability appeared again, her reaction to his words squeezing his heart. But she swiftly wrestled her reaction into submission. "What you're really saying," she said, "is you regret kissing me, and that until this case is resolved, we'd best keep it professional between us."

He nodded, the gesture wooden and empty. "Yeah."

"And on that day, you'll leave."

He didn't answer, focusing on his horse's rig, any possible response clogged in his throat.

"But I'll have my story," she added. "And then we'll both have what we want."

SOPHIE KEPT the low-throbbing headache to herself. She didn't want McKay to hover over her like a nursemaid, pretending to care. But he did care a little, didn't he?

You're young, you're beautiful, and you're smart, Sophie. You're going to do great things.

The compliment had shot through her like wildfire, making her burn white hot. But after such a declaration shouldn't the man have scooped her into his arms and kissed her senseless? When he hadn't it was clear as a hammer between her eyes that the compliment was meant as a barrier, a way of putting her off. A way of saying goodbye, in a sense.

And this was why her head was hurting.

They mounted their horses and were soon backtracking through the events of the night while she did her best not to think about McKay's kiss, since it made her heart race and her limbs feel weak. How in the world did a woman get anything done when she was in love?

But she wasn't in love, she reminded herself. Lust, maybe. Something she'd read about in her books. And that was surely all McKay had felt in return.

But was lust so bad? It didn't require commitment. It didn't require longevity. And in the short-term, it would quench this longing she'd developed for Benton McKay.

A glance at him sitting so tall and assured on his horse ignited her hunger anew. If they were alone, she could remove his shirt and admire his muscled frame, visible the night she'd picked a bullet from his shoulder. Granted, lust hadn't been on her mind then, but how quickly things could change.

She could learn his mouth more thoroughly than she had during the night, she could press her body against his and show him she was feeling as much physical attraction as he was.

He was, wasn't he?

But he wanted to keep things professional.

Get a hold of yourself, Sophie.

She used the kerchief on her neck to wipe off the perspiration on her brow.

After inspecting the area around her attack and finding nothing useful, she had followed McKay to the edge of Pecks Lake. There were fresh tracks of horse and wagon.

"So Bromley came out here to dive in the water," she said, scanning the swollen waterway from the recent heavy rainfall. In the distance were Indian ruins.

"Seems possible." Ben's gaze was unreadable as he scanned the area.

"It's so open. Why would the Spanish have hidden their gold here? Retrieving it from the lake would be so difficult."

"Maybe the water was shallower back then, or even nonexistent. Maybe they planned to come back for it, and then these plains flooded."

She tugged her hat low as a gust of wind blasted them, the horses dancing in response. The thunder from the night had left the morning sky filled with dark, puffy clouds, and Sophie had already resigned herself to returning to town in the rain.

"We should head back," he said.

They hadn't ridden far when Sophie noticed a boot protruding from the shadow of a rocky escarpment.

"McKay!"

He turned his horse and rode back to her as she dismounted and rushed over to the body.

"Sophie! Careful!"

McKay hastily put himself between her and the unconscious man, his gun in hand, blocking her from getting any closer. He knelt beside the gray haired and filthy older man.

"What is it about this area and knocking people to the ground?" she muttered. "Is he dead?"

McKay checked his pulse. "No."

The man stirred.

Sophie peered over Ben's shoulder. "Are you all right?"

With an unfocused gaze, the man said, "What happened?"

"We found you lying in the dirt." McKay helped the man sit upright.

"Did someone attack you?" Sophie asked.

The man sighed and shook his head. "No. It's Mabel. My mule. She must've tossed me again."

"We'll help you find her," Sophie said, but then she gasped as McKay pulled the man to his feet. He'd been lying on her notebook.

"That's mine!" She snatched it up. "Where did you get this?"

"I found it."

She flipped through the book, dirty, but her notes were intact. When she got to the location of the map in the back, only a torn page was present. She exchanged a glance with McKay, understanding in his eyes.

"Where's the page you ripped out?" she demanded.

"I didn't remove nothin'. I just found it. In fact, I was riding toward it when Mabel threw me. I guess I landed on top of it when my lights went out."

His story was unbelievable, but she had to admit that this old man with his well-worn clothing hanging from a stooped frame likely didn't have the strength to knock her from a horse and then drag her to a hole.

"Did you see anything out of the ordinary yesterday?" McKay asked.

The man dusted off his clothes. "Nope. Just business as usual out here."

Sophie tucked her book into her satchel. "What does that mean?"

"I'm just prospectin'." He shifted his gaze between them. "I'm Harry."

"Ben Lewis." McKay met her eyes with another unspoken exchange. *Stick to my cover.* "I'm a bird watcher. This is Sophie Ryan. She's a reporter."

"Are you two sightseein'?"

"Something like that," McKay answered.

Harry chuckled. "I'm wise to it. The canoodling, I mean."

Sophie's cheeks heated.

"You've seen right through us, Harry," McKay said, and Sophie glared at him. It might be partially true, but McKay didn't need to confirm it. The man had the audacity to grin, and he was wickedly handsome, igniting the annoying lust that she'd developed for him. He shifted his focus back to Harry and asked, "How's the prospecting out here?"

Harry scanned McKay from head to toe. "A man can't divulge all his secrets now, can he?"

"No, I suppose not."

"Where do you think your Mabel might've gone?" Sophie asked, wondering if the animal existed at all.

"Prob'ly toward the lake."

Sophie could read McKay's mind. He didn't want to backtrack, but they hadn't gone far. "We'll help you find her," she suggested. Maybe they could trip up Harry in his story.

"Miss Ryan can ride with me," McKay said. "Harry, you take her horse. His name is Roger."

"That's kind of ya."

Sophie was soon tucked behind McKay, crammed into his saddle with him, their bodies touching more intimately than during the night when his kiss had opened a vault of need inside her she'd had no idea existed.

How was she supposed to endure this?

With her arms wrapped around him, she peeked past his shoulder as his horse went back to the lake, inhaling the scent of him, a mix of musk and an underlying smell of lye soap, the sharp acrid smell somewhat muted by the past day of outdoor endeavors. She committed it to memory.

"Do you trust Harry's story?" she asked.

"Of course not. Could he have been the man who attacked you?"

"I don't know. I never saw him. From what Olivia said, he wasn't a frail old man."

McKay twisted at the waist to meet her gaze. "Do I smell?"

Embarrassed that he'd caught her sniffing him like a dog, she said, "No more than I do. Why?"

He frowned and faced forward again. "I think it's clear that whoever it was wanted that map, so it's likely they aren't associated with Bromley."

"And what does that mean?"

"We know Bromley is connected to the Weavers," he said. "So there's someone else playing in this game."

"Harry?"

McKay shrugged. "Maybe." He glanced over his shoulder, his gaze landing on the old man riding her horse behind them. "I'll admit he's not much of a threat."

But a thought occurred to her. "What if Mabel the mule is a lie? What if he plans to steal Roger much the way he stole my notebook?"

She swiveled her torso as much as she could to look behind them. Harry lagged about thirty feet behind, but he hadn't tried to sneak off. Yet.

With her breasts pressed more firmly against McKay's back, a pleasant sensation went through her. When McKay didn't try to lessen the contact, she felt emboldened. She brought her mouth close to his ear. "Might you slow down so we don't lose him?"

She couldn't see so much as sense the change in McKay and his awareness of her. His spine stiffened, and his shoulders rose and fell in what she was certain was frustration. She wanted to tell him she understood, that she felt same, but she held her tongue. Instead, she basked in the knowledge that he wasn't immune to her.

"Don't worry, Soph," he said, casually using the nickname that Lucas did, "I won't let him take Roger from you."

CHAPTER 18

McKay slowed his horse to let Harry catch up. If he didn't, Sophie might start nibbling on his ear and while he was fully aware she was goading him, part of him didn't much care what her motivation was and instead his mind was sinking into all the ways he could get her into his bed.

She wasn't a saloon girl, and he damned well had no intention of treating her like one, but she was so willfully playing with fire that his resistance was stretched thin, ready to snap.

Harry pulled too hard on Roger's reins once he was close to McKay's horse, causing Roger to bob his head in annoyance.

"Easy, Harry," McKay said. It would seem Mabel likely had a reason to dump the old man.

"You two could just get a room at one of the saloons instead of coming all the way out here," Harry said, ignoring McKay's admonishment.

McKay cleared his throat as Sophie gasped quietly behind him. Harry's solution was on point, but no need to openly agree.

Harry leaned back in the saddle to peer at Sophie. "Women like to be romanced." He grinned at her.

"I'll remember that," McKay replied. Probably best to change the subject. "How long have you been in these parts?"

"I pitter patter around. I come to this area at least once a season."

"How long do you stay?"

"Weeks, I s'pose."

"Have you seen any strange activity out here lately?" McKay asked.

"You ain't no bird watcher, are ya?"

"There seems to be stories floating around about Spanish gold," Sophie cut in.

Harry laughed, derisive and dry and loud as a dog bark. "Is that what you're lookin' for?"

"I'm doing a story for the newspaper," Sophie chimed in. "Mister Lewis is helping me track down the details."

Harry let out a grunt expressing his obvious skepticism. "Those are just tall tales."

"Would you know any?" Sophie prodded.

Harry considered her question. "I've heard a few, but I consider it fodder for the weak."

"Why is that?"

"Some folks don't like to do the hard work. Prospectin' can be backbreaking, with little reward. Ain't it nice to pretend there's some giant stash out there waiting to be discovered by some poor fool lucky enough to find it?"

"If it's true," McKay said, "then they wouldn't be a poor fool any longer."

"True 'bout that."

As they crested a rise in the terrain, a mule appeared. Presumably the ornery Mabel.

"There she is," Harry muttered.

Sophie gasped once again, and McKay knew it was at the sight of the poor animal. Her hide was a patchwork of bald spots, and her frame was far too gaunt.

Harry dismounted and approached her. She seemed placid enough and accepted his taking her reins. His gear was still intact as well as his ratty saddle.

"We have to do something," Sophie whispered, and McKay couldn't disagree.

Her hand gripped his arm as she dropped to the ground. "Mabel doesn't seem too angry," she said to Harry.

The old prospector shifted a wad of tobacco in his mouth. "She can be moody."

Starved, more likely.

"Why don't you bring her to the livery in Jerome," Sophie suggested. "The boy, Trent, is good with animals. He'd give her some tender loving care."

"What're you sayin'?" Harry asked, his hackles clearly up.

"I'm saying that Mabel needs a good grooming, and her shoes need reshod." Sophie's ire seemed to rise with each word she spoke. "And I'm guessing she wouldn't mind a good rest and a stall filled with hay for a few days, even a few weeks. It's the least you can do for an animal that has clearly done much for you."

"You're an opinionated little thing, aren't you?"

McKay moved his horse closer, ready to cut off Harry should the man decide that Sophie had crossed a line. Which she had, but McKay couldn't blame her.

"I'm not stating opinion," she said. "Only the facts, Harry."

He looked at Roger. "What about him?"

"He's not mine. He belongs to the livery."

"So you can't trade him for all time, but how about for a few days? You take Mabel and baby her, then I'll come for her by say ... Monday."

"How do I know you'll keep your word?" she asked. "And that you'll treat Roger well?"

"You want the story of the gold, right? I'll give it to you."

Sophie went quiet, then said, "And some actual gold."

Harry guffawed. "You're loco. Why would I do that?"

"Insurance. I'll return it when you return Roger. And you promise to take better care of your mule."

He swore under his breath, but said, "All right, it's a deal."

McKay helped Sophie change her gear with Harry's, saying quietly, "I hope you know what you're doing."

"We're getting information, aren't we?"

"That remains to be seen. And I don't think you should ride Mabel."

"I agree. I'll walk."

"No, you won't. I will."

She smiled at him. "I knew you were a gentleman."

Once the switch was complete, Sophie focused on Harry. "Now, the story."

"Let's go to the overlook." He guided Roger down the path until they reached the expansive view of the valley that encompassed Pecks Lake.

Big billowing dark gray clouds decorated the landscape with an ominous touch, but slanted sunlight broke through, reflecting on the water, causing it to shimmy and sparkle.

Having walked The Belgian, McKay positioned himself between where Sophie and Harry now stood.

"There weren't always water here," Harry said. "When the Spaniards came through, the Conquistadors they was called, it would've been the 1500's. This place was known for its ore deposits even back then, and the local Indians, the Yavapai, would mine the copper, makin' trinkets and what-not. Those Spanish fellas were lookin' for El Cibola—some city of gold that was part of their lore—and the Indians and their trinkets was too promisin' not to pursue. It's said they found a vein of gold as long as Hull Avenue and as wide as a horse. They mined it and then they hid it, some say in Sycamore Canyon."

"Where's that?" Sophie asked.

"'Bout ten miles north."

"But you don't think so?"

Harry shrugged. "It ain't ever been found. You'd think it would've by now."

McKay had no doubt Harry had done his share of scouting Sycamore Canyon. Probably with poor Mabel in tow.

"But that's not all of it," Harry continued. "This lake here is cursed."

"How's that?" McKay said.

"Well, the story goes that some fifty years ago, a prospector found somethin', they say around Sycamore. So maybe it was the Spanish gold. But he went to great pains to hide it, and no one can say for sure where it is. But then he came here and lived for a time up around that bend."

"Where the ruins are?" Sophie asked.

"Yep. They call it Toozigoot. So this fella was said to hide the gold around here somewhere."

"In the lake?" McKay said.

"Why do you say that?" Harry asked.

McKay bit back an explanation and exchanged a look with Sophie.

"Well, that wouldn't make sense, now would it?" Harry said. "Why would you throw it in the lake?"

"Because you prospectors seem to be a paranoid bunch," Sophie said under her breath. Then she added more loudly, "It would be a good hiding place."

Harry considered the suggestion, watching the water beyond as the wind picked up.

"But how would you get it out?" he murmured. "Well, I steer clear of this lake. The curse and all."

Sophie tightened the stampede strings of her hat against a gust of air. "And what is this curse?"

"That fella I told you about drowned in this lake."

"That's terrible," she said. "But how is that a curse?"

"It's the Spanish gold. He took it, and then he died."

"That seems a bit farfetched," she said.

"Irregardless, the gold ain't here." Harry made the statement with confidence. "It ain't *anywhere*."

"I've heard there was a man," McKay said, "who was hired to bring crates to this area from a distillery in the hills."

McKay could feel Sophie's questioning gaze on him, as if she'd said aloud *why didn't you tell me this*.

"Crates?" Harry's face pinched into a look of skepticism. "I've never heard 'bout that. It must be men braggin' about doing somethin' darin', is all."

"What's so daring about stashing crates of liquor?" Sophie asked.

"Sounds to me like someone was *stealing* said liquor." Harry bookended his statement with a raised brow.

They were getting nowhere. Harry was talking in circles now.

"Who told you the story of the gold and this lake?" Sophie asked.

"That'd be Rosie."

"Rose Palmer?"

"Yep."

CHAPTER 19

While McKay had offered to walk, Sophie saw no reason for that. She rode behind him once again while Mabel trailed behind his horse. It was comforting to lean into him since her gut was twisted in a knot over Harry having Roger. She prayed the old coot wouldn't mistreat her horse. And that's when she knew—Roger *was* her horse. When she had enough money saved, she would ask Trent to convince the owner of the livery to sell the animal to her, and she would take him with her wherever she ended up. And if she couldn't take him, she'd send him back to Texas and Dove Crossing. Her pa would take good care of him.

It helped that Harry had given her a small bag of gold dust. She was certain he wouldn't have parted with such a treasure if he had no plan to return to town in a few days. Instead, his face was bright with the knowledge that he would have a strong animal over the next few days to accomplish whatever it was he had planned. Was Roger about to be involved in something sinister?

She would need to convince Trent to take Mabel in while Roger was "away" for a few days. With hope, he would be agreeable. And eventually, she would need to convince Harry to give up Mabel permanently. The poor girl needed help. That knowledge helped Sophie make peace with the uncertainties of the situation.

Maybe it was Sophie's imagination, but the mule already seemed happier, walking behind McKay's horse without much prompting, gaining more pep to her walk with each step she took away from Harry.

But then the rain came. It was inevitable. They'd been lucky to have avoided it for as long as they had. The visibility was terrible, so McKay insisted on stopping. They huddled together, man, woman, horse, and mule.

"Has Rose told you the same story she apparently told Harry?" McKay asked, his face far too close to hers.

"No," she said, letting the brim of her hat bump his, creating a shelter for their faces from the buckets of water unleased on them. She wondered if they could get to the mine adit. Were there still blankets and food stashed inside? But she estimated they were too far to get there quickly. "I never thought to ask, to be honest. Do you think she had an agenda in spreading that tale to Harry?"

"It's crossed my mind."

Sophie was thinking the same. "I'll question her when we return. Don't worry, she loves me. I remind her of her daughter who passed away. She's been married three times and owns land outside of town from her last husband. Believe it or not, she used to run a distillery and make whiskey."

"She made whiskey?" McKay asked. "Was the distillery on this land she inherited?"

"I'm not sure, but if I had to guess I would say yes."

"And where is this property?"

"I'm not sure," she said. "Why? Do you think she's hiding something? Does this have something to do with those crates of liquor you told Harry about?"

"Maybe."

"I'll see if I can find out."

"No. I'll take care of it."

"Why won't you let me help?" she asked.

"Because Marty Ennis has already been bothering you, and he's related to Rose. And Lucas and I believe he's involved in whatever's happening here at Pecks Lake."

"He's the crate man." *Interesting.* But she knew McKay well enough by now that she would get nowhere arguing with him, so she said what he wanted to hear. "I'll leave you to it then."

"Why are you being so agreeable?" he asked, suspicion in his tone.

"I have no interest engaging with Marty," she answered truthfully.

"All the more reason you should move to the Bromleys'."

She frowned. "Are we back to that?" There was something presumptuous about moving in with Olivia even if Lucas did plead on Sophie's behalf. And Sophie wasn't convinced that Lucas's opinion was going to matter much to Olivia now.

"Then move to the hotel."

"I can't afford it," she said reluctantly. "Rose has been gracious enough to give me a discount since I was new to town and alone."

"What's the catch?"

"There's not always an ulterior motive," she countered.

He held her gaze.

"Okay, fine. She wants me to pursue prospectors in the area and write about them in the paper."

McKay frowned. "Why?"

Sophie shrugged. "I'm not sure. And after meeting Harry …. Wait." She pulled out her notebook and retrieved the paper Rose had given her with the list of names. "There's a Harry Lesar on here. Do you think that's our Harry?"

"He did say he knows her."

"But Harry's not out there cracking the prospecting business wide open, and besides, he'd never agree to an interview. His paranoia was very clear."

"He did give you that gold dust. It surprised me. He must really want Roger."

"Has he struck it big?" she asked. "Maybe we should follow him."

McKay sighed. "As he's not my prime suspect, I can't prioritize that, and I presume a man like Harry knows these hills better than most. He could probably shake a tail easily."

She glanced at the mule. "If only Mabel could talk. What has she seen, I wonder?"

The onslaught of rain abated, and Sophie shivered, unable to stop.

He pulled her to her feet. "I need to get you back to town."

Beneath light sprinkles and intermittent thunder, they made good time and entered Jerome by early afternoon. He dropped her at Rose's Place.

"I'll take the animals to the livery," he said. "I'll make sure Mabel is groomed, fed, and given a warm stall."

"You'll tell Trent about Roger?"

"I'll take care of it. Don't worry, Sophie. And I'll find Lucas and have him smooth the way with Olivia."

"What will you say?"

"Your head injury oughta do it," he said. "Get some rest. Tell Rose to check on you hourly, at least."

"And I tell her I fell?"

"Off your horse," he said. "In this rain."

Rose appeared at the front door, then rushed down the porch steps. "Sophie, what on earth? You're soaked. Mister Lewis, I'm not sure what you think you're accomplishing by keeping her out in the elements for so long, but she's going to catch her death of cold."

She put her arm around Sophie, then she paused and looked at Mabel. "Where did you get that mule?" she asked.

"From the livery," Sophie said, glancing at McKay as she told the lie. "Why? Do you know her?"

"Hmmm." But Rose didn't say anything more, ushering her inside.

———

SOPHIE SAT in the boarding house parlor with a blanket around her shoulders. Rose had taken one look at her and insisted she have a hot bath. Thankfully, she had left Sophie alone in a room near the kitchen while she bathed, so Sophie had been able to clean the welt in private. And then Rose had tucked her onto the sofa.

Rose came into the room with a tray, set it on a nearby table, and poured Sophie a cup of tea. There was also a plate of chicken dumplings.

"Drink this," Rose commanded. "And when you're ready, you need to eat something."

In truth, Sophie was exhausted, and Rose's mothering was welcome if not a bit overbearing.

With the aroma of the food reaching her, Sophie could no longer hold back her hunger. She set the teacup on the saucer and reached for the plate, balancing it on her lap as she dug into it. She was starving.

Rose sat across from her, her cheeks glowing pink and her apron sporting wet patches from the bath she'd labored over for Sophie.

"Sophie, I feel it's my place to say that you shouldn't be gallivanting around with Mister Lewis. It's unseemly, but even more, he's putting your poor health to the test. No man is worth that."

Sophie couldn't reply because her mouth was full of food, so she nodded her acknowledgment. What could she say anyway? McKay wasn't really her beau, so his actions weren't ungentlemanly no matter how they appeared.

"And what's more, he's not properly courting you," she continued. "So I'm offering my services to act as your chaperone since your own mother and father can't be here."

Sophie swallowed and took a big sip of tea. "Thank you, Rose."

Now that she was starting to feel better—she was clean, warm, and dry, and no longer famished—she felt equipped to broach the subject of Harry's story, but then Deborah Gibbons strode into the room, a strong waft of perfume accompanying her.

"Deborah," Rose said. "I want you to meet Sophie Ryan."

The woman set a glass of sherry on the side table, took a seat, and fluffed her maroon skirt. "We've met," she said with a condescending nod.

"It's nice to see you again," Sophie said somewhat grudgingly.

"Miss Gibbons and her son have moved in."

That took Sophie by surprise. "How nice," she murmured.

But it wasn't. Would Sophie, would all the tenants, have to worry about this woman possibly drawing a gun on them?

"Is Ned here?" Sophie asked.

Deborah took a sip of her sherry, then said, "He's upstairs doing his schoolwork."

Sophie went back to her food, but her appetite was waning. "And where were you living before?"

"Outside of town, but with Ned in school it was becoming too difficult. This arrangement will work better."

"They'll have the room beside yours," Rose added, taking up her embroidery.

Sophie stretched her lips into a smile. McKay's directive that she reside with the Bromleys was starting to sound better.

"Oh, now I remember that mule," Rose said, pushing her needle through the fabric. "It belongs to Harry Loser."

Sophie frowned. "That's his name?"

"No," Deborah answered. "It's Harry Lesar."

Rose chuckled. "It sounds like loser, which he is. How did Mister Lewis get the animal? Is Harry dead?"

"No, we ran across him out by Pecks Lake," Sophie answered.

"What were you doing out there?" Rose demanded.

Thinking fast, she answered, "Well, he's on your list, Rose. I thought to interview him."

The reply seemed to please the woman. "And what did you learn? What big finds has he discovered?"

Was that it? Was Rose trying to track claims in the area?

"Well, it can hardly seem surprising that he had no intention of sharing such information," Sophie said. "But he did tell us of the curse."

Deborah's nose wrinkled. "Curse?"

"That a man had died at Pecks Lake because he found Spanish gold, or else he put it there after finding it in Sycamore Canyon. Harry said you told him the tale, Rose."

Rose shrugged, taking up her sewing again. "A little tall tale to keep the riffraff away."

Riffraff? The caretaker Sophie had met at Nighthawk Ranch two days ago had said something similar. What was his name? *Buzz.*

"Why are you trying to scare people away from the area?" Sophie asked.

"Oh no, I'm not," Rose replied, a tad too swiftly. "Others tell the story too. Harry is probably misremembering where he heard it."

"If someone were to find gold out there," Sophie said, "wouldn't the United Verde Mine Company have ownership? Joe Atkins mentioned the mine uses it for runoff from the smelter."

Rose shook her head. "No. Whoever finds it would keep it. It's the common law of the Rule of Finds."

"I believe there's also a federal antiquities law," Sophie added.

"That wouldn't apply here." Rose's rebuttal was fierce. "It wouldn't belong to them, because it was found and moved, and the man who did it is now dead. It would be finders keepers."

Rose's passionate and somewhat confusing response made it clear Sophie had tripped a nerve with the woman. "I suppose such a find would have to be sorted out in the court system."

"I would take care, Sophie, about spreading these stories in the newspaper," Rose said, a slight tremble in her hands as she focused on her stitching. "It would distract the miners."

So Rose wanted her to dig up the activity of the prospectors but leave the storytelling out of it.

"Do you think those men actually read the paper?" Sophie asked skeptically. From what Joe had said, most of the miners worked grueling hours and when they had time off, they were in town finding respite in the saloons and down on Hull Avenue with the working girls.

"She's got you there, Rose," Deborah muttered.

Suddenly tired of dealing with Rose and the appearance of Deborah, as well as the discomfort of Marty being so close, Sophie blurted, "The Bromleys have invited me to stay with them."

The surprise on Deborah's face was hard to miss. "What for?" she asked.

"Olivia would like the companionship." Sophie mentally crossed her fingers. With hope, Olivia wouldn't say no.

Rose's affront was obvious as she made a dismissive sound. "That's ridiculous. Olivia is quite fine with her own counsel. You'll stay."

Sophie set her plate aside. "I'm afraid I've already agreed."

"You're moving out?" Rose's ire was apparent. "Now?"

"Yes. I'd thought of leaving in a few days, but I can see that with Deborah and Ned moving in, you could use my room for him. Then he would be beside his mother. I'll just gather my things and leave shortly. I'm paid up through the week, and you may keep it in lieu of my short notice."

"Well, I ...." Rose was flustered, and Deborah's brow had frozen in a permanent furrow.

"Might I have Ned run a message to Mister Lewis?" Sophie asked.

"What for?" Deborah's only response seemed to be on repeat.

"To remind him that he promised to help me move my things."

Deborah shook her head. "Ned is busy."

"I'll do it." The boy entered the room, obviously eavesdropping. "What will you give me for it?"

Sophie cast an annoyed look at him, but she couldn't fault his logic. "A silver coin."

Ned grinned, plopping down on the settee beside Sophie.

"Let me just write the note," she said. "And then you can go immediately." She went to the small desk Rose kept in the corner and wrote a quick note, then folded it and handed it to Ned. Once he was on his way, she said, "I'd best be getting upstairs to pack my things. Thank you for the tea and supper, Rose. Good evening to you both."

Sophie took the stairs to her room at a glacial pace, rewarded when Deborah began talking quietly. "What now? I can barely get around Olivia as it is. Now there'll be *two* of them."

"You went too slow with Bromley," Rose replied. "What happened to that charm of yours, Sally?"

Sally?

"Coltrane beat it out of me. And Bromley doesn't want to get married again!"

"I thought you were going to discredit his mind."

"It doesn't work like that, Aunt Rose," Sally replied in a fierce whisper.

Sally and Rose are related?

"Don't worry," Rose said. "We'll deal with it. We still have Habison as backup."

Habison? Did she mean the town marshal, Scott Habison?

"What if Bromley never finds it?" Sally asked.

"He will. We're almost there."

Sophie hustled upstairs before the two women caught her listening. She opened and closed her door in one swift movement, then leaned against the door, closing her eyes, her heart beating fast.

Did they expect Bromley to find gold in Pecks Lake? And by Rose's own admission, he would have automatic ownership of it. If Sally were his wife, would she then take it from him? This plan had so many holes in it, and when it fell apart, because surely it would, then what? Would Sally start shooting everyone?

Sally the sharpshooter had a certain ring to it.

And how were the Weavers connected?

CHAPTER 20

McKay went to Sophie's boardinghouse and removed his hat as he stepped through the entrance, a bell ringing to announce his arrival.

Rose came from the kitchen, wiping her hands on a towel, and gave him a look of clear disdain when she saw him. "Sophie is upstairs," she said flatly. "I'll let her know you're here."

He gave a nod of acknowledgement.

"You're a bold one, aren't you, Mister Lewis?"

"I'm not sure what you mean."

"Sophie's a young woman alone in a town she hardly knows. Are you the one who convinced her to stay with the Bromleys? If I didn't know better, I might think you were taking advantage of her."

"I'd never do that, ma'am."

But the woman's admonishment pricked his conscience, because it was true he was intruding in Sophie's life.

Rose went upstairs to get Sophie, who soon appeared with two packed bags, which McKay took from her.

Rose looked visibly upset. "You can return anytime, Sophie dear." She pulled her into an embrace.

"Thank you," Sophie said into Rose's shoulder, her voice muffled.

Once McKay was outside with Sophie, she asked, "How's Mabel?"

"She settled in right away."

"What did you say about Roger?"

"I gave Trent an extra dollar to give us a few days to get the horse back. He said he'd smooth it over with the livery owner."

He had brought a buckboard to make it easier to transport Sophie's things. He helped her to the bench seat, sat beside her and released the brake, then flicked the reins to get the horse moving.

Sophie glanced back at the boarding house. "Any word from Lucas?"

"He's headed to the Bromleys' now."

"I hope this works, because I don't think I can return to Rose's."

"Had enough?"

"Something like that," she muttered.

"Want to talk about it?"

He guided the wagon down Main Street.

"Because we're partners." But her tone was deadpan. "I'll think about it."

"Did you tell her about Harry?"

"She guessed we'd seen him," she answered. "She recognized Mabel. His last name is Lesar, so he was on the list she'd given me."

McKay sensed Sophie was holding back.

"Let me ask you this," she said. "Are all the Weavers men?"

"Yes."

"No women?"

"Not that I'm aware of. Why?"

She shrugged. "Just a thought."

They fell into an awkward silence as McKay concentrated on the dark road out to the Bromley homestead. Lucas's horse was still tied to the hitching post in front of the house as McKay brought the buckboard to a stop.

"Here's goes nothing," Sophie said as she stepped down before McKay could assist her.

He grabbed her bags and followed her up the porch steps as Sophie knocked on the door.

Olivia answered with a smile that didn't hide the strain she was obviously feeling. "Sophie, it's so nice of you to come. Please come in. You too, Mister Mc ...." She caught herself. "Mister Lewis."

"Miss Bromley."

Olivia pushed open the screen door and they stepped inside. McKay set the bags down. In the parlor, Lucas sat with the elder Bromley, tea service on the coffee table.

"Uh, Mister Lewis and Miss Ryan, do you know Mister Smith?" Olivia was struggling to remember everyone's names, stumbling through the introductions.

"Of course," Sophie said. "It's nice to see you again. Mister Bromley, thank you for having me in your home."

The older man frowned. "It seems you're staying with us."

"I've explained that you're not happy at Rose's," Olivia clarified. "And we're always here to help our employees."

Sophie nodded. "I appreciate your hospitality." But she also looked slightly baffled.

Too late, McKay realized that he'd forgotten to tell her that, according to Lucas, Olivia hadn't discussed anything with her father yet regarding the man's involvement with the Weavers.

Mister Bromley looked at McKay. "You the bird man?"

"Yes, sir. Pleased to meet you."

"You're studying the nighthawks. George Jenkins had quite the love of them. You been down to Nighthawk Ranch yet? It's not far from here."

"I have."

Sophie swung her gaze at him. "When?"

"It was a few weeks ago." The day he'd arrived. He'd wanted to speak with George but when he'd learned the man was dead, he'd gone anyway, wanting to see the place where he'd lived as a child. It had been bittersweet.

"So you met Buzz?" she asked.

"No. Who's that?"

"The caretaker," she replied, her brow furrowed.

"A lot of men come here looking for gold," Bromley said, changing the subject, "or silver."

Sophie shifted her attention to the man. "I thought all the mines were copper."

Bromley nodded. "They are. That doesn't stop the opportunists." His gaze landed on McKay again. "We don't abide opportunists around here."

"Papa!" Olivia admonished. "Are you threatening Mister Lewis?"

"I'm just being clear on the boundaries, son. Birds better be all you're looking for."

The air was thick with intimidation.

"I understand the boundaries, Mister Bromley." McKay's voice was low, almost as lethal as the other man's.

Lucas stood. "I should be leaving."

"As should I." McKay gave a nod in Sophie's direction. "Ladies."

Lucas rode beside the buckboard as they headed back to town.

"How did you convince Olivia to stay quiet?" McKay asked.

"She gave it some thought and decided on her own. What now?"

"We need to find this land Rose Palmer owns."

Sophie followed Olivia upstairs, each of them carrying a valise.

"The room is small," Olivia said, "but the bedding is freshly laundered. Lucas said the injury from last night is concerning. I'm next door if you need anything during the night. My father is at the end of the hall."

They entered the modest room with a lavender quilt on the bed and an oil lamp glowing on the nightstand. "If you would just wake me periodically," Sophie said.

"Of course. I'm a light sleeper."

Olivia deposited the bag in a corner of the room, and Sophie did the same. Now that they were out of earshot of Mister Bromley, Olivia quietly closed the door. "Do you trust them?" she whispered.

"Lucas and McKay?"

Olivia nodded, her blonde hair starting to fall free of the pins.

"I .... Well, I don't know McKay very well, but Lucas is a good man."

Olivia's face dissolved into relief.

"Did you tell your father that you'd followed him to Pecks Lake?" Sophie asked.

"No. After considering everything, I decided that I should wait. Is that why you're here? To help me spy on him?"

Sophie paused, then silently agreed. "I'm thinking yes. But I *was* happy to get out of Rose's boarding house. Deborah Gibbons has moved in."

Olivia scoffed. "Well, that's a relief. She's been trying to live here ever since I hired her."

"I think she wants to marry your father."

"Yes, I know. What last tendril of influence I have over him has managed to delay it."

"That's good," Sophie said.

"Why don't *you* like her?"

Sophie considered telling her everything—that Deborah had tried to kill McKay, that she was Rose's niece and had neglected to share it for some reason, that she was likely trying to marry Olivia's father to steal the gold "Sally" and Rose seem certain he would soon find—but she held back, unsure if trusting Olivia with this information was wise. She hadn't even shared it with Lucas, or all of it with McKay.

Seeking something true, Sophie said, "She's been very rude to me."

Olivia started laughing, spurring Sophie to join her.

When it finally ebbed, Sophie added, "And while Rose has been kind, she's inserted herself in my love life far too much."

"She does like to be in the thick of gossip," Olivia admitted. "You and Marshal McKay, huh?"

Sophie's stomach did a somersault. "Yes."

"I guess we're hopeless."

"I guess we are."

From the look in Olivia's eyes, it was clear that McKay had been right. There was more between Olivia and Lucas than just this case. Sophie knew Lucas. He wouldn't dally with a woman under the pretense of using her to gain information. His feelings must be sincere, and it was obvious that Olivia felt the same.

Envy grabbed hold of Sophie. She wanted the same with McKay. But she needed to take care with such yearnings. They would only lead to disappointment.

"Can I ask you something?" Sophie said.

Olivia nodded.

"Rose said she owns land outside of town that she inherited from her husband. Would you know where it is?"

"Yes."

CHAPTER 21

Sophie rose early and slipped out of the Bromley house once Olivia had gone back to bed. She had woken Sophie twice during the night, and the third time Sophie had decided to remain awake. She was feeling much better, and the welt was now half the size.

Since she had no horse of her own, she was forced to borrow the mild-mannered mare the Bromleys kept in a small shed beside the barn where Bromley housed all his inventions. She had her saddled quickly enough, and they headed west toward the Haynes Camp where a rare gold vein had been found according to Olivia. Dawn was just breaking, and with luck Sophie would be back before Olivia or her father knew she had been gone.

Locating Rose's property proved a challenge despite Olivia's directions. Sophie didn't know what a distillery would look like but when she found a wooden building tucked into a depression in the land, and a well-used road leading to it, she suspected this was it.

The building was padlocked, but before she fiddled with it, she walked the perimeter, pausing at the back of the building when she heard another horse approach. Should she hide? But she'd left the

Bromley mare ground-tied. Whoever it was would know someone was here.

The toe of her shoe hit something hard, a bright flash in the dirt. She leaned down and was shocked when she pulled a misshapen coin from the dirt. Was it possibly ....

Spanish gold?

"What're you doing here?"

Sophie jumped at the sound of the voice.

Marty Ennis.

"You startled me," she said, fisting her hand with the coin at her chest.

"I saw a horse. Didn't expect to find you out here, Sophie. Why are you skulking around?"

She had to think fast. "I was on my way to the Haynes Camp, but I'd heard that you work a distillery for Rose, so I thought I'd stop and say hello."

"You really shouldn't be out here alone. And why are you going to the camp? Doesn't that other reporter cover such things?"

"That's true, but I'm an inquisitive sort. Since I was out this way, I thought I should stop by. I've been wanting to come out here and see what this was all about." She waved her hand to encompass the building they stood beside. "But then I saw that it was locked, so of course I knew that I should come and see you. But here you are, so that was fortunate."

Marty seemed to lose his edge a bit, and Sophie forced a smile onto her face.

"You shoulda asked before coming out here," he said, adjusting his hat.

"You're right." She stepped back, prepared to scoot around the side of the building and away from him. "I should go."

"No! Wait."

She stopped, still clutching the coin.

"We could meet later," he said. "And I could tell you more about the whiskey and such."

The clench of Sophie's stomach was a clear indication of what a bad idea this was, but she nodded anyway, eager to flee. "That would be lovely," she agreed.

"What about that Ben Lewis? What's he gonna say about this?"

"Oh, well. This is just work. There's no reason to tell him."

Marty seemed to like that, making her heart pound in her chest, and for all the wrong reasons.

"I'll fetch you from Rose's since we both live there. How about six o'clock? We could have supper at the English Kitchen. I like their chop suey."

"I'm not staying at Rose's any longer, so what if I meet you there?"

"You've moved?" His face pinched in concern. "To where?"

"The Bromleys'." She could think of no reason to lie, since he could easily find it out.

"It's so far out of town," he said. "Why would you do that?"

"Rose's is too busy. I can't get a good night's sleep. Olivia Bromley offered to let me stay with her and her father, and it seemed like the right move."

He nodded. "Yeah, sounds like it could be. I guess I could come there and get you."

"No, that's fine. I'll be at the newspaper all day, so I can just walk over. I'll see you then."

She spun on her heel and shuffled away, all but running to the mare, and was mounted and riding before Marty decided to detain her further. Somehow, she would need to get out of their supper date.

Since she'd told him she was here to visit the Haynes Camp, she rode west on the main road to make her cover look convincing, the early morning sun bathing the land in golden light. But after a time, she turned back, and caught sight of Marty on his horse headed to town. On impulse, she returned to the wooden building, knowing she'd never get a better chance to investigate.

When she arrived, she took a moment to examine the coin, since she'd had to stash it in a rush. It was misshapen with a Jerusalem cross on one side with the words 2 *eskodos* and a shield on the other. But it was bright yellow. If it were three hundred years old, wouldn't it be more tarnished? She stuck it in her boot to hide it, then hobbled the mare behind the building in case Marty returned. It would buy her a little time at least.

She retrieved her tools from her satchel and immediately went to work unlocking the padlock. It was tricky, trickier than Mister Bromley's front door, which was surprising considering he was an inventor. But maybe inventing an unpickable door lock hadn't been high on his list of projects.

In addition to tinkering with locks with her cousin, Travis, Sophie also had learned about handcuff mechanisms from her Pinkerton cousin Kate. This padlock never stood a chance. She removed the chain and slipped inside, leaving the door slightly open to let sunlight illuminate the dark interior.

Right away she sensed this was no distillery, although she wasn't familiar with the parts and pieces of a still. Chopped wood occupied one corner, nearly six feet tall and as wide. A thick iron pot hung from a tripod made of the thickest iron rods she had seen, and a tool to grab the pot was nearby.

Marty wasn't making liquor, he was melting something. There were empty crates and piles of hay, and then she found the molds. Coins. And it appeared to match the one she had in her boot. She hadn't found Spanish treasure. Marty was melting gold and turning it into coins. Coins that could be mistaken for Spanish gold.

En route to the office, Sophie discussed her Marty run-in with Olivia, and they agreed Olivia would accompany them on their supper date. Sophie was relieved, but she had kept the existence of the gold coin to herself. All morning, she pretended to do work at her desk while ruminating over what to do. Should she tell McKay? Lucas? Or Olivia?

Joe was in this morning, and when Olivia stepped out for a meeting with Mayor Sterling, Sophie grabbed her notebook, still stained with dirt, and sat in a nearby chair.

"Can I ask you some mining questions?" she said.

"Sure." With gray at his temples, he was much older than both Sophie and Olivia, but despite his more extensive experience, he'd been supportive of Sophie as she'd learned the ropes of putting out a weekly paper.

"How easy is it get gold out of the ground? Like up at the Haynes Camp?" She thought it best to start with a generic question.

"Well, it's the same as with copper. The miners chisel out the ore, it's brought to the surface, and then it's processed to extract the metal, whether it's gold or copper."

"Why isn't there more gold found around Jerome?"

Joe shrugged. "I'm not sure. Gold is often found side by side with copper. The Haynes Camp is a bit of a peculiarity, however."

"What about the tales of Spanish gold around these parts? What do you know about that?"

Joe laughed. "Been listening to the stories, have you? There are men that like to gamble, who like the faro tables, and then there's men that like the speculation of a huge stash of riches, and they cling to the tales as if they're real."

She sighed, not bothering to hide the sarcasm in her voice. "Well, tell me how you really feel, Joe."

"I'm not saying there isn't merit to it, but it's hard to weed out the facts from the fabrications." He leaned back in his chair. "But ask me what you wanna know."

"If the Spaniards left gold behind, in what form do you think it would be?"

Joe considered her question, his slight frame somewhat engulfed by his chair. "It would depend on whether they brought it with them, or if they processed gold found along the way. I suppose if they had it with them, it would be in the form of coins or jewelry. Maybe a brooch or a clip, something like that. If they made contact with the Indians here and used their techniques, it would probably be ingots, probably small so they could be transported and dispersed among pack animals more easily."

"Would there be any way to verify a find?"

"A find?" Joe frowned. "Do you know something?"

"No. But ... all right, I'm writing a novel," she blurted out the deception. "It's something I'm doing on the side, so I don't really want anyone to know."

"Ah," Joe said with a knowing nod.

"There's some great lore around here. I thought it would make for a compelling story, so I was thinking ... what if my hero finds, say, a gold coin in the dirt somewhere, and it has Spanish markings. That would be proof the Spanish were here, right?"

"I suppose so."

"Would there be some way to test the coin, to ascertain its validity?"

"Maybe. You could, or rather your hero, could see an assayer in town and ask them about it."

She took notes as if it were for her fake novel, but also because she wanted to keep track of the information Joe was giving her. Could she take the coin to a local assayer? How would she explain how she'd gotten it?

"But I think it highly unlikely the Spanish would have left gold behind," he added.

"Why?" Sophie asked.

"The Spaniards came to the Americas, initially South America and Mexico, specifically for gold. They plundered the Aztec and Inca civilizations for it. They stole and looted and took over existing mines with the sole intention of sending the riches back to Spain. They would hardly leave it behind. They were brutal and would have simply taken what they wanted from the Indians."

"What if some of the local population fought back?" Sophie asked. "What if they hid the booty?"

"I suppose it's possible."

"How would I know, or rather how would my hero know, if what he has is gold and not something else?"

"Well, you could melt it down. A fire assay looks at the weight of the gold before and after removing impurities, and that would give the purity. But it's destructive. If you had an actual coin, you wouldn't want to destroy it. But you can put it in a glass of water. If it sinks, that's a good indicator it's gold. Pyrite, which is fool's gold, will float because it has a much lower density."

Joe then reached for a pile of papers and began to flip through them. "I had a friend down in Phoenix who claimed to have seen a Spanish coin that had surfaced at an assayer's office. He sent me a drawing of it."

He found it and presented it to Sophie.

"The Spaniards would gather as many gold trinkets as they could from the local populations in South America and melt everything down, then make ingots, and sometimes coins too, for easier transport and to pay the troops. These types of coins were called escudos."

The drawing looked remarkably like the coin she had found.

"Do you notice anything?" Joe asked her.

She shook her head.

"Look at the words 2 *eskodos*. It's a misspelling. It should be *escudos*. I don't think the Spanish would make a mistake on their own coins. This piece was a counterfeit."

"Oh, I see. But it's still gold?"

"Probably."

"Can I make a copy of this?" she asked.

"Sure. Even if this coin was somehow legitimate, it still doesn't prove the Spaniards came through this area. Historical accounts show them to have stayed to the east. Francisco de Coronado fought the Zuni and the Hopi as he made his way into New Mexico Territory."

"You seem to know a lot of the history around the Spaniards."

"I told you the stories were bunk, but that doesn't mean they aren't interesting."

When Joe stepped out of the office, Sophie pulled the coin from her shoe and compared it to the drawing of the piece that had been sold in Phoenix.

They matched.

She hurriedly filled a glass with water from the pitcher Olivia kept near her desk and dropped the coin into it. It sank with a hard thunk to the bottom.

Gold. Not pyrite.

Since going to an assayer was too risky, these assessments would have to do.

And if Joe's information was correct, there were other coins like this one already in circulation.

She supposed it was hardly a surprise that Marty had managed to botch the job with a mistake in the Spanish word, making these counterfeit coins stick out. Did Rose know about them and about the error?

Either way, the big question was—where was this gold originally coming from?

CHAPTER 22

McKay headed to the survey office, intent on learning the location of Rose's property, while Lucas would try to find one of the men who may have been hired to dump crates at Pecks Lake.

As McKay crossed the street, Deborah Gibbons and Rose Palmer entered the land office together, so he waited. They spent twenty minutes inside before exiting, followed by a man using a cane and sporting a handlebar mustache that was much darker than his thinning hair. He must use dye on it, and he must be the agent, Arthur Sewell, the name painted on the glass window of the office.

Inside, a clerk was still present. McKay lingered for several minutes and then went inside.

"I think I'm late," McKay said. "Is my aunt Rose still here?"

"No, sir," answered the young man, looking through his spectacles. "You've just missed her."

"Oh no. Was she able to get the paperwork completed?"

"Yes, sir, I believe so." He shuffled some papers, found what he was looking for, and handed it to McKay. "Is everything in order, Mister Weaver?"

Mister Weaver?

McKay froze. In another life he would've been Benton Weaver. But there was no way this clerk could know that. He scanned the document.

And there it was on the deed of sale—Russell M. Weaver.

"Since you already signed and had the document notarized, we can move forward with recording the deed." The clerk stared with such intensity that McKay felt a surge of unease.

What was he missing?

"Your name will, of course, be changed for the recording," the man said in a low voice. "And rest assured that the notary will be discreet."

Russell was buying land and trying to hide the transaction. And Rose Palmer and Deborah Gibbons were aiding him.

"I appreciate the assurance," McKay said. "May I jot down the description of the parcel? I want to make sure I've got the details correct when I'm setting the boundary fence."

"Of course." The clerk handed him a pencil and a piece of paper.

The document had been notarized yesterday, presumably at the bank in town. The seller was Walt Jenkins. Was this Nighthawk Ranch? McKay didn't ask, not wanting to press his luck with the clerk. He copied the definition of the plat as well as the size—150 acres. He hadn't realized George Jenkins' place was so large. Mining companies tended to absorb as much land surrounding their operations as they could. How had this slipped through United Verde's fingers? And why hadn't the mine made an offer to Walt?

McKay returned the deed to the clerk. "Thank you."

"It's been a pleasure doing business with you and your partners."

"Yes, my partners. I hope they haven't given you any trouble," he hedged.

"Well, there was an issue with payment. Mister Ennis wasn't agreeable initially, but he did come around."

McKay nodded. "Yes. Marty. He sometimes steps out of line."

"I'll say." The clerk cast a disapproving look his way.

"Was everything resolved to your satisfaction?" McKay asked, trying not to trip himself up.

"Yes. Mister Sewell was simply getting nervous. Fixing documents can get tricky. While the town marshal will look the other way, it's not always the case with the mayor. And of course we had to hold off the other offers. So please know the higher fee was nonnegotiable."

A bribe. And *other offers* were probably mining companies.

"I understand."

McKay left the land office. The clerk was chattier than he'd anticipated, which meant Russell had likely never made an appearance before either of the men.

He went to the survey office as originally planned and asked to see a public map of Jerome. He located Rose's land and then using the information he'd gotten from the deed, he also found Russell Weaver's new purchase.

It was Nighthawk Ranch.

OLIVIA RETURNED, snapping Sophie out of her ruminations over the coin, and hung her coat on a hook. She waved Sophie over to her desk and laid out a Wanted poster, her hands still stained with ink from the typesetting she'd done this morning.

"I just got this from the mayor," Olivia said. "Apparently, Scott Habison was supposed to give it to me days ago, but he forgot."

"The town marshal?" Sophie said.

"Yes. I've questioned his civic duty before, and I think he's held it against me."

Sophie read the notice.

Proclamation – Governor of Texas – Wanted Dead or Alive –

Notorious Badmen – The Weaver Gang. Reward of $10,000. Additional $5000 for the leader, Russell.

"That's a big reward," Sophie muttered.

"Do you recognize this Xander Weaver who supposedly met with my father?" Olivia asked, the desperation in her voice hard to miss. She must want Sophie to disavow McKay's claim that Charles Bromley was in cahoots with the gang.

Sophie examined the two small sketches of Russell and Alexander Weaver. The drawings were poor, but ....

She studied Russell. It was Buzz. She was sure of it.

McKay *had* been right about her. She could lead him straight to the gang.

"Well?" Olivia prompted.

"I'm sorry," Sophie said. "I never got a good look at Xander. I can't say if this is him or not." *But it probably is.*

Olivia sat down, looking defeated.

"It doesn't say exactly what they've done," Sophie said.

"Well, as Lucas and Ben said, they rob trains. I guess they've taken thousands of dollars' worth of gold over the years. But the bigger crime was a train conductor was killed during the last one, sometime earlier this year. So now they're wanted for murder."

Sophie recoiled, making her way back to her desk to sit.

She'd all but stumbled into Russell Weaver, alone, in the middle of nowhere. How easily he could have disposed of her.

She grabbed the glass of water she'd used for the gold coin and took a big gulp, grimacing from the metallic taste, and choked it down.

She needed to find McKay.

CHAPTER 23

It was early afternoon when McKay came to the outer perimeter of Nighthawk Ranch. Although the United Verde mine was nearby, the sulphur smell was vastly decreased due to a steady wind blowing to the east. Much of Jerome was high desert, dry and barren, and the ranch was no exception, but with it tucked down in a valley it afforded privacy from not only the townsfolk but the mining activity as well.

In short, the perfect property for a retired train robber to live out his days in peace.

Is that what Russell was doing? Even an outlaw had to pull back at some point.

But why Jerome? Did Russell know that Benton's mother was buried in the town cemetery? Was he somehow sentimental over Moira McKay, who had left him nearly twenty-four years ago to raise Benton away from a criminal father? Did Russell regret losing Benton?

As personal as this was for McKay, he'd left a message for Lucas that he was heading out to the Jenkins' Ranch to have a look around. He knew he had to follow protocol, although he made sure to leave before Lucas might consider accompanying him. He'd already been here a few weeks back and had found nothing to indicate occupation, so it was likely he would again find nothing.

When the homestead and surrounding corrals came into view, he stopped and hobbled his horse in the barely-there shade of a shrub and took up a position of surveillance. Using a spyglass, he watched for over an hour but there was no activity. The homestead appeared abandoned, as vacant as it had been on his last visit. Apparently, Russell hadn't moved in yet despite the finalized paperwork, and a deed that was to be doctored before its public filing. Once Russell and Xander were apprehended, McKay would submit a report with charges against Arthur Sewell.

Movement caught his eye.

There was a man moving about. Tall. Wearing a duster and a ten-gallon hat.

Russell Weaver?

McKay couldn't be certain, but who else? Maybe Xander. He decided to move closer on foot.

It was tricky approaching without being seen since there was little cover, so he waited until the man went into the barn before making his final approach at a run. With the house as cover, he watched the man emerge from the barn.

Not Russell, based on eyewitness accounts and wanted poster sketches. And McKay's own assessment that he would resemble the man since they were kin. Even the side glimpse he'd seen of Xander in the Bromley barn had been a familiar profile, matching his.

It was clear the man was on the prowl. Was he also searching for Russell, or something else? McKay backtracked to the front of the house and the man's horse. The animal snorted and McKay froze, willing the beast to be silent. The sound of footsteps alerted the man's approach and McKay barely moved to the other side of the building before being caught.

The man aggressively tried to open the front door, and when it refused to budge, he swore to himself and kicked it in, going inside.

McKay eyed the saddlebags on the man's mount. He holstered his gun and quietly edged closer, using the horse as cover, the animal skittish. He quickly flipped open the nearest pouch and retrieved a leather billfold and returned to the cover of the house to inspect the contents.

Money. A wanted poster of the Weavers. Identification—John Coltrane, Pinkerton Detective. McKay relaxed a bit. This man was on the same assignment. But then he unfolded the final paper—a hand drawn map of Spanish gold that led to Pecks Lake.

It was the page torn from Sophie's notebook.

Sonofabitch!

This was her attacker.

McKay debated his options. Confront and arrest the man? The map, unfortunately, was flimsy evidence, however damning it was. Or maybe he could ferret out what Coltrane knew.

He made sure the way was clear and he returned the billfold to the saddlebag, then he adjusted his hat and kept his gun holstered as he stepped onto the porch and knocked on the open door, eyeing the etching of a bird beside it. A nighthawk.

"Hello! Is the owner here by chance?"

Coltrane came out of the back room, gun cocked and pointed at McKay. "Who're you?" He had a rough look to him, but his gaze was shrewd.

McKay lifted his hands. "Whoa. My name is Ben Lewis. I'm an ornithologist and I'm tracking a nest of nighthawks on this property, and I came to ask the landowner for permission to camp overnight. No need to point a gun at me."

Coltrane assessed him then slowly lowered his weapon.

"And you are ...?" McKay said.

"Not the owner. The name's Coltrane. I'm a Pinkerton, and you're impeding an investigation, so I suggest you depart now."

"What kind of investigation?"

"What did you say you do?"

"I'm a bird watcher."

Coltrane released a derisive snort. "Sounds like a job for a woman."

"I've heard tell there are women Pinkertons."

The man released a breath of frustration. "A big mistake, if you ask me," he muttered. "Have you been here before?"

"Here?" McKay glanced around. "No."

"And you haven't met the owner? You don't know where he is?"

"No. Is he the one under investigation?"

Coltrane holstered his gun. "I'll tell you what, Mister ...."

"Lewis."

He nodded. "Mister Lewis. I'll let you go on your merry way on one condition. You'll let me know if you see anything suspicious in these parts, or if you see the owner arrive, since you'll be camped out and all. Can you do that?"

"Sure. But without permission, I'm technically trespassing, so until I can clear that, I'll stay beyond the property line."

"You're one of those do-goods." The comment wasn't complimentary. "If you see something from afar, then please report it to me." He enunciated the words like he was speaking to a child.

"And how would I do that?"

"You can find me at Jennie's Place."

Unlike Rose's establishment, Jennie's Place was a brothel, and certainly not a hotel. Coltrane must be paying premium to keep a room there, or else he had something over the madam, Jennie, to let him stay indefinitely. A good place to hide. Upstanding Pinkerton, indeed.

"Are you looking for the gold?" McKay said, throwing out a little bait.

Coltrane stilled.

Bullseye.

"And what gold is that?" Coltrane asked.

"Spanish, of course. It seems to be the talk of the town. I've been out in the wilderness these past few weeks, and I frequently come across prospectors looking for it instead of veins." Somewhat true if he included Bromley and Harry. "Seems a bit preposterous to me."

"I agree, but men will go to great lengths to hide their fortunes." Coltrane narrowed his eyes. "A bird watcher who's looking for gold. Maybe I've underestimated you and your benign cover."

McKay smiled. "Don't worry, I'm no treasure hunter, just a scientist trying to keep my footing in a mining town. Not everyone has a moral backbone, if you know what I mean."

Coltrane remained silent, his face impassive.

"Well, I'll leave you to your investigating, Mister Coltrane."

As McKay left, he noted the interior of the house appeared recently occupied if the general cleanliness was any indication. Wouldn't there be a layer of dust on the counters and furniture if the place had been vacant for many weeks?

He cut around the house and to the back of the corrals, so he wasn't in line of sight of Coltrane as he made his way back to his horse.

Someone had been living here and was likely of the Weaver variety. And for some reason, Coltrane's presence had scared them off. McKay couldn't deny that a Pinkerton would do that. But a Pinkerton who was also hunting gold?

SOPHIE WENT to the Connor Hotel, but McKay wasn't in his room, and after a minute of knocking at Lucas's door, she left and scanned the afternoon bustle on Main Street. Jennie's Place to her right and the bowling alley to her left, reminding her she needed to be back in time for her supper date with Marty. Her energy flagged at the thought.

She dodged a wagonful of ore on its way to the smelter and went to the mine office where she inquired about Nathan Smith, shoe salesman, and got lucky when the man sitting at the desk said he'd just left. She took a guess and found her cousin exiting the livery with his horse.

"Where's McKay?" she asked. "I need to find him."

Lucas adjusted his hat. "Go back to the paper, Sophie. Let us handle this."

"Handle what?"

He gave her a hard look that said *let it go*.

She huffed in frustration. "I have reason to believe Russell Weaver is living at Nighthawk Ranch under the alias of Buzz."

That caught her cousin's attention, but his poker face held. "Duly noted," he said. "I have work to do."

Without further discussion, he mounted and left her where she stood.

"So do I," she said under her breath.

She found Trent mucking a stall. "I need a horse," she said.

He frowned at her and chewed his lower lip. "Where's Roger? I thought you had him."

Sophie inwardly groaned. She'd forgotten about the horse and Harry. "Crumb," she mumbled. "I'll get him back, I promise, but right now I need another horse."

"I don't have anything available. Just Mabel."

Sophie's heart sank.

"She's been eating well and is getting stronger," Trent said. "It would do her good to get some exercise, if you wanna take her."

Sophie's forehead scrunched together. "You think so?"

"Just don't overdo it. Where you fixed on riding?"

"To the Bromleys'," she replied. In truth, she planned to follow Lucas.

"That'd probably be all right."

Trent was too slow in saddling Mabel, so Sophie pushed his hands aside in impatience, the boy throwing irritated looks her way.

She grabbed the reins and headed past the stalls. "I'm in a bit of a hurry."

"I'll say. When will you be back?" he yelled after her, but she ignored the question.

She climbed into the saddle and set off in the same direction as Lucas, which happened to be toward Nighthawk Ranch.

Mabel started out agreeable, and somewhat docile, but then she began to chomp at her bit, trying to take the lead. Sophie constantly had to correct her to keep her on course, and at one point the ornery girl swung her head around and tried to nip at Sophie's leg.

Sophie gasped, tightening her grip on the reins. "You've got a little demon in you, don't you. Can't say as I blame you, sweetheart, but I mean you no harm. I promise."

As they neared the ranch, Mabel became more choppy-strided and harder to control. When the animal took a turn in the wrong direction, nothing Sophie did could get her back on track. The mule picked up her pace and Sophie was unable to dismount without risking injury and besides, then Mabel would run off, and after trying to help her Sophie wasn't about to lose her in the back country.

She pulled on the reins repeatedly, but Mabel shook her head, and it was all Sophie could do to hang on as the girl ran to the west in a burst of energy, taking them into the hills, following a path of sorts. When Mabel finally slowed her gait from a gallop, Sophie breathed a sigh of relief, but the animal didn't stop until she came to a dead end in an alcove surrounded by boulders.

Sophie dismounted, needing a moment to collect herself and ran a hand along the mule's neck. "We'll discuss your behavior later."

Mabel snorted and pawed at the ground.

Enlightenment hit Sophie. "You've been here before, haven't you?"

She glanced around, noting a narrow pathway between two tall boulders. She secured Mabel then squeezed her way through. It ended in a protected area that the recent rains had turned into a watering hole.

Like my dream.

But that was silly. Mabel was likely attracted to the water, like any animal in this barren landscape. And her dream had probably been for the same reason.

Still, Sophie removed her coat and pushed her dress sleeves high on her arms. Leaning as far as she could, she ran her hand through the water. Nothing. She went deeper. Still nothing.

Shifting to a different spot, her hand hit something.

Burlap.

There was a bag in the water hole. She tried to lift it, but it was too heavy.

She considered her options and then took off her shoes, skirt, and blouse, leaving only her camisole and bloomers. Gingerly she stepped into the murky liquid. Her feet sank into the silty bottom and mud oozed between her toes. She paused, hoping it wasn't quicksand, but she soon stopped sinking.

She waded over to the bag and was able to get a good idea of its weight and girth now that she was beside it, and she found two more bags, equally as heavy as the first. She struggled to untie one, but it wouldn't budge.

She had a knife in her satchel. She climbed out of the water hole and carefully retraced her steps through the narrow opening in bare feet.

And then came face to face with McKay.

CHAPTER 24

When McKay had come across Mabel, he'd assumed that Harry had reacquired her and was lurking about somewhere. The last thing he expected was to see Sophie emerge from the rocks wearing nothing but her undergarments, wet and clinging to her like a second skin, leaving nothing to the imagination. She was perfect, and his mouth went dry at the sight of her, his eyes dropping to her breasts, her nipples dark and puckered beneath the flimsy material. He forced his gaze back to her face.

"What are you doing here?" he said, his voice strained with panic.

"Looking for you." Her husky response ignited a need in him that he'd been doing a fair job of suppressing. How was he supposed to keep her at arm's length now?

"How did you even get here?" He tried to keep his eyes from drinking in every inch of her curves now on full display.

She crossed her arms to cover herself, but it did little to appease his imagination. She was beautiful in every way possible.

"It was Mabel." She pointed to the mule nearby, exposing her breasts again, and his mouth went even drier.

"She brought me here," Sophie added, "pretty much against my will."

He needed to keep his priorities straight. The fact that he was alone with a nearly naked Sophie shouldn't be a deterrent, but right now all he could think about was touching her. "Where are your clothes?"

"Back there." She pointed behind her, revealing dips and curves that beckoned.

"Sophie—"

"I came to tell you that I've found Russell Weaver. He's at Nighthawk Ranch."

"I know."

"You do?" She stepped closer.

"You shouldn't be out here alone."

"I told you. I was looking for you." Another step forward. Her wet hair framed eyes clouded with raw longing. Hunger. "You're driving me mad, McKay," she whispered.

He closed the distance between them and kissed her, knocking his hat to the ground. It was unprofessional, the timing couldn't have been worse, and he was crossing a line he vowed not to after the last time he'd kissed her, but Sophie had been taking up space in his mind and his heart for days now.

He devoured her mouth, cupping her face between his hands, resisting the urge to remove the thin fabric barely hiding her body that had been tormenting his dreams. Her lips met his, eager and open, and his desire rose to a flashpoint.

He stopped, holding her less than an inch away, his breath mingling with hers. "I'm not myself, Sophie," he whispered. "And you tempt me far too much."

"I know." She pressed against him, and his body shuddered in response. "I want this."

"You don't know what you're saying."

"Because I'm young? You're wrong."

He was quickly losing his mind. "What are you saying?"

"I'm saying you can have me. Right now."

She kissed him, her innocence apparent, but there was also a frantic need that matched his own. His hands dropped to her hips and then to her buttocks, and he wanted nothing more than to bury himself in her. She clawed at his shirt, pulling it over his head. He pushed the camisole from her shoulders and once her breasts were fully exposed, he lowered his mouth to one nipple and sucked, causing her to whimper and arch against him. He held her tight, then let his lips taste her skin upward, capturing her mouth once again.

She was a fever in his blood, his arousal straining his control. When she tugged at his trousers, he caught her hand. "No. We can't do this the normal way. You could get with child."

"I know." She kissed him, her breathing hitched, desperate. "At least, I know it in theory. How would it work?"

"I can use my hand or my mouth instead of ...."

She paused, breathing heavy. "I thought you would be ... with me. Can't we just ... for a short time ...." Her teeth grazed his jawline.

He was beyond any temptation he'd ever had for another woman. This was a bad idea, but maybe just a brief joining and then he'd stop. He removed his pants while she did the same with her bloomers, then he spread his discarded shirt on the ground so she wouldn't have to lie in the dirt.

As she lay back, a flash of worry in her eyes caused him to pause. He held himself above her. "This doesn't have to go any further," he said.

She nodded, but she kissed him, her hands slowly exploring his face to his shoulders to his ribcage, and then lower. She smiled and shifted to allow him access.

"Are you sure?"

"Yes."

He pushed into her, hesitating from the resistance, but her gasps had nothing to do with pain, and she took him more fully. Her convulsions around him caught him by surprise, and before he could stop it, he was gone, too.

———

Sophie held tight to McKay, clutching his shoulders, inhaling the scent of him.

What had just happened?

She was pretty sure they both had lost their minds and hadn't prevented a possible baby. She shut her eyes, holding him close, reveling in the pleasure still coursing through her body. They may have made a terrible error but a part of her simply didn't care.

She pushed aside the thought of her mother's dismay. She would dwell on that another time.

"McKay," she whispered into his neck.

He raised his head. "I'm sorry, Soph. I didn't have time—"

"I know." She kissed him. "It'll be fine. It was this one time. Maybe if I stand up."

"Yeah, yeah." He lifted himself off her and then easily pulled her to her feet.

She swayed a bit from rising too quickly. And then, of course, there was McKay's nakedness, his frame lean and strong. She was dizzy with fascination over this man who had just taken her virginity.

McKay grabbed his shirt from the ground.

"Use this," he said, offering it to her.

"No. What will you wear? It'll ruin your shirt."

Fluid ran down her leg, carrying a trace of blood. She wasn't shocked, her mother had educated her about this, but it was clear she could never have a follow-up conversation with her mama. The discourse had been in reference to the marriage bed.

Sophie glanced at where she and McKay had made love in the dirt.

My marriage bed.

Except she and McKay weren't married, and there was a good chance they never would be.

A breeze caused gooseflesh to ripple across her skin as McKay rummaged through his saddlebags, and Sophie enjoyed watching every inch of his muscled backside. As soon as he turned back to her, however, she averted her eyes.

He'd found a bandanna. Kneeling before her, he gently cleaned her.

"I can do that," she said, feeling a bit embarrassed.

"Don't be shy, Sophie," he said, as if he'd read her mind. "And this wasn't your fault. I was impatient. I'm sorry."

She was looking down at him, his dark hair moving in the breeze, and her body responded to his closeness, and it made her feel strong. Desirable. As if she held a new power between them. She wanted to kiss him, to explore him.

"If we did this again," she said, "would it be as fast?"

His gaze jerked upward, meeting hers. He looked so stunned. Had she said the wrong thing?

"You want ...." He swallowed, his Adam's apple moving up and down. "Now?"

"Well ...." Her nipples reacted of their own volition, and his eyes drifted to them, and the wanting in them was heady.

He stood. "Hell, Sophie. It's no wonder I have no willpower around you. And you're cold." He grabbed his coat and put it on her, pulling the lapels together as he kissed her. It was chaste, no hungry devouring, but desire swirled in her abdomen. "Where are your clothes?" he murmured against her mouth.

"Oh, I have something to show you!" she exclaimed, suddenly remembering what she had been doing before he'd arrived. Before he'd completely overwhelmed her senses, apparently giving her short-term amnesia. "But I need a knife."

She went to Mabel and retrieved the item, then picked up her wet undergarments as McKay pulled on his trousers. She led him through the crack in the rock to the water-filled hole. She was about to shed his coat when he stopped her.

"Let me do whatever it was you were planning," he said.

She nodded. It did save her from plunging into the water as naked as the day she was born.

"It's there," she said, pointing to the spot where the bags were submerged. "There are at least three burlap sacks tied off."

He got into the water up to his waist and walked over. Once he located the bags, he spent several minutes trying to cut the rope on one. When it finally gave free, he rummaged underwater and then lifted a handful of gold coins.

The gooseflesh this time had nothing to do with being chilled.

McKay HAULED all three bags from the water and Sophie helped move them out of the protected alcove. When she attempted to clothe herself, her undergarments still damp, McKay distracted her. Or she distracted him. She wasn't sure, except that she was enjoying the ability to touch him at will. She knew that coupling in the way they had was unwise, so instead of a repeat, he did other things to her, delightful and pleasurable, and her body craved more.

When they were finally satiated with each other, he said, "That's a helluva lot of gold." With one final kiss, he retrieved her clothes, and she was soon dressed, as was he.

They sat side by side and inspected the coins.

"So the Conquistadors were here?" McKay said. "And they left this amazing treasure behind?"

Sophie made a sound of skepticism.

"What?" he asked.

She pulled the coin from her boot. "I found this on Rose's property where she supposedly keeps her distillery."

"There's no still?"

"No." She compared her coin to one from their discovery. "These are the same, and I believe they're counterfeit."

He took the pieces from her. "Why do you think that?"

"First off, if these bags had been left behind by the Spaniards, wouldn't the burlap have disintegrated by now? And these coins are too shiny. Wouldn't they be dirtier from the elements after a hundred and fifty years or more? Second, the word *escudo* is misspelled. And third, I found smelting tools in Rose's shed and molds for the coins."

"Why didn't you tell me about this?"

"I'm telling you now. I only found this piece this morning."

"So Rose is behind this?" he asked.

She shrugged. "Maybe."

McKay looked at her. "Did you trespass?"

"A little," she said a bit sheepishly. "There was a padlock—"

He held up his hand. "Don't tell me. How did you find the alcove?"

"Mabel. Trent told me to exercise her, and she pretty much went straight here."

"She knew the place," he murmured.

"Harry," they said at the same time.

"So he's working with Marty?" she asked. "Not to put too fine a point on it, but neither of them seems intelligent enough to pull this off."

"I don't disagree with you, but it appears they have. Although ...."

"You think this is related to the Weavers somehow," she stated.

He nodded. "How did you know Russell Weaver was at Nighthawk Ranch?"

"I met him."

The shock on McKay's face took her aback. Her mind scrambled over what she possibly could have done wrong. Was McKay frightened for her safety as she had been when she'd realized Buzz was Russell? Or was it something else?

"When was this?" he asked, still looking stunned.

"Three days ago. I didn't know it was him. He said his name was Buzz and that he was a caretaker for the ranch while the land agent was trying to sell it. I only realized it today when Olivia showed me the wanted poster."

"What was he like?"

Sophie hesitated over the strange question. "He was gruff and seemed irritated that I was there, but then he offered me coffee. I said no. He told me he had known George Jenkins, that they'd been friends, and I had the odd sense that maybe he wanted to buy the property. He knew about the Spanish gold stories in the area and about George's own obsession with searching for the treasure. And he said a nighthawk plaque hanging near the front door had been carved by a woman named Moira."

McKay's gaze snapped to her.

She reached for him. "Are you all right?"

His face had paled. He looked lost in thought, but he nodded and said, "Yeah, I'm fine."

"How did you know Weaver was at the ranch?" she asked.

"Your intuition was right. He's been trying to buy it. Or he already has. I think the land agent is forging the documents, and that Marty Ennis is somehow involved."

"Then your case is done," she said. "You can arrest them all."

"Weaver wasn't at the ranch. There was a Pinkerton named Coltrane searching the premises. He must've scared Russell away."

She frowned. "Coltrane, you say?"

He seemed to recover himself, the color in his face returning. "What do you know, Sophie?"

"Last night I overheard Rose and Deborah Gibbons talking. Turns out Deborah's real name is Sally. That's why I asked if there were any female Weavers. You do have to admit that she looks a bit like Russell and Xander."

McKay's expression became shuttered. "You're the only one who has seen each of them. I don't know of a Sally Weaver, but I suppose it's possible."

"Sally mentioned something about a man named Coltrane abusing her. And she called Rose her Aunt Rose."

"You're saying Rose is possibly a Weaver as well?"

She shrugged. "I don't know. They seem to be pursuing a marriage between Bromley and Sally, I think in the event he finds the gold that Xander wants him to. Sally would own it if she were his wife." She considered the situation. "I doubt Russell is really gone. He wouldn't leave without *his* gold."

At McKay's questioning look, she clarified, "The gold that Marty has converted for him." She pointed to the bags. "These. *We* now have the Weaver gold." She noted the sun's position low in the west. "I have to go. I'm supposed to meet Marty for supper."

That seemed to bring McKay out of his stupor. "What?" Then he shook his head. "You need to stay away from him. Especially now."

"I agree, but he caught me on Rose's property, and I had to come up with a good reason why I was there, so I told him it was to see him. Olivia said she would accompany me. Maybe I can learn something useful."

"I'll meet you there."

"It's the English Kitchen at six. What about these?" She indicated the gold coins.

"Don't worry. I'll take care of them."

CHAPTER 25

Sophie barely made it to the restaurant in time after stopping at the Bromleys' to change into a dry maroon dress. It had been a busy day, and she was still flushed with energy from her afternoon in McKay's arms, as giddy about him as she was about the gold they'd found. But when she entered the adobe building, she was jarred by the dark and heavy atmosphere.

Opium dens.

While not obvious, she was sure some of the closed doors along one side of the room housed them. This was a bad idea. She turned to leave when she bumped into Marty wearing a clean shirt and his hair combed back.

"Is something wrong?" he asked, grabbing her shoulders.

She stepped out of his reach. "No. I thought maybe I was in the wrong place."

"This is the right place."

A Chinese man greeted them with a bow and led them to a table. Marty held her chair out so she could sit.

"Thank you," she smiled politely, regretting not waiting for Olivia, but she hadn't had time to check the newspaper office and instead had come straight here.

And McKay had said he would come as well.

Sooner would be better than later, you two.

Marty took his seat across from her. "You're looking very lovely, Miss Ryan."

His manners were on high, making Sophie even more uncomfortable. He obviously thought this was a courtship meal, and she searched for some way to shoot this down as swiftly as possible.

Except, Marty was up to no good. She would be stupid to waste this opportunity.

"Thank you," she said again.

They were handed menus written in broken English, but Marty waved them away and said, "We'll both have the chop suey."

She was perfectly capable of ordering for herself, but she nodded her assent and decided to dive right in. "How long have you been making whiskey for Rose?"

Confusion flashed in his eyes, but he recovered quickly. "A while."

"It must be backbreaking work."

"Yep."

"Do you know a man named Harry Lesar? Rose and Miss Gibbons seemed to."

Marty shrugged. "He's an old fart." He cleared his throat. "Apologies. He's just an old man with aimless pursuits."

Hardly. His *pursuits* were likely to make him very rich.

She settled her napkin onto her lap. "What do you think about all the tales of Spanish gold?"

He shifted in his seat, as if he wasn't comfortable. "Whaddya mean?"

"I keep running into people who are searching for it."

He took a sip of water, exposing a crooked canine. "Like who?"

"Well, Charles Bromley for one. And I heard that George Jenkins had been searching for many years before his death." She leaned forward, adding in a low voice, "I heard the treasure can be found in Pecks Lake."

Marty choked on the water he'd just swallowed.

"Oh dear," she said. "Are you all right?"

"I'm fine," he replied in a strangled voice.

"But I've also heard the treasure is in the hills near the Nighthawk Ranch, stashed in an anonymous alcove, waiting to be discovered."

A look of terror froze Marty's face.

"Sophie!" a voice called from the entrance. It was Joe from the newspaper. He hurried to the table.

"What's wrong?" she asked, concerned about the alarm on his face.

"We're having a newspaper crisis. Olivia needs you at the office. Now."

She stood. "What's happened?"

"Bromley found the Spanish gold."

"What?" Marty exclaimed.

Joe cast a look of exasperation toward the man, then said to Sophie, "That's not all of it, and I'm not sure which news is more distressing to Olivia. Charles has married Deborah Gibbons."

Sophie grabbed the next sheet of paper as Olivia tossed it her way and went to work expanding the woman's reporting while also cleaning up the hastily written prose.

She'd followed Joe back to the office, abandoning Marty and the chop suey that had just been delivered to the table, the bowl of noodles, vegetables, and meat smelling more appetizing than she'd anticipated.

"It's a headlining story," Joe had said as Sophie was running to keep up. "The bigger papers are going to pick this up, and we need to get something out there as soon as possible."

Olivia was writing, Sophie was editing, and Joe was typesetting.

"He married her!" Olivia huffed to herself. "I just ...." She shook her head. "He didn't even tell me beforehand."

"Did he say why it was so fast?" Sophie asked, keeping her voice low in case she didn't want Joe to hear.

"She's pregnant," she whispered, her face flushed.

Shocked, Sophie didn't know what to say. Before she thought better of it, the words tumbled from her mouth. "Are you certain?"

Olivia went still. "Why would she lie?"

"Why wouldn't she? Isn't it strange that he married her the same day he found the gold?"

And at Pecks Lake, no less, the very spot on his map, a map that perhaps Deborah had given him.

"It wasn't the same day," Olivia said. "He found the gold the day before."

Interesting. "Where is the find now?" Sophie asked.

"The jail. Marshal Habison is keeping watch while ownership can be determined."

Finders keepers. Deborah, or rather Sally, was trying to lay claim to the find.

When McKay couldn't find Sophie at the English Kitchen, he stepped outside, not liking the location on Hull Avenue, a general lawlessness permeating the area. Despite the name of the restaurant, the proprietor didn't speak English, so it had been impossible to learn if Sophie had even been there. Ennis wouldn't do something stupid, would he?

As McKay made his way to Main Street, a frisson of expectation seemed to fill the townsfolk passing by. It was certainly more populous than usual considering the lateness of the day, well past dusk.

Lucas materialized from across the street, heading for him. "Good, I found you," he said, slightly out of breath. "We seemed to have missed each other at Nighthawk Ranch." His tone had a slight accusation to it.

Ignoring it, McKay asked, "What's happened?"

"Bromley found Spanish gold in Pecks Lake. I'm headed to the jail now."

"What for?"

"To see it, of course."

SOPHIE PUSHED her way into the front office of the jail. Upon hearing that Bromley's treasure was on display, the townsfolk had turned out in droves. Gasps and chatter and the smell of too many bodies crammed together accosted her.

The deputy raised his hands and said loudly, "One at a time. Once you look then please step outside."

Her heart leapt when she saw McKay in discussion with Marshal Habison in the corner. Lucas was here too. She jostled her way over to him.

"What's going on?" she asked.

While they were only supposed to be acquaintances, with so much chaos would anyone notice her speaking to him?

"Habison has decreed Bromley's find must go to Phoenix until ownership can be determined," Lucas said.

"Why? Who owns it?"

"Well, technically, Bromley does. He found it. He keeps it. There's no owner about to show up. The Spanish are long gone. But Habison is being obstinate about some thirty-day rule, so everyone is clamoring to see it before it's gone."

She peered into the cell—the door shut and obviously locked—where Charles Bromley's discovery was currently being kept. She was surprised to see spikes protruding from the floor. *So the rumor is true.* The cell had been outfitted for difficult detainees.

She said into Lucas's ear, "Wouldn't it be better off at the bank?"

"Habison is convinced someone might steal it."

The Weavers maybe? But was Bromley's find the real deal or was it part of the counterfeits she had already found? She wished she could get closer to examine one of the coins, but from her vantage point she was struck by how little treasure there was. Just a small pile. There had been far more in the bags in the alcove. Harry's stash.

"Are they sure it's Spanish gold?" she asked.

Lucas frowned at her. "What else would it be?"

She was surprised that McKay hadn't shared the discovery of the counterfeit coins with Lucas. She should tell him, but not here.

"I'm being discerning," she said. "Olivia wants me to gather the facts."

"I heard about Bromley and Miss Gibbons. Is Olivia okay?"

Sophie shook her head. "No. She's still at the newspaper. You should go and see her."

Lucas looked at McKay.

"I'll tell him where you are," she added.

With a silent acknowledgement, Lucas disappeared into the crowd and left the building. Sophie made her way over to McKay. She caught his eye and offered a half smile, her heart bursting from seeing him.

"What do you want?" Habison said to her, annoyance in his voice, cigar smoke and whiskey emanating from him.

"Can I see the find up close?"

"No."

"But I need to inspect it for the newspaper article I'm writing," she said.

"Bromley found it. He owns the paper. Have him write the article." Habison turned away from her.

He had a point, but she bristled at the man's rudeness. McKay's jaw clenched and he offered a sympathetic look her way from beneath the brim of his hat, but he said nothing.

She should probably return to the Bromley homestead, if only to check on Bromley and his new wife. Olivia was overwhelmed by everything that had happened.

"He's right," she said to McKay, as if they were chatting about the weather. "I'll find Bromley to get the information." Then she added, "Mister Smith has gone to check on Miss Bromley."

McKay nodded, but he gave her nothing more. With her topics of conversation exhausted, she had no choice but to turn and leave.

Sophie bypassed the newspaper since Lucas was with Olivia. The typeset was complete on the issue for tomorrow, and Joe was planning to stay late and handle the printing. Sophie would get to the Bromley homestead without delay. Maybe she could help Olivia with this mess between her father and Sally.

She ran into Trent on Main Street. "I was coming to see you," she said. "How's Mabel?"

"She's fine. She seems to like Roger."

Sophie went still. "Roger is back?"

"Yep. Tonight. Have you seen the treasure? Everybody's talking about it."

"Yes, I know." Why didn't Harry come and see her? Didn't he want his pouch of gold returned? But maybe he didn't care since he had bags of coins hidden away.

"Everybody wants to get to Pecks Lake now," the boy continued. "They think there's more out there."

Sophie hadn't thought of that. Pecks Lake, as well as Jerome in general, was likely to be overrun with prospectors and treasure hunters in the coming days.

"Where are you going?" she asked. "Aren't you on duty?"

He flashed a silver coin. "I'm gonna have a quick supper."

"Who's watching the animals?"

"They'll be fine for a bit."

"Well, if it's all right with you, I'm going to take Mabel for the night. And I'll check in on Roger."

"Suit yourself. He's in the stall beside her."

She was relieved that Harry hadn't taken his mule, but feared Roger may have been mistreated—Trent's silver dollar smelled suspiciously of a bribe—so she picked up her pace.

With no one minding the store, she slipped inside and headed to the back stalls. Mabel greeted her, and then Roger stuck his head out over the stall gate.

With relief, she stroked his snout. "Hi there, boy."

A shadowy movement behind the horse startled her. "Harry?" she said incredulously.

He waved her inside. She glanced around, unsure whether to follow his instructions, then unlatched the gate and stepped around Roger.

"Are you hiding?" she asked.

"Did you see anyone out there?"

"Like who?"

"Anyone?"

"No," she said. "The livery boy is getting supper. I came alone. Thank you for returning Roger." She reached into her satchel and retrieved the bag of gold dust, then handed it to him. "I wanted to ask if I could keep Mabel."

He pocketed the gold and shook his head. "Nope. Sorry. I need her."

"What if I buy her from you?"

"Why would you want her? She's stubborn and ornery—"

"That doesn't bother me," she interrupted.

Harry was breathing fast as if he'd been running. He pulled off his hat and wiped the perspiration from his brow, his gray hair matted to his head. "I need to leave town," he said.

"Not just yet," said a man's voice, and Sophie startled for the second time since arriving. The click of a gun conveyed the gravity of the situation with lightning speed.

"Is this her?" the man asked. It was Buzz, or rather Russell Weaver. And then Marty Ennis appeared.

"Yep. And I shoulda known you was in on it too, Harry."

"What's going on?" she asked.

"We meet again, Sophie Ryan," Buzz said. "We need you both to come with us."

She stood her ground. "I'll do no such thing. I know who you are, Mister Weaver. You'll never get away with this." Whatever *this* was.

Marty was surprisingly fast as he yanked her arm behind her and started tying her wrist with a rope, adding the other hand to it.

"Marty, he's a criminal," she said. "You'll be in trouble if you help him."

"I thought you were a pretty one." He cinched the rope tight, causing her to wince. "But you stole from me too. You and Harry. I guess I'm a fool."

"A lazy fool," Russell muttered. "We're in this mess because you couldn't do your job."

Marty grabbed Harry from where he was cowering in the corner of the stall. "It's not my fault," Marty said with a whine. "I trusted Billy, but then he said *you* were helping him," he said to Harry, then he looked over his shoulder at Sophie. "I never woulda believed you were in it too if you hadn't told me so at supper tonight."

Maybe she had gone too far in dropping that bait. Would Russell kill her? Would he kill Harry?

"I don't know what you're talking about," Harry said. "I don't know any Billy."

"You're lyin', Harry," Marty said. "Billy already confessed. All you have to do is show us where the gold is, and we'll let you go."

CHAPTER 26

McKay didn't trust Habison. The town marshal had been smug and dismissive of McKay's concerns, wondering why a bird watcher was questioning the security surrounding Bromley's coins. McKay considered revealing his true identity, but he'd held back, sensing it would take away whatever small edge he might still have.

It seemed unlikely this gold would be transported to Phoenix with proper documentation and recourse. It would be surprising if it were still here in the morning. As such, he went looking for Lucas. He found him at the newspaper, where McKay had also hoped to find Sophie.

"She never returned," Lucas said when they stepped outside.

Joe and Olivia were getting the edition ready for tomorrow, although Lucas planned to take Olivia home shortly. The woman looked exhausted.

"She probably went back to the Bromleys' to check on the sudden marriage," McKay said, referring to Sophie. "Olivia have any clue why they did it so quickly?"

"Apparently Miss Gibbons, or rather Mrs. Bromley, is with child."

Memories of his afternoon with Sophie came back to McKay. Could she be with child? It had only been the one time. He'd been careful after that. But if she were pregnant, would McKay do the right thing as Bromley apparently had?

The idea didn't fill him with trepidation, as he'd always imagined it might. And he wanted to think that his mother would have approved of Sophie, that they would've had a close relationship.

According to Sophie, Russell knew that Moira had taken Benton to Nighthawk Ranch all those years ago, had known she was there. Had known she'd made the plaque. Even Benton hadn't been aware of that fact. He wondered if he could take it without anyone noticing. A Weaver intent on theft. The apple never falls far from the tree.

"We need to watch the jail tonight," McKay said. "I'll take first watch so you can get Olivia home and spend time with her. Tell Sophie I'll see her tomorrow. You can relieve me at three a.m."

"Understood," Lucas replied. "You think the gold will move?"

"I do."

SOPHIE'S FERVENT wish that someone would see her and Harry being led away from the livery was soon squashed. The town was abuzz with excitement over Bromley's find. The saloons were overflowing with excited chatter and music, and foot traffic was headed down to Hull Avenue in a steady stream. No one looked twice at them, with her hands bound behind her and her mouth gagged with a kerchief as she sat atop Roger, Russell leading them.

Had she been clear to McKay that she was headed back to the Bromley homestead? Would he come looking for her? And if he did, would he realize something was wrong when she wasn't there?

Her hopes sagged. No one would likely know she was missing until tomorrow.

Harry was to lead the men to the gold coins he'd stolen from Marty, and while Marty believed her also to know the location, it was Harry they were leaning on. And given the direction they were headed, Harry was caving, about to give them exactly what they wanted. He'd folded his cards almost immediately.

But the gold was no longer there. McKay had moved it, to where she didn't know. He'd said at the time that it was to protect her, but it was looking more as if it would now condemn her. She and Harry wouldn't be able to give Russell what he wanted, and when he realized it, what would he do?

As McKay HEADED BACK toward the jail, a boy ran up to him.

"You're that bird guy, aren't you?" he said.

"And you are?"

"Ned. Ned Gibbons. You know Miss Ryan, don't you?" he asked, his hat pulled low.

"I do know Miss Ryan. Are you related to Deborah Gibbons?"

"Yes, sir. Could you do a favor for me?" Ned asked.

"Depends what it is."

The boy pulled a book from his coat pocket. "Can you give this to Miss Ryan?"

It was a copy of *Oliver Twist*.

"Why don't you do it yourself?" he replied.

"I don't have time to keep lookin' for her. I'm leavin' tomorrow. She loaned it to me, and I promised her I'd return it."

"Why are you leaving?"

"Deborah," and then he mumbled, "my ma, said so. She's done somethin' bad again, and we have to go."

"Are you in trouble?" McKay asked.

"Nah. She just told a whopping lie to get hitched, and now I think she wants to take it back, so she said we gotta head south to Phoenix."

"Where's your ma now?"

"With her new husband, but I expect she'll be back soon," Ned answered. "It's all right. I'm with my aunt."

"That'd be Rose Palmer?"

"Yes, sir. Anyway, tell Miss Ryan that I liked the book. I think I understand why she gave it to me." His face took on a determined slant. "I think I want to be more like Oliver."

McKay wasn't familiar with the story. "And how's that?"

The boy lifted his gaze. "Just because I'm born into thievery doesn't mean I have to become one. By the way, my name isn't Gibbons. It's Ned. Ned Weaver."

Stunned, McKay watched the boy run off into the darkness.

SOPHIE SAT atop her horse while Harry took Marty to the water hole. At least Russell had removed her gag.

It was dark, and Marty lamented, loudly, the lack of light.

How long would Harry search for the coins before realizing the entire stockpile was gone? How long would Russell let this drag out?

Could she kick Roger into a run and get away before Russell shot her? All she needed was a lag in his attention.

"I guess you're no reporter."

"No, I am one," she replied. "I figured out who you were, didn't I?"

"You saw my wanted poster."

"Why do it?" she asked.

"And what's that?"

"Robbery. Is it worth it?"

Russell chuckled. "Sometimes the path you start on is the one you end on."

"How prophetic," she murmured. "You're an inspiration, Mister Weaver. How long have you been hiding in Jerome?"

"Longer than you'd think."

"But you left Nighthawk Ranch," she countered.

"Come back to see me?"

"Of a sort."

"I've got myself a thorn. *Of a sort*," he added with a bit of irony in his voice. "His name is John Coltrane. Did any of your investigative digging find *him*?"

"No. Who is he?" she asked, pretending McKay hadn't already told her.

"A Pinkerton detective who betrayed me."

"I would imagine that's a risk in your line of work."

He chuckled again. "I like you, Sophie."

"Enough not to kill me?"

He considered her question. "Maybe. I seem to have a reputation for killing, don't I?"

"They say you murdered a man in Texas."

He made a noncommittal sound, then said, "You say you're a reporter. What if I told you I wanted to tell my story, that maybe I'm looking for a writer?"

"I could do that." If it would buy time, buy her life. And maybe she'd have that gritty, no holds barred piece the Dallas Morning News was looking for, if she could somehow convince Russell to release her once it was all done. "We could go now to Nighthawk Ranch and get started."

"Tempting, but I do have to take care of my gold problem first."

His statement confirmed that Marty was using Russell's stolen gold to make the coins. Honestly, it was a clever scheme, a way to hide the true origin of the spoils.

"So the plan was to 'discover' it as if it were left here hundreds of years ago by Spanish Conquistadors?" she asked. "Is that what Charles Bromley found? Your gold?"

"Bromley," Russell repeated with a sigh. Then he said in a sarcastic tone, "His contribution has been almost as good as Marty's."

"Why bother with either of them?"

"The art of deflection. And Marty's family." He scanned the darkness.

Marty? That meant Rose was a Weaver, and ....

"You have a sister, don't you?" she said.

Russell pushed his hat back as his mount shifted. "Careful. The more you know, the more reason I'll have to get rid of you."

"Sally," she said quietly.

"I guess you *have* been paying attention around town."

"Why did she shoot a man in the hills two weeks ago?" Sophie pressed.

"She thought it was Coltrane."

"Aren't you worried about who she did shoot?"

He spit tobacco juice onto the ground. "Believe it or not, I don't condone indiscriminate killing. I looked into it. A body was never found. The man somehow lived."

If he found out it was McKay, would Russell finish the job since McKay could incriminate Sally Weaver?

Russell focused on her. "You know who it was, don't you?"

She didn't reply.

He grinned. "You're loyal. I can respect that."

Marty and Harry returned soaked from head to toe.

"What happened?" Weaver demanded.

Marty bent forward, hands on his knees, and tried to catch his breath. "There was nothin' there."

It was enough of a distraction for Sophie to kick Roger hard as she leaned forward to compensate for not having the use of her hands, and the horse leaped into the darkness.

CHAPTER 27

I t was well after midnight when two men on horseback approached the jail and quietly dismounted, then led the horses around the back of the building. McKay watched from his vantage point on the roof of the blacksmith's shop.

He'd been ruminating over Ned's admission of his true surname. Who was Ned's father? Xander? If it was Russell, then McKay and Ned were brothers. The boy had run off before McKay could question him further, and McKay was forced to let him go, needing to remain close to the jail.

The Weavers had been under his nose the entire time.

But now it was time to act, to finally rectify all the wrong turns he'd taken on this case. He slipped to the ground and kept to the shadows.

The men, wearing heavy dusters and hats pulled low, brought out a bag that was most assuredly the gold. They mounted and headed along a back alleyway. McKay followed on foot. He was certain one of the riders was Marshal Habison. Was the other a Weaver? Russell or Xander?

They headed out of town toward Perkins Road. McKay quickly

grabbed his horse from the livery and trailed them. He thought maybe they were headed to Nighthawk Ranch, but he soon realized he was wrong. The destination was the Bromley homestead.

AT FIRST, Sophie let Roger have his head, unconcerned about where he was taking her, her only goal to get as far from Russell and Marty as she could. She and her sisters had often played riding games as girls where they didn't use their hands, so she wasn't without some practice, but she did have to concentrate on matching Roger's gait to avoid falling off. By leaning and using her legs, she was finally able to control his direction.

They came to the backside of the Bromley barn, and she slid to the ground, her legs buckling. She struggled to a standing position and said in a low voice to Roger, "Stay here."

As she rounded the building, the house came into view, light spilling from the parlor window. She slipped into the barn, intent on getting the rope off before she went any further, not wanting to ask Bromley or "Deborah" for help.

She had to wait a few seconds for her eyes to adjust to the darkness, then she found a hacksaw on a worktable, but after a few minutes of fumbling it was clear she was going to slice her hand open. She moved deeper into the barn, searching until she found an axe. It was heavier, so she'd be able to anchor it better. She dragged it to the barn wall and propped it up, then peered over her shoulder as she attempted to cut the rope, careful to avoid her own tender flesh.

Slowly it worked, the pressure of the binding lessening. When she was finally able to move her wrists, she pulled and yanked until she had one hand free, then shed the remaining rope. Rubbing at her wrists, she relished the freedom.

Then she heard voices coming toward the barn.

She quickly looked for a place to hide, startling as she turned toward Bromley's underwater apparatus. Hanging from a hook, it resembled a man staring at her. She stepped behind it, but she couldn't possibly get into the rubber suit in time, especially with her skirt. Instead, she stuck her head into the helmet and positioned her shoulders behind the body, standing perfectly still. She was too short to view through the clear glass in the helmet, but that also meant no one could see her in return.

The barn door opened, and light filled the space.

"I don't know what's happened." It was Harry. "It was there. I put it in the water myself. It wasn't easy, the bags were heavy and I—"

"You've told us," Russell interrupted. "You can stay here until you remember the name of your partner."

"It was Sophie," Marty whined. "She all but confessed to me."

Harry snorted. "She's not my partner. I never told her nothin'."

"Then why did she run away?" Marty demanded.

"I suppose she didn't want to get shot," Harry whimpered, "and neither do I. I'm sorry, okay? I swear to you everything I took was there until three days ago. Maybe it was five. I can't remember exactly the last time I checked. I've only taken a few coins. Sold them to a dealer in Phoenix. Just so I could eat, you know? I'm not greedy. Someone was there. Someone else has taken them. You should be lookin' for *them*."

Russell released a sigh that sounded frustrated. "Maybe if I string you up in town your partner will show up."

"Someone's coming," Marty said in a low voice.

After a slight pause, Russell said, "It's fine. It's Xander and Habison."

Russell's brother and the town marshal.

The barn doors creaked open.

"You have it?" Russell asked.

"Yep," Xander said, Sophie recognizing his voice from her previous surveillance in this barn.

Something heavy was set on the worktable and the clink of coins could be heard as they were dumped out.

"I gotta tell you, there's way too much interest in this," Habison said. "I'm gonna get a lot of questions when this is missing from the jail tomorrow."

"Just tell everyone you sent it off to Phoenix like you were told," Russell said. "This isn't near enough to match what I gave Rose."

"You think Rose double-crossed us?" Xander asked.

"With Harry?" Russell's question was skeptical.

"And Marty." Xander's statement sounded grim.

"What're you sayin'?" Marty's voice rose in a panic. "I didn't steal it. I promise. I just ... parceled out the work is all. Who knew I would be double-crossed?"

"I told you this was a bad idea six months ago when Sally and Rose came up with it," Xander said.

"Be that as it may, we're stuck now," Russell said. "And for God's sake, can someone find Coltrane and get rid of him? Habison, I'm losing confidence in your ability to police this town."

"I can't be everywhere," the marshal rebutted, annoyance in his tone. "Just take the gold and leave. Coltrane will run out of steam when he can't find you."

"He already has," Russell replied in anger. "My oasis of Nighthawk Ranch has been breached. Hell, even that reporter girl found me there."

"Be careful," Habison said. "I heard she lives here now."

"Here?" Russell said. "With Bromley?"

"She works with Olivia Bromley and moved in a few days ago."

"Then she'll return," Marty piped up. "And we'll nab her then, and then we'll torture the location of the gold from her."

Sophie shrank back in her hiding place. She hadn't liked Marty all along, but now she realized her assessment of him had been too kind. There was something methodical about the way Russell Weaver conducted himself, giving her some sense of how he'd managed to keep his criminal activities alive for years. But Marty was the kind of lawless individual who lacked impulse control. And that made him far more dangerous. It made her sick to think how close she had been to him, and more than once. How easily he could have acted on those impulses.

"We're not torturing anyone," Russell said. "Exactly how much gold did you steal, Harry?"

"I ... well, there were two bags, like I said."

A bold lie, Harry. He was still hoping to salvage some of that booty with the third bag.

Russell swore. "If you're telling the truth, then Bromley didn't fail at Pecks Lake. He got everything that was there. Who else knew about your hiding place?"

"No one! Except ...."

"Except who?" Russell prodded.

"Mabel," Harry said in a whisper.

"Who the hell is Mabel?"

"My mule."

"You're telling me your mule has my gold?" Russell said.

"No," Harry said. "But Mabel is smart as a tack. She knows the way to the alcove, and I gave her to that Sophie a few days ago. Mabel must've taken her there."

"See?" Marty interjected. "It's been Sophie Ryan all along. We need to find her."

A horse whinnied.

Roger!

The men went quiet. Sophie held her breath in vain hope her horse wouldn't be found, but footsteps around the back of the barn yielded the inevitable. Roger was brought to the entrance.

"That's her horse," Harry said.

Thanks, Harry.

"She's here." Marty's voice was low and ominous.

"Search the barn," Russell said. "Habison, go inside the house and see if she's there. Whoever finds her first, bring her to me."

CHAPTER 28

S ophie remained as motionless as possible but damn Marty and
his tenacity.

"What the hell is this contraption?" he'd said as he started
manhandling the diving suit, then grabbed her arm so fast she had
no chance to run. "Gotcha! I found her!"

She fought him, her head still inside the helmet, but it was to no
avail. Marty pulled her free and dragged her to the front of the barn.
The look of reproach on Russell's face made her feel as if she were
being brought before her pa.

"Let's get her in the house," he said.

Marty's grip was painful as he hauled her behind Russell,
Xander pushing Harry forward.

In the foyer, Habison said, "It's empty." When his gaze landed
on her, he swore.

His disgust made her stomach clench. She knew too much and
could identify any of them. This was bad.

"This place is a mess," Xander said, shoving Harry onto the sofa
beside Sophie. "Where's Sally?"

Ignoring Habison, Russell searched the house again. "No one's
here," Habison reiterated.

It was surprising since it had to be around two a.m. Where was the newlywed couple? Where was Olivia?

"I forgot to tell you," Habison added. "Bromley showed up earlier demanding his gold. He said he and his new wife would take it to Phoenix themselves."

"What the hell?" Xander said. "That's not the plan, and Sally knows it."

"I told him no," Habison said. "And to come back tomorrow. He must still be in town. Sally must be with him."

"All right, we'll worry about that later," Russell said.

"I need to leave." Habison's gaze swung her way. "And these loose ends need to be taken care of."

That would be her and Harry.

A wagon approached outside, and then the front door opened. Ned ran into the parlor, then stopped abruptly, taking in the scene, his eyes growing big when he saw Sophie.

Rose was behind him. "What's going on?"

McKay didn't need his spyglass to recognize Roger being led to the front of the Bromley barn. His fears were validated when Marty Ennis dragged Sophie from the building, her burgundy dress streaked with dirt, and led her to the house. Harry was with them, and Xander. That meant the remaining man was Russell Weaver. For the first time since he had been a child, McKay laid eyes on his father. He wasn't quite as tall as Xander, but he had broad shoulders and a solid build that was echoed in McKay's own frame.

Familiarity accosted him, as if this scene had played out at another time and another place. He and his mother had lived with Russell until McKay was two years old. There were surely memories of that time buried inside McKay's head, and he couldn't help but wonder if there had been any happiness between Russell and Moira.

A wagon rambled down the road and delivered Rose Palmer and Ned Weaver, who entered the house.

McKay considered his options. None of them were favorable, especially with Sophie and Ned now inside.

Like an owl, Lucas Blackmore appeared silently at McKay's side, giving him a start.

McKay released a silent huff. "How did you find me?"

"I went to relieve you by the jail, but you were gone. Then I saw Rose headed this way."

"Sophie's inside the house."

Lucas swore under his breath.

"And I'm guessing Olivia and Bromley," McKay added.

"Not Olivia," Lucas said. "She's in my room at the hotel, asleep."

McKay didn't inquire further, considering the progression of his relationship with Sophie. At least Lucas had his woman tucked away, an outcome that McKay wished were true for him, because if something happened to her ....

"Who else is inside?" Lucas asked, remaining calm but the strain in his voice was discernible.

"Harry Lesar, Russell Weaver, and his brother Xander. I also saw Habison enter and leave. I believe he brought Bromley's gold here. And Rose and the boy Ned, who are both Weavers as well."

"We need a diversion."

McKay could think of only one.

"I have something to tell you, Lucas."

Rose's gaze settled on Sophie, confusion in her eyes, but she said nothing more, her coat buttoned to her neck and her hair stuffed entirely into her hat. Her skulking around outfit, Sophie concluded.

"It's about time you got here," Xander said from where he sat with a pistol resting on his lap, ready to shoot Harry or Sophie should they decide to bolt.

With a nod toward the kitchen, Rose silently beckoned Russell to follow her. "And you," she said to Marty, not bothering to hide her displeasure with him.

The murmur of voices could be heard as they discussed the obvious changes in their plans.

Ned edged his way into the parlor. "Hi, Uncle Xander," he said. "Are they prisoners?"

Ned was a Weaver. Of course.

"Something like that," the man said.

Ned stopped near the sofa. "I gave your book back to the bird watcher," he said to her.

McKay?

"Thank you, Ned," she said quietly.

"Did you make my pa mad?"

"Who's your pa?" she asked.

"Russell."

"Russell is married to Deborah?" she asked with alarm. Was the woman now a polygamist?

"Nah. She's my aunt. She just pretends to be my ma since my own died."

Sally Weaver: bogus mother and sharpshooter.

"She's not really pregnant, by the way," Ned added.

Add fraudulent wife to the list.

"Be quiet, boy," Xander admonished.

Ned scowled at his uncle, then flicked his gaze between her and Harry. "Why are you here?"

The others returned to the parlor, and Ned backed away.

Rose focused on Sophie and Harry. "So the two of you have our gold. It seems we're at a standstill."

"Did you really think this arrangement would work?" Sophie asked, the reporter in her looking for motive.

"It would have," Rose replied with a sigh. "If not for you."

"Deborah won't be able to get the gold from Bromley," Sophie said. "Everyone knows the marriage is phony."

"Of course it's not," Rose said, her tone admonishing. "They're in love."

"In love with gold," Ned said under his breath with a smirk.

"You must be itching for a whoopin', Ned," Rose warned.

The boy went contrite. "No, ma'am."

"Why did you want me to report on that list of prospectors you gave me?" Sophie asked.

"Is that why you were following me?" Harry exclaimed.

Sophie shook her head. "I never followed you, Harry. The biggest failure was Marty's laziness. If he'd dumped everything in Pecks Lake like he was supposed to then Bromley's discovery would be complete, and the marriage would yield the results apparently expected."

Marty took a step toward her. "You need to watch your mouth."

Russell raised an arm, stopping Marty across the chest. "You've done enough. She's not wrong. Rose, this has been a debacle from start to finish."

With hands on her hips, Rose said, "You're going to blame me for this?" She huffed. "Perhaps I should've kept a closer eye on the boy. Why are you such a twit, Marty?" She turned her attention back to Sophie. "I've underestimated you, Sophie dear. I'd like to think my own Henrietta would've been as sharp. I'm truly sorry to do this, but you need to confess."

She grabbed Xander's pistol, her speed impressive, and before Sophie could react, she was staring down the barrel in shock. She'd underestimated Rose. Sally wasn't the only one with hidden skills.

"Tell her," Harry whispered, his voice frantic. "Tell her now!"

"That's enough!" *McKay!*

Russell pulled his weapon as Rose shifted hers to the man standing at the entrance to the parlor. He also had a gun drawn.

Sophie held her breath. McKay took one quick look at her.

"They don't know where your gold is," he said.

Russell narrowed his gaze, scrutinizing McKay. "And why's that?"

"Because I have it."

"The bird man?" Rose said skeptically. "Why should we believe you?"

"Because I'm a Weaver, too."

CHAPTER 29

The room went deathly quiet.

What had McKay just said? Sophie couldn't believe it. He must be lying. Not about the gold, but ... *he's a Weaver?*

"I'll take you to it," McKay said to Russell. "But first, you let Sophie go."

"What about me?" Harry sputtered as Rose spoke over him, saying, "Why should we believe you?"

"You don't really have much of a choice," McKay said. "Bromley's find is small. You need me."

"Are you really a Weaver?" Ned asked from across the room.

"No," Rose answered. "It's a trick."

"It's no trick." McKay's voice was steady, sending a tendril of unease through Sophie. His calmness said more than any of them realized.

It's true, then.

Why hadn't he told her? He'd hidden his true motives from her the entire time. Did Lucas know?

Russell took a step forward, closing the distance between him and McKay. "Then explain to us who you are."

"I think you know," McKay replied, a sadness in his eyes.

"Benton?" Russell's voice was filled with astonishment. And anguish.

"What?" Rose demanded. "This is your son?"

Sophie closed her eyes. It was worse than she'd thought. McKay had been chasing the Weavers not for justice but to find his father?

Why didn't you tell me, Ben?

"You're Moira's boy?" Xander said. "That was a long time ago. It doesn't mean he's yours, Russell."

Moira? The woman who had carved the bird at Nighthawk Ranch? Sophie's head was spinning.

"How old are you?" Russell asked.

"Twenty-six," McKay answered.

"What happened to her?"

"She died when I was four. Here in Jerome, in fact. She's buried in the cemetery."

"I know," Russell said. "I wanted to find you. George told me no."

"George?" McKay asked.

"George Jenkins. We'd been friends a long time. When she left, she went to him for help, and he kept her hidden from me. And you. Much later he told me, and I didn't forgive him for some time. I'd wanted you back, but he said Moira's dying wish was for you to go to a better family and he wouldn't tell me where. He loved you, and I hated him for it. But now you're here." Russell looked amazed.

"Well, this all very touching," Rose interrupted, "but the bigger question is, how did you get our gold, Benton?"

"I found Harry's stash, so I moved it," McKay said. "Sophie's innocent. And Harry too."

"Hardly," Marty interjected. "Harry's been stealing from me for months."

Harry shook his head decisively. "No, no. Not *that* long. A few weeks, at most."

He was lying, and Sophie suspected everyone in the room knew it.

"Well, if you're a Weaver," Rose said to McKay, "then do the right thing and tell us where it is."

"First, release them." McKay's gaze swept over her, emotionless, and his lack of response to her, his apparent lack of remorse, made her feel cold.

He'd used her, more thoroughly than she'd thought possible. But he was at least trying to free her, although she feared she was about to forfeit her life in service to a man who had never been truthful with her.

"And then I'll take Russell," McKay added. "Only him."

The wonderment on Russell's face was almost embarrassing to witness, making Sophie feel like an interloper in this bizarre family reunion.

Russell looked from Rose to Xander. "Let them go."

They both refuted the command.

"Enough!" Russell's command blasted the room. "I'm still in charge. Let them go."

"Why?" Rose whispered aghast.

"Because he looks like her."

Moira.

"I hope you know what you're doing," Rose said, her displeasure evident. She nodded at Sophie and Harry. "It seems you're free to go."

Harry hopped up and ran for the door. Sophie rose more slowly, daring to glance at McKay, but he wouldn't meet her eyes. Walking past him was the hardest thing she'd ever done.

She would likely never see him again.

As soon as she was outside, Lucas was there, dragging her away from the house and into the darkness.

Rose's face was a mix of panic and pride as she faced McKay. "You got what you wanted. Drop your gun," she demanded.

McKay complied.

"Search him." She waved Xander forward, who conducted a rough search of McKay's person, finding all three of his extra weapons.

Rose's hostility amped up a notch. "You're well-armed for a man who studies birds all day."

Russell looked amused. "He's no bird watcher. Weaver blood always runs true. Let's get saddled up, boy."

Xander shook his head. "You're not going alone with him."

"Can I come?" Ned asked.

Russell laid a hand on Ned's shoulder. "Not this time."

"Is he really my brother?" The boy's expression was hopeful.

"I am," McKay said.

"We let your friends go," Russell said to McKay.

Friends. Harry was hardly that, and Sophie was so much more.

"Now you'll honor your word and return what belongs to me," Russell added, then said to his brother, "I'll be fine, Xander. He's weaponless."

McKay shoved thoughts of Sophie aside. She was safe. That's all that mattered. Her reaction to his true parentage was inconsequential, despite the look of anger—horror even—she'd given him. He knew he'd failed her, and he wanted nothing more than to chase after her and bare his soul, explaining everything, but the truth was, deep down, he was a Weaver. He'd always be a Weaver.

He anticipated the outcome of this to go one of two ways, and neither presented the possibility of a life with her. He hadn't realized how hard it would be to watch her walk away from him, how much he'd want to pull her close, to feel her against him one more time. To tell her he loved her.

But she was alive, and it was all that mattered. That would have to be enough.

Xander eyed McKay. "At least let me tie him up."

Russell silently agreed.

SOPHIE PUSHED AGAINST LUCAS. "Let me go!"

"No!"

"They'll kill him!"

Lucas held onto her. "He was very clear. I was to get you back to town."

"You can't believe the lie he's told," she said, grasping for a different truth. "He said he's Russell Weaver's son."

"Soph, he is."

She stopped fighting, and her body went limp with defeat. Lucas released her. "You knew?" she asked, feeling hollowed out.

"Yes."

"For how long?"

He didn't answer.

"Why didn't you say anything?" she demanded.

"It was part of my assignment. To make sure he didn't do anything stupid."

"He's doing something stupid right now!"

"Maybe," Lucas admitted. "But right now I have to worry about you, then I'll deal with him."

She'd felt so humiliated moments ago, but now that she was out of danger, a surge of hysteria for his safety had overtaken her. Despite everything, she didn't want him to die. Despite everything, she loved him.

Lucas had dragged her some distance from the house. He'd retrieved Roger and Mabel and had them waiting, and as soon as Harry had caught sight of his mule, he'd jumped on her and lit out like a man on fire.

She calmed herself. This wasn't over, and Lucas was about to jump into the fray. "You don't have to escort me back to town."

"I'm not leaving you alone."

"I'll find Olivia," she said. "And I'll look for Bromley and Sally Weaver."

"Can I believe you?"

"Yes!"

"Sophie, please don't lie to me."

"I'm not," she said. "You should follow McKay and Russell but promise me you'll be careful."

He nodded. "Not that it's any of your business, but Olivia is at my hotel. She was exhausted and upset about her father's new marriage. She didn't want to go home, so I took her to my room."

"Thank goodness you did."

"Yeah, thank goodness."

"Go." She pushed him away from her.

He mounted his horse, and the night swallowed them up. She climbed atop Roger and managed to catch Harry despite his frantic escape.

"I can't believe you gave all of it to him," Harry huffed. "Are you so addled by love that you let him convince you that you could trust him?"

"What are you talking about?"

"He tricked you," Harry persisted.

"It's not what you think," she said. "McKay is a U.S. Deputy Marshal."

Harry barked out a laugh. "He admitted he's a Weaver. They just rode off together with all the gold I worked so hard to steal."

"You're wrong."

But as she pushed Roger back to town, it played out in her head. First McKay romanced her. Quite thoroughly. Then she readily shared what she had found. Then she let him take it from her.

Was it true? Had she been played for a fool after all? Was the entire scene in the Bromley house a ruse that had been concocted by all of them, McKay included?

With her emotions a jumbled mess, she considered what her next move should be. She'd told Lucas she wouldn't follow him, but he could very well be riding into a trap.

CHAPTER 30

Benton's hands were bound at the wrists, resting in front of him, and Uncle Xander had tied each foot to a stirrup.

It was a foolhardy move, surrendering himself, and one of the possible scenarios he'd considered was him not surviving. But when Rose had pointed that pistol at Sophie's head, there'd been no question of him entering the Bromley house and playing the best card he had. And it worked. With hope, at this very moment, Lucas had Sophie safely tucked back in town.

Now it was time for Benton to play the long game.

Never mind that a part of him was relieved to be in the company of his father. For so long he'd wondered about this man who had cast a long and wide shadow over his life, beginning in earnest when Benton had been twelve years old and his aunt and uncle had given him a letter written by his mother, who had instructed that Benton read it when he was of an age to want to know more about Russell, and why Moira had left him. She had described their early courtship and the flush of their young love. The quick marriage. Her almost immediate pregnancy. And then the slow but steady realization that Russell wasn't who she had thought he was.

His mother had been an only child of a traveling preacher, her own mama dying during an epidemic of yellow fever, and then her father had taken a fall from a horse. She'd met Russell shortly after her pa had died, in a café in Fort Worth where she'd been able to get work, and she'd been utterly alone, with only a few distant relatives in California with whom she was barely acquainted.

Russell had seemed the answer to her prayers.

But the criminal activity began to take its toll. At first, she hadn't understood the extent of it. And then, she had tried to reason it in her own mind, that it was necessary for their survival but would eventually stop. She gave birth to Benton, but her conscience was heavy, and she stayed as long as she could, finally fleeing in the night when Benton was two years old.

She had included his father's name—Russell Weaver—because she had wanted Benton to know who he was, to understand that there was no reason to ever find him, that he would likely be dead by the time Benton was old enough. But she also shared the name so Benton would know if the man ever came for him. Not to be caught off guard, to know exactly who he was.

But as Benton came of age a hatred slowly took root, a simmering emotion over his father's failure to give his mother a life she deserved. He had failed to protect her, to simply love her enough, an act that might have helped her live despite her failing health. If only his father had done what was right.

And then there was the brewing resentment for the man himself. Had Russell given any thought to his son in all these years? Was it true that George Jenkins had kept Benton's whereabouts a secret until the man's death? Was it true that Russell had mourned losing his firstborn?

It was the tiniest of thorns—this hope that his father would've wanted to know him—and it was buried deep in Benton's heart.

It made him angry even to want such a thing.

And when he had rushed in to save Sophie, he was ashamed that saving her hadn't been the only reason. A part of him had wanted Russell to know he was there. He'd wanted Russell to acknowledge he was his son.

He'd always wanted it so damned bad.

Russell brought his horse in line with The Belgian. "How long have you known about me?"

"Since I was twelve," Benton answered. "My mother left a letter."

"George never told me where you went after Moira died."

"I called them aunt and uncle, but they were her second cousins. We lived in California."

"Did you have a good life?" he asked.

"Yes."

Russell watched him. "I recognize a lawman when I see one. Sheriff? Ranger?"

"U.S. Deputy Marshal."

Russell smiled as if he were proud, and McKay couldn't stop the pleasure he took in it.

"Damn, boy," he said. "You did that for me? I'm honored." Then he quieted and said soberly, "Moira must've hated me. She must've made you hate me."

"Why didn't you try to change for her? Why did you let her go?"

Silence filled the space between them, their horses picking their way through the calm night as McKay guided The Belgian to Nighthawk Ranch.

"Pride is a devil," Russell finally said. "And I never knew any other life. You get told enough that you're no good, you start to believe it. And then I found something I *was* good at, and no one was gonna take that away from me." He shifted his hat. "I truly believed she'd come back to me. I didn't think He would take her so soon after." His voice rasped on the last sentence.

"And you didn't come for me?"

"I wanted to," Russell answered, his voice firm and tinged with bitterness. "But then there was George. My friend," he added softly. "He helped her when she had no one else, and I suppose I must be grateful for that. And he kept her confidence for years after. I know what you're thinking, and I thought it too, that he loved her. That he took her from me. But he said no. He was a decent man, and he knew me well enough to know that I wasn't.

"But one day he finally confessed it all, knowing that I'd been mourning her leaving me. I didn't believe him at first when he said she'd died. That hit me hard. Not even Xander knows how hard. George told me to let you go, that she'd wanted it that way. She'd wanted you to have a life I wouldn't be able to give." He cleared his throat. "She was right, so I slowly let it go. You just stop thinking about it, and after a while you can convince yourself that it never much mattered.

"And now here you are, and you've got my gold. There's got to be some irony in that somewhere. You stole from me what I'd already stolen. You've got more Weaver in you than you think."

"Maybe," Benton said. *Probably.* Dare he believe that Russell had, in his own way, cared about his wife and son? "Were you going to buy George's ranch and live your end days there?"

Russell shrugged. "I was thinkin' about it. Robbing trains isn't a restful lifestyle. And George always wanted me to get out of the business, as it were, and live more respectably. Buying the place seemed like a way to honor him. And Moira. She'd left her mark here. I guess I hadn't accounted for a son out to end me."

"You have to pay for the crimes you've committed. If not me, it would've been somebody else."

"Then I'm blessed it was you who found me."

Benton would be hard pressed to consider any of this a blessing.

Once in town Harry disappeared, and Sophie let him go. She went to the Connor Hotel and pounded on Lucas's door until Olivia answered, half asleep and still wearing her day dress.

"What's going on?"

"Lucas might be in trouble," Sophie said. "We have to do something."

Olivia came awake. "What time is it?"

"Three a.m."

"Come inside."

Olivia shut the door, and Sophie quickly caught the woman up on what had happened, including that Deborah, alias Sally Weaver, wasn't pregnant, and McKay's admission to being a Weaver.

Olivia was speechless on both points, but then she said, "I can't believe my father *married* a train robber. And do you really think McKay stole the gold *for* the Weavers?"

Tears welled in Sophie's eyes. "I don't know." Then she squared her shoulders. "We need to go to Nighthawk Ranch. Russell has been using it as a home base, and maybe he'll return. But we need a weapon."

"I have none."

"I still have the gun McKay gave me," Sophie said. "It's in my satchel, and my satchel is in your father's barn." It had been tossed aside when Marty had discovered her.

"Are you sure my father isn't there?"

"I think he's somewhere in town. We'll look for him at first light."

Olivia nodded. "Okay. We can take a back way to the barn in case Rose, Marty and Xander are still trespassing."

As they neared their destination, Russell asked, "Nighthawk Ranch?"

The outline of the ranch could be seen in the distance. Everything was dark.

"The gold's here," McKay said.

"You don't say."

"Hide in plain sight. It seems to be the Weaver motto."

Russell halted his horse, and McKay did the same. "I concur with the motto, but this isn't the best hiding place. Coltrane has been sniffing around. We'd best not ride in announcing our presence."

"I met him a few days ago. What's he doing here?" He didn't mention the attack on Sophie. The less she was involved, the better.

"Sally is my younger sister. She's always been a smart one, but that all went to pot the day she met Coltrane. She fell hard for him and urged us to bring him into the fold, so we did. Xander did some digging on him, and what he'd told us seemed to align with it. He used to be a U.S. Marshal but was caught dealing in stolen bonds. How he avoided jail time for that, I was never sure. Sally said it made him as hungry for our next job as we were, and he'd be an asset, so we let him in.

"Turned out he was a Pinkerton, hired by a businessman we'd targeted a year before. He was to infiltrate and bring us in, except he decided our take was far more than he was being paid as a spy, so he cut a deal with us, but it was more like blackmail. He's the one who killed the train conductor, but it's been pinned on me. Sally confronted him, and he beat her. Somehow, she managed to get away and tell us, so we came here. We were careful, but somehow, he found us."

"I was the one Sally shot a week ago."

"Sonofabitch," Russell muttered. "She thought it was Coltrane. He makes her skittish, and when she's skittish her trigger finger gets itchy. You're lucky to be alive."

"I can't believe she shot me from the distance she did," Benton said. "Her skill is ...."

"Unmatched."

"Is he after the gold as well?"

Russell nodded. "Seems to think we cheated him out of it. Which, of course, we did. How did you know we were here?"

"A tip came to the marshal office in Tucson that Xander had been seen in a stage headed out of Phoenix."

"Coltrane must still have friends among the marshals," Russell said. "And he used it to track us down. Although Sally told me recently that she'd mentioned George's ranch once in passing to him. Did you know it was Moira who named Nighthawk Ranch?"

Yes. Sophie told me. That moment seemed so long ago, their passionate tryst near the alcove when the barriers between them, not only physically but emotionally, had dissolved. For the briefest time, Benton had been happy.

But he'd lied to her, and to Lucas, until tonight. He was under no illusions that his actions would be forgiven if he managed to survive.

"She told me stories about the birds," Benton said, thinking of his mother.

"Back in Texas, they were her favorite. She said her mother taught her to listen to them at night. She suggested to George that he call his place Nighthawk Ranch, and she did a carving by the front door."

Benton would like to see that carving one more time, to remember the woman who had given him life and then left him far too soon. Was he letting her down, leading the man she'd tried so hard to escape to the doorstep of her final sanctuary? Should he give the gold to Russell as he'd promised? Or act now and arrest him?

Unfortunately, Benton was at a disadvantage. He had no weapons, and Russell was no weakling. A physical altercation could go either way.

And despite Russell's admission of regret over losing Benton, would that stop the man from acting in violence against him? Against his own kin?

Russell had said it was Coltrane who'd murdered the conductor, but he could be lying.

Weavers were good at that.

CHAPTER 31

Sophie suppressed a squeal as she tripped over an anvil at the same time Olivia ran into a table. The Bromley barn was dark, and they had rushed inside too quickly to avoid being seen since Rose's wagon still sat in front of the house.

Olivia cursed, then said, "You don't think Sally will do anything to my father, do you?"

"Nah." They both jumped at Ned's voice, Olivia stepping on Sophie's toe, causing her to hiss. "Don't worry," Ned added. "I won't snitch on you."

Sophie lifted her foot, trying to shake off the pain. "How did you know we were here?"

"I was looking out the window and saw you. Rose told me to sleep but I don't like being in someone else's house."

Olivia crouched so she was face to face with Ned. "Have you seen my father?"

"No, ma'am."

"Your mother?"

"Like I told Miss Ryan, she's not my mother. But no. Sally's missing, too. Aunt Rose ain't too happy 'bout it. That's why we're still here. We're waiting for her."

"Did Russell ever come back?" Sophie asked.

Ned shook his head. "Are you gonna go look for him?"

"That's none of your concern."

"Uncle Xander and Marty are gone, probably lookin' for my pa, so you should take me with you. I could help with all the male folk."

That hardly seemed like a good idea, not the least because he was a child.

"I always wanted to be called Snake Eyes," he continued. "But now I want to be like Oliver Twist. I want to be better than my circumstances. I want to make somethin' good of myself."

Sophie didn't know what to say. Had she truly gotten through to the boy? Would the course of his life be changed from here on out? This boy who was McKay's brother.

"I'm glad, Ned," she said, giving his arm a squeeze. "But you should get back to the house before Rose notices you're missing. That would help us tremendously."

"Fine." The boy accepted his defeat with more grace than expected. "Did you know we were livin' at Nighthawk Ranch when we first came here?"

It didn't surprise Sophie.

"That was before Sally got scared bein' out in the middle of nowhere," he continued. "And she decided to move to town with me."

"Why was she scared?" Olivia asked.

"A man named John Coltrane. He hurt her real bad back in Texas, and she was convinced he was here. You should watch out for him. I wouldn't want him to hurt you, too."

"Thanks for the information, Ned," Sophie said. "The next time I see you, I'll let you have my spyglass."

"No joke?"

"No joke."

He left them, and her heart felt heavy. What would happen to him when the Weavers were caught? Would he go to jail? He was just a boy. He never picked his life circumstances, the same path that could've easily been McKay's if he hadn't gotten away thanks to his mother. Or was that just a story too?

Had McKay cared about her? Even a little? Or had she simply been a means to an end?

"I DON'T SUPPOSE you'll just tell me where the gold is," Russell said as he cut the ropes securing Benton's feet and hands. "Then you could stay and let me confront Coltrane if he's here."

Was Russell giving him a chance to escape? Or was the Coltrane story a lie? Maybe the two of them were working together after all.

"Your manners are certainly a surprise," Benton said, considering his newfound freedom from Xander's handiwork. He needed to get hold of one of Russell's guns. He'd caught sight of a shoulder harness earlier, but the one at the man's hip was the most accessible.

"I'm not a monster, Benton. And you must know you can join us. Although I take pride that you broke the cycle for the Weavers. Maybe Ned has hope."

"What happened to *his* mother?" McKay asked.

"She died too," came a voice from behind with an accompanying hammer click. *Coltrane.*

The Belgian shifted, giving McKay a glimpse of the man. He was on foot, which explained why they hadn't heard him. And he was downwind to avoid alerting the horses. Russell turned, his hand gripping The Belgian's bridle.

"You just can't keep your women alive, can you, Russell?" Coltrane added.

"She died giving birth to Ned," Russell said to Benton. "I did everything I could to help Cora."

Coltrane waved his pistol. "Let's get on down to the ranch and you can show me where you hid your daddy's treasure. Leave the horses. We'll walk."

McKay dismounted.

"Drop your guns, Russell."

Russell unbuckled his gun belt and let it fall to the ground.

"And the coat," Coltrane added.

Russell shed his jacket, revealing the shoulder holster. He removed it as well.

"And that knife you just used."

Russell slid it from his shirt sleeve where he'd hidden it. In the dark, McKay hadn't noticed. He added it to the pile of weapons.

"Now we walk," Coltrane said.

With reluctance, Benton left behind Russell's weapons and his last hope of changing the rules of this night.

As Sophie and Olivia neared the ranch house, they came upon two saddled horses. One was The Belgian and the other was likely Russell Weaver's mount. No sign of either man.

She scanned the ground. Three sets of boot prints went toward the house. Someone had found them. Lucas? Or was Ned right, and it was Coltrane?

"Now what?" Olivia asked.

"Secure the horses."

They hobbled not only theirs but McKay's and Russell's too. Sophie noticed a pile of something nearby. Weapons. And Russell's duster.

Olivia came beside her. "Why are these here?"

"I don't know." Sophie pulled the pistol from the shoulder holster and checked it. It had bullets.

"Take this." She handed the holster to Olivia, who stared at it

237

with confusion. Sophie lifted Olivia's arm and looped the leather around it, then buckled it as tightly as she could. "Do you know how to shoot?"

"I …." She shook her head. "No. I'm a writer, Sophie."

"Then just hold the weapon and point. That you *might* shoot should be enough."

Sophie buckled the gun belt around her waist, but it was also too big and hung loose. She added McKay's gun to the other holster. "These weapons must be Russell's."

"Why would he leave them behind?"

"Something must be wrong." She put the knife in the waist of her skirt. "Come on."

But Olivia didn't move.

"We need to get closer to see what's going on," Sophie added.

Olivia's distress was pronounced but there wasn't anything Sophie could do about it. She waved her forward with impatience.

When they were closer, three men could be seen in the front room of the house.

Russell.

McKay, her heart skipping a beat at the sight of him.

The other man must be Coltrane. And he held a gun.

"LET'S MAKE A DEAL, JOHN," Russell said from his seat on the sofa beside Benton.

"That time has passed."

"Nah." Russell seemed relaxed for having no weapons and a gun pointed at him.

Benton was running the options through his head. Hand over the gold. Or don't. What would Coltrane do? Benton had told Lucas to take care of Sophie and to secure things in town, telling him he would deal with the Weavers. There'd be no backup coming.

"There's three bags that Rose converted into Spanish gold coins," Russell said. "We'll split them three ways."

Coltrane frowned. "Three ways?"

"We'll cut in Benton." Russell nodded toward him. "My son. And a U.S. Deputy Marshal. He can cover our tracks with the law."

Benton's refusal was ready, but he held back as Coltrane uttered, "Bullshit. I'll take it all. You have no bargaining power here, Russell."

"I understand, but you made things more difficult for me when you took out that conductor. Benton will smooth that over for us, won't you, son?"

Benton didn't answer.

"But it'll cost you," Russell added to Coltrane.

Coltrane laughed. "This has been a pain in my ass from beginning to end. You thought you could cut me out. You were mistaken."

"I didn't like what you did to Sally." Russell's voice was low. Lethal.

"You're too soft on her," Coltrane said. "And you let the women run things. It's why you're in this mess to begin with." Coltrane motioned for them to stand. "All right, enough talk. Bring out the gold, *Benton*, and I'll decide whether to leave a donation for the father-son reunion."

Russell gave a silent assent.

"It's outside," Benton said and led them to the horse trough along the corral. He pulled out the three bags that had been submerged in the water, dumping each one on the ground with a thud.

The whistle of a bullet hit Coltrane and he fell back.

Benton dropped down, wedging himself behind the water receptacle. Coltrane was motionless. Russell crawled over and took the man's gun. For a long moment, they remained in this suspended state, silent, waiting for more gunfire, or perhaps for Coltrane to wake up.

If he wasn't dead, that is.

"Must be Sally," Russell murmured. "She's the only one who could've taken this shot. It's time to go, Benton."

"You know I can't do that."

"You don't have a choice, and you know it. Your Weaver blood is humming. If it'll make it easier, I'll hold you at gunpoint."

Benton left the safety of his cover. "There's no need for that."

Xander appeared with three horses. He took one look at Benton, and said, "You sure about this, Russell?"

"It's about time my son learned the family business."

Benton grabbed his hat from the ground. It was the long game, the possibility he'd hoped to avoid, because the path ahead, littered with unknown obstacles, might offer no way back.

Forgive me, Sophie.

WHEN COLTRANE DROPPED, Sophie stopped abruptly and scanned the hills. Dawn was approaching, and in the growing light a woman's figure ran along a ridge and then disappeared.

Sally!

Gunfire erupted to the north. Lucas? And she thought she caught a glimpse of Marty. Back at the ranch, Xander, Russell, and McKay were loading the bags of gold onto horses.

"Lucas is in trouble!" Olivia took off running in the opposite direction from the ranch.

Indecision gripped Sophie. If she confronted the Weaver gang with Russell's weapons in hand, could she stop them? Could she save McKay and help him take custody of the men?

But Olivia's impulsive move might get the woman killed. Marty was too unpredictable to be deterred by the simple waving of a gun as Sophie had instructed.

When McKay mounted one of the horses alongside his father and uncle, she blinked hard. Her eyes must be deceiving her. He wasn't being detained. Or coerced.

They departed, heading west.

And then they were gone.

Stunned, Sophie stumbled after Olivia.

CHAPTER 32

Three weeks later

Sophie squinted at the morning sun as she entered the newspaper office and removed her satchel.

Olivia looked up from her typesetting, her face aglow and her blonde hair less severe in its usual twist. It was the look of a woman in love. "Good morning, Sophie. I can't believe it's your last day." Her happiness dimmed slightly. "We're sure going to miss you."

Sophie removed her coat along with the blue scarf McKay had given her, unable to toss it in the trash after that night at Nighthawk Ranch when he'd chosen a life on the wrong side of the law. When he'd chosen a life without her.

She hung both on a wall hook. "It's not forever. I'm sure I'll return to visit since Lucas has decided to stay."

It was the source of Olivia's happiness, Sophie knew. Word had come from Tucson that the U.S. Marshal office had been happy with the outcome of the case in Jerome and had supported Mayor Sterling when he offered the position of town marshal to Lucas since Habison and his deputy had been arrested. And to Sophie's surprise, her cousin had been amenable to resigning his brand-new U.S. Deputy Marshal position for one that would keep him near Olivia.

And while there had been additional charges served—notably to Arthur Sewell and his clerk for document forgery, and Marty Ennis for handling and tampering with stolen gold bars, as well as several instances of bribery of town and mine officials—it confounded Sophie that the case was considered a success.

Lucas had managed to nab Marty that night with the help of Sophie and Olivia, but all the Weavers had escaped, including a few that hadn't been known—Rose, Sally, and Ned. And of course, McKay. By all accounts, the entire job had been an abject failure.

And Sophie had done her best to ignore her broken heart.

"Are you packed and ready to go?" Olivia asked.

"Yes. My pa will arrive later, and we'll depart first thing tomorrow." He was accompanying her back to Texas.

"I look forward to supper, and meeting Uncle Logan," Olivia said, referring to Sophie's father. "Lucas speaks very highly of him."

Sophie sat at her desk, pushing aside a pang of sadness. She would miss this place, along with Olivia and Joe, who asked, "Are you ready for the big time?"

The Dallas Morning News had made her an offer she couldn't refuse after the story of the Weavers and the counterfeit Spanish coins broke. Olivia had been much too kind in allowing Sophie to have the byline to herself.

"All I did was edit," Olivia had said. "You wrote it."

The story had gone wide, and the Dallas paper had reached out to her.

"I think so," Sophie replied in response to Olivia's question, pulling her trusty notebook from her satchel, more from habit than anything. The pages were still wrinkled and stained in places from when Coltrane had stolen it from her, that bit of news shared with her via Lucas.

Joe smiled. "Maybe you'll write that novel after all."

"Maybe."

They fell into a companionable silence as they each resumed their work, although Sophie had nothing to do since it was her last day. She would get a new notebook once she assumed her position in Dallas, since they had requested a lengthier piece on what had occurred here in Jerome. She opened the well-worn book that had accompanied her throughout her time here and began reviewing her notes to make sure she hadn't missed anything while it was all fresh in her mind.

She considered again her interrogation of Lucas when the dust had settled. While he'd shared many details such as Coltrane's involvement with the gang—the man was unfortunately deceased, Sally's aim having been true—and the surprising audacity of Rose receiving shipments of gold via packages delivered to Walt's mercantile, reminding Sophie of the heavy parcel she'd abandoned that day Ned had stolen her spyglass—Lucas had been vague when she had questioned him about McKay. He'd simply said the case still was ongoing, and he couldn't discuss specifics. Especially since Sophie wanted to write about it.

It had been frustrating, and she'd gone from shock to misery and finally to anger, all concerning Benton McKay. Had he truly defected? She'd been checking the wanted posters every day that came through the mayor's office, expecting to see his likeness beside Russell and Xander, along with Sally and Rose, now that their identities were known. But there had been nothing. Had his new family turned against him? It was the not knowing that gnawed at her.

Her monthly had come, so there was no baby. She had been both relieved and surprisingly sad, mourning a possible connection with McKay. She was such a fool. At least she wouldn't have to confess to her mother how easily she'd fallen for a handsome face.

When there was nothing else to occupy her time, Sophie collected her things. "I've got some goodbyes to say in town, so I think this is it."

Joe stood and gave her a hug. "Don't forget about us little people."

"Never." She turned to Olivia, determined not to cry. "I'll see you later, but will you give my regards to your father?"

"Of course."

After Sally's disappearance, it hadn't been difficult for Bromley to dissolve his hasty marriage considering the situation. He'd been cleared of any charges despite his work with the Weavers since he had honestly not known he was engaging in criminal activity. Using the map they had had given him via Sally, they'd convinced him he was searching for real Conquistador gold, using it as bait so he would perform the task of discovering the coins, making the stolen goods "respectable."

Bromley had gone into seclusion among his inventions, shaken by the entire turn of events, according to Olivia. He still harbored a belief there was Conquistador gold in the area, and Olivia feared he would sink back into his obsession.

As Sophie walked down Main Street she thought of Harry, unsurprised by his disappearance, but still concerned for Mabel. Moving all that gold had taken a toll on the animal, and she hoped he would take better care of her. Sophie had arranged with Trent to buy Roger with funds her pa had sent her, and the horse would have a permanent home at Dove Crossing.

She entered Walt's mercantile, and his face became crestfallen the moment he saw her. "Is it time for goodbyes already?"

"Yes. I'll be leaving in the morning."

He abandoned the condensed milk cans he'd been stacking. "We're gonna miss you, Sophie."

"It's been an adventure, I'll say that. Any interest in buyers for Nighthawk Ranch?"

"Maybe. Of course, the mine wants it, but they'll raze the property and exploit the mineral rights, so I'm rather disinclined to entertain any offers from them." He scowled. "The Weavers hadn't really needed to bribe any officials to prevent it. I can't believe I almost lost the place to such a bad lot."

"Don't be hard on yourself," she said. "Apparently, George and Russell Weaver had been friends."

Walt shook his head. "I'd no idea. George kept a lot of secrets. But no reason to dwell on that. I guess you haven't heard, and maybe I should keep it to myself, but your cousin Lucas has inquired about the ranch."

"He has?" If he was looking to put down roots, he must be more serious about Olivia than Sophie had realized. She tried to ignore the swell of envy.

"Don't tell him I told you," Walt added.

She nodded, then said, "Would it be all right if I went out to the ranch?"

"Today?"

"I wanted to take one last look around."

"That'd be okay," he said. "You sure you want to go alone?"

"It's probably the safest it's ever been," she said with a smile. "The Weavers are gone. And John Coltrane. And Marty Ennis is in jail. Things have calmed down."

"Not for the treasure hunters," Walt said. "More seem to arrive every day. It's good for business, though. And all thanks to your newspaper piece. You've got big things in your future. I'm sure of it."

"I'm grateful for your faith in me." She purchased a pack of Juicy Fruit gum and tucked it into her satchel.

"Don't be a stranger."

"I won't. I'll return this later," she said, referring to the key he'd handed her. Then she headed to the livery.

"You still need Roger ready to go in the morning?" Trent asked.

"Yes, but I'd like to ride him now for a bit."

"Sure thing, Miss Ryan."

He saddled the horse and brought him to her. "I'm gonna miss this boy," Trent said, "but I'm glad he's goin' to a good home."

"My folks will take good care of him."

"I think he misses The Belgian. He was sweet on her."

Xander had managed to retrieve McKay and Russell's horses before escaping with them and the gold, including Bromley's "find" from Pecks Lake. All the bars that Marty had melted down were gone, no doubt supporting McKay and his "new" family.

Sophie waited for the melancholy to pass from Trent's comment, having had to do it numerous times in the past few weeks. She'd wept enough over McKay during many sleepless nights at the Connor Hotel, where she'd moved to be closer to Lucas, as well as to give Olivia and her father their privacy. In honor of the national exposure Sophie had brought to Jerome, the hotel had graciously given her a greatly reduced price on the room.

Sophie rode Roger down Main Street, her hat shading her eyes, and her duster buttoned over her day dress to ward off the October chill. In such a short time, the town had grown on her, and her homesickness for Texas was now replaced with Jerome. Never mind that everywhere she looked, memories of McKay accosted her.

She didn't bother to cover her nose with McKay's scarf, hardly noticing the sulphur smell, mildly shocked that she could ever become accustomed to it. Once she had passed the last reminders of civilization, she let Roger have his head, reveling in the feeling of freedom as he raced along Perkins Road and then down the path that led to Nighthawk Ranch.

Once there, she stopped where she and Olivia had found The Belgian and Russell's horse along with the pile of weapons. In the late afternoon sun, she let the warmth fill her as the wind gently caressed her face. It were as if the land, the ranch, was saying, *Farewell. Arizona will miss you.*

It was here that she'd seen McKay for the last time.

Why had he done it? She'd gone over it again and again in her head, and every time it made no sense. He had honor. She was sure of it. But somewhere, deep down, he also must've desired a connection to his father. She was close to her own pa, so she understood, but perhaps she could never truly comprehend what it had been like for McKay to have been abandoned by Russell for his entire life.

She had gone to the cemetery a week ago and after much searching had found the headstone for Moira McKay, and it had filled her with heartbreak. And not for the first time did a fierce longing grip her to see Benton again, to speak with him, to touch him. To be a friend as he worked through this.

But he hadn't wanted that. If he had, he wouldn't have left.

She was pining for something that had never been hers to begin with.

She took her time walking the perimeter of the ranch, leading Roger behind her. In the peacefulness, she imagined that George, and Moira and McKay during their short time here, had found the quiet and solitude a boon. As she looked around, she decided it suited Lucas. One day he and Olivia would have a passel of kids running amuck. It brough a wistful smile to her lips, for the children she would never have with McKay.

She passed the coop where she had first met Russell, but the chickens were gone. And the water trough where McKay had hidden the gold was dry. Almost as if it had never happened.

She tied Roger to the hitching post and stepped onto the porch, running her fingers over the nighthawk etching near the door. Moira's work. The young woman had wanted to keep her son from Russell, but in the end had failed, and anguish pressed into Sophie on the woman's behalf.

She opened the door with the key Walt had given her, glad she didn't have to do any lock picking today. Scanning the room, she searched for evidence of a latching mechanism described to her by Olivia shortly after she'd found her father in town, blindsided by Sally's lies and manipulations. He'd told her that some time ago, before they were estranged over the search for Spanish gold, he and George Jenkins had been friends, and Bromley had built a secret cubbyhole in Nighthawk Ranch, and that it had been near the front door.

Ever since, the detail had been bugging Sophie.

But there was nothing near the door.

The room was sparsely decorated since Walt had recently removed some of the finer pieces of furniture to resell through his store. Her gaze kept returning to a small wall hanging with an embroidered bird. The material was faded and obviously old. It reminded her of the kerchief McKay had shown her when they'd been in the adit together.

She inspected the edges and found the initials MM.

Moira McKay.

She lifted the hanging and behind was a faint outline of a square border.

A secret panel?

CHAPTER 33

Immersed in her find, Sophie didn't hear boots on the porch until the last second. She barely had the panel closed before twisting around and hiding the sketchbook she'd found behind her.

The door opened and McKay entered, his cheeks ruddy from the cold October air and his eyes bright. He removed his hat and ran a hand through his hair, which had grown longer, and his face was covered in a beard and mustache, as if he'd been lost in the wilderness living like a fugitive. Which he had.

She stared, stunned.

"Why .... Why are you here?" she stammered.

"I was looking for you."

She glanced out the front window. The Belgian stood beside Roger, happy to see her old friend. There were no other horses. McKay was alone.

"Walt told me you were here," he said. "And that you're about to leave town."

"Ben, you should go. You'll be arrested." So much for letting him lie in the bed he'd made. Seeing him now made her heart ache. And despite that he'd chosen his family over doing the right thing—over *her*—she didn't want to see him in jail.

Maybe someday I'll write about love and ethical dilemmas, she thought rather cynically. She forced herself to stay rooted in her position when all she wanted was to rush into his arms, to hold him once more, even if it would be the last time.

"I know what you must think," he said.

She didn't answer, her throat tight, her heart pounding.

"I spoke to Lucas," he continued. "He filled me in on the last three weeks."

Lucas? Why?

"What's going on?" she whispered.

"I had to make a decision that night Russell had you and Harry. I needed to get you out of there. Promising him the gold seemed the best way. And while it had been a possibility that I would embed with them, I never believed it would go that far."

She frowned. "Did Lucas know this?"

"Not at first, but that night I told him."

"He never said anything to me."

"Well, in his defense, it wasn't something we wanted in the press."

"And you think I would've shared it?" she asked in a rush. "I'm not without discretion."

"I know. I think the bigger reason was he had doubts about my return. That either Russell would kill me, or even more concerning, that I'd embrace my new circumstances."

She pressed her lips together. "That's what I thought happened."

"I won't lie. That night I had a chance to talk to Russell, and he wasn't what I expected. The time I spent with him wasn't without a certain amount of internal conflict."

"What happened?" she asked, hungry to know. Hungry for him. Was there still a chance for them?

"We went into New Mexico. Russell had a place he could hole

up. They were all there—Xander, Sally, and Rose. And Ned, my new brother."

"Oh God," Sophie said. "Ned."

McKay held up a hand. "He hasn't been charged. The judge gave him leniency."

"Where is he?"

"His mother had family. He's been sent to them."

"Like you," Sophie said quietly.

"Russell seems to have a knack for losing his sons."

"How did you do it?" she asked. "How did you bring in all the Weavers?"

"Well, I didn't. I only got Russell. And Ned. Rose and Sally never trusted me, and they slipped away rather quickly. Xander defected soon after. I should've moved faster, but ...."

"You wanted more time with him."

He nodded. "Yes. I always wanted to think I wasn't compromised, that I could do the job without any emotional entanglement. I'd convinced my boss of it, but he hadn't believed me, and he sent Lucas not only to help, but also to monitor my actions."

"Then why did Lucas let you run off? It made you look like an outlaw. Why didn't he set the record straight?"

"Because it was classified. Letting that information out could've possibly exposed me. There were leaks in the marshal office. I also wanted you out of it. The less you knew, the better, and Lucas agreed."

"That's admirable of him, but I can take care of myself," she said. "And he can't tell me where my heart lies."

"And where is that?" His voice was quiet.

"With you." Her voice faltered. "Always with you. It broke me in half when you left." She stood, setting the sketchbook on a nearby table, and stepped closer, stopping before him. "Why didn't you tell me Russell was your father?"

"I couldn't in the beginning. It was sensitive information, and I thought you were part of the gang."

Her eyes widened. "Oh God, did you think I was your sister or something?"

The corner of his mouth lifted with a hint of a smile. "No, and I was relieved when I learned your nosiness was part of your natural personality."

"I'm not nosy." She moved closer. "I'm helpful."

"And I'm grateful. I'm hopelessly in love with you, Sophie. I have been since the moment I met you."

"When I pulled a bullet from your shoulder?" she whispered.

He kissed her, feather light, gently cupping her cheeks. She returned the gesture, and with each kiss she demanded more, until he took her mouth with as much fierce desperation as she was feeling.

"I have a lot to atone for," he said, his breath hot against her lips. "Will you let me?"

She nodded, indulging kiss after kiss, his mustache scratching her face, but she didn't care. She ran her fingers along his beard and then down his chest.

He leaned his forehead against hers. "Why are you here?"

"It was the last place I'd seen you," she answered.

He leaned back and looked at her with surprise. "You were here that night?"

"Olivia and I both came."

McKay swore under his breath. "Sally could've shot you."

She shook her head. "No. Her aim was true. You of anyone should know that. Besides, I found Russell's guns, and had them in hand, but then I saw you leave with him and Xander."

He took her hand and led her to the sofa in front of the fireplace. Despite a layer of dust, they both sat.

"It must've been difficult turning in Russell," she said, facing him, still in disbelief that he'd come back to her.

"In a twist of irony, it was Russell who pushed me to do it. He told me he hadn't expected to live as long as he had, that one of the reasons Moira left him was because one of her fears had been that he would die, and she might never know. He'd been pursued by other agents in the past, and he had no doubt there would be more in the future. If he was going down, he found it rather fitting it be by my hand. We spent time together, and I think he knew I was wavering, that there was a part of me that was considering staying with him."

"Buzz had a conscience after all," she said.

"It would seem. He's in custody in Dallas since the initial charges were filed in Texas. I hear you're headed to the Dallas Morning News. Congratulations. You deserve it."

"You could've spoken to me there," she said. "You didn't have to come all this way."

"No. But I needed to tell you in person that I'm sorry for lying to you. I was required to go to Tucson for a debrief, and my boss told me Lucas has decided to remain in Jerome."

"It's Olivia, of course."

He took her hand. "Sophie, if we could have a second chance, I'd be willing to do the same."

"Stay in Jerome?" she teased.

"Only if you're here." His gaze was raw and vulnerable, stripping away the last of her doubts. "What I meant was, I'll request a transfer to the U.S. marshal office in Dallas."

"Okay," she said, her mood serious. "Then I'd like to try." She reached for the sketchbook and handed it to him. "There was another reason I came today. This belonged to your mother. Her name is written inside. George had kept it all this time."

McKay opened it, the pages filled with drawing after drawing of nighthawk birds.

"She was talented," Sophie said, admiring the intricate artwork. She stopped him on a particular page. "This one I think says it all."

It was a nighthawk nest, built on the ground with little protection. Moira had written her thoughts beside it.

Nighthawks consume with abandon, swallowing their prey whole, but they have such steely nerve to nest in the open, relying on their camouflage to confuse predators. I can't help but admire their audacity to protect their young in such a way. Russell had told me that hiding in plain sight had given him an edge to avoid detection while he committed his dreadful crimes. Those pursuing him never believed he would be so obvious. So now I'm here at George's ranch. He's been a good confidant to me, but he's also Russell's friend, and I know his help has come at great cost to that loyalty. But I took a page from Russell's book. I took cover in plain sight. Russell would never have suspected me of going to George.

George has promised to send Benton to my second cousin, and I'm at peace that this is the appropriate course of action. That Benton will find a true and right path without Russell's influence. That he will find a true and right love, one that will guide him and not lead him astray, as my love for Russell did.

But my lost path gave me Benton, so I cannot grieve it. To my strong, curious son who is like his father in so many ways, I love you with all my heart. It was this love that gave me the strength to leave Russell, a man for whom I still pine today.

McKay was silent, then he looked at her. "Thank you. Where did you find this?"

"I learned that one of Bromley's inventions was a hidden wall panel and that he'd installed one for George to store valuables. At the time, George was heavily invested in looking for Conquistador gold, and in fact, it was he who ignited the desire in Bromley. But with them eventually being in competition for the treasure, George announced he wouldn't use the secret hideaway for anything important, believing that Bromley would sneak in and steal whatever was there. The story made me curious."

He smiled. "Nosy."

She scoffed. "Do you want to know what I found or not?"

"There's more?"

She went to the wall hanging beside the fireplace.

"This was stitched by your mother, I believe," she said. "It matches the one you have."

He crouched to have a better look. "I think you're right."

She lifted the material and opened the panel. "And it would seem George adhered to hiding in plain sight as well."

McKay peered into the interior of the cubbyhole. "Is that what I think it is?"

She grinned, then released a giddy laugh. "Yes."

McKay removed the wooden box, the coins inside covered in grime. She'd already examined the contents although she hadn't removed them from the box, but now she helped McKay set several on the table to examine. They were dirty and irregularly shaped, but some patterns were visible.

"He was smart not to clean them," she said. "It would've ruined the engravings. The marks seem more in line with what Joe told me. For instance, look here. *Escudo* is spelled correctly."

McKay sat back. "If this is Conquistador gold, then these belong to Walt. It'll be up to him how to proceed. But I'd like to ask if he'd let me have the sketchbook and the hanging."

"I'm sure he would." She placed the coins carefully back into the box. "We need to go."

"You're not leaving for Dallas now, are you?"

"No. My father will be here in time for supper, and I'd like you to meet him."

"I'd be honored, Sophie."

CHAPTER 34

Dallas
November 1899

Hunched over her typewriter, Sophie didn't notice her sister's arrival at the Dallas Morning News until Anna was sitting across from her desk.

"Anna!" Sophie exclaimed. "What are you doing here? I wasn't expecting you until next week."

"My plans changed, and I decided to surprise you."

Sophie's normally stoic sibling, a striking twin to their mother with the same blonde hair and love of medicine, was smiling, and she looked ... relaxed. She'd spent the last four years studying at the Women's Medical College in Kansas City, and while she had been home over the summer assisting their mother with her practice, she'd been rather moody. Anna was never one to show her emotions, but Sophie had overheard her folks discuss her sister's angst over wanting to break out on her own and finding several obstacles in her way. Their mother, Claire, was happy to partner with her, but Anna's ambitions were burning brighter than that.

"I'm almost done here," Sophie said, indicating the piece she was finishing up.

"Is it the Russell Weaver story?"

"Yes, the second part. I've still got a third section to write." Benton had accompanied her to the Texas penitentiary in Huntsville to interview his father. Since it was almost two hundred miles to the south of Dallas, they'd spent several days visiting with Russell. Her boss had been keen on an in-depth look at the life of an outlaw, and it was the only thing she was working on at the moment. "Give me twenty minutes and I'll meet you at the café down the street."

Anna glanced around the busy newsroom, then threw Sophie a proud smile from beneath her straw hat and left. Within the hour, she was sitting across from Sophie once again, a pot of tea and a plate of sweetcakes between them.

Sophie frowned at a stray hair that had come loose when she'd removed her wool hat and tried to stuff it back into the bun. "Are you still interviewing?" she asked.

"Yes, I have one appointment next week at a private hospital."

"I thought you had several."

Anna pressed her lips flat. "Female physicians aren't placed on staff. The other interviews were cancelled."

"I'm so sorry."

"I'm optimistic for the remaining one, but I came early because the Texas Medical Association is holding a meeting tomorrow and the topic is diphtheria antitoxin. I didn't want to miss it." At the last statement, the joy from earlier returned to her face.

Sophie added cream to her tea. "Riveting, Anna." But she was happy her sister was jubilant about something.

Anna scoffed. "You should be glad I haven't told Pa that you've been interviewing a criminal."

Sophie sighed. "He'll know soon enough. Part one will be in print in early December."

"Will Benton continue to see his father?"

"I'm not certain." Benton's relationship with Russell was complicated and ever evolving.

Anna took a sip of her tea. "Has there been any word on the remaining family members?"

"No. They're still at large, but we received a letter from Ned and he's doing well in California." His path had become eerily similar to Benton's. "I sent him my copy of *Frankenstein* and my spyglass."

Anna's eyes widened. "Those are prized possessions. You must be very fond of the boy."

"I am."

"And perhaps you'll become a true sister to him soon." Anna's expression was hopeful.

Sophie laughed. Her family loved Benton, thankfully, and were waiting for an engagement announcement any day. She took a bite of cake, then leaned forward. "I'll tell you a secret. Benton *has* proposed."

Anna gasped. "Sophie, that's wonderful, but Pa never said anything."

"That's because Benton hasn't asked him yet. But we're also delaying an announcement because of Lucas and Olivia."

Anna's questioning look indicated her lack of knowledge on that piece of gossip as well. Sophie hoped she wasn't spilling too much news. "Olivia is with child. They plan to marry soon, probably at Christmastime, so Benton and I might announce after the new year."

"Well, of course I'm happy for Lucas, and I look forward to meeting Olivia—you've spoken so highly of her—but can you delay until after the holidays? *You* could be with child."

Sophie shushed her, glancing around. "We're careful," she whispered. *Mostly.*

Anna grinned from behind the rim of her cup. "Where will you live? That room at the boarding house is tiny."

"I know. Benton has been looking for a modest bungalow."

Anna set down her teacup. "I'm happy for you, Soph. If you hurry, you can produce a cousin close in age to Sarah and Jack's little bundle." Their sister, Sarah, was expecting next summer.

"What about you?" Sophie countered.

Anna paused as a rumbling sound signaled an electric streetcar passing outside the café. "I don't have time for romance. I've got big plans."

"I still don't understand why you don't want to practice with Mama."

"I know she would welcome me in a permanent capacity, but I'd like more experience in a hospital as well as surgical opportunities."

Sophie didn't cover medical reporting for the Morning News, but she knew women weren't allowed to perform surgery, at least not in an official capacity. Her ma carried out minor operations, but her practice was rural, and those procedures were borne of necessity. Claire Ryan would have as difficult a time as Anna in the medical community in Dallas, but for some reason, Anna wanted to follow the "proper" path as dictated by the American Medical Association, despite the many roadblocks that stood in her way.

If only Anna had been present the day Sophie had "operated" on Benton's shoulder. Sophie was still a bit shocked that she'd done it, forever grateful the wound hadn't somehow festered. From now on, she was happy to leave such things to her mother and sister, and thankfully Benton's work was less risky. Since moving to the U.S. Marshal office in Dallas, he spent his days serving subpoenas, summonses, and warrants, and transporting federal prisoners to and from court.

"Well, I'm happy to have you here for a bit," Sophie said. "We can attend the theater and have supper at the Oriental Hotel. And you'll stay with me."

"No offense, but your accommodations are cramped. I have a room nearby."

Maybe it was just as well, since Benton liked to sneak into her room several nights a week. On the heels of that thought, he appeared at the café entrance looking distinguished in a black wool coat, and her heart did a delighted little jig. She smiled and lifted a hand to catch his attention.

"What are you doing here?" she asked as he came to their table.

"The newspaper told me where you were." He took Anna's hand and offered a peck on the cheek. "It's good to see you, Anna."

"Likewise."

He took a seat, and a waiter brought him a place setting, then poured a cup of tea.

"Has something happened?" Sophie asked. He didn't normally visit her at work.

"It has, and as I was nearby, I thought to stop and tell you. Sally Weaver has been sighted in the company of a man named Alfred Hardy in Oklahoma Territory."

Anna's teacup froze halfway to her mouth. "Hardy, you say?"

Benton nodded. "Do you know him?"

"Alfred Hardy owned land near the Rocking Wren," Sophie said, referring to her Uncle Matt's ranch in North Texas. "His son, Roy, got into trouble in a land dispute with the Callahans a few years back. My cousin Eli's wife, Cassie, was a Callahan. The Hardys are a no-good lot."

"Not Malcolm," Anna said quietly, then finally sipped her tea.

"Oh, that's right," Sophie said. "You were sweet on him when we were at the fair in Denton. When was that? Five years ago?"

"Seven."

Anna's adamant response surprised Sophie. Had her sister's affection for him been that strong? It was so long ago.

Sophie decided not to press the issue, instead addressing a more urgent one. "Are you going to Oklahoma?" she asked Benton.

"No." But then he added, "At least, not for now, but maybe I should visit the Hardys still living in Texas."

BENTON LAY in Sophie's bed with her curled against him. He hadn't planned a rendezvous since her sister was in town, but after they'd taken Anna out for a late supper and dropped her at her hotel, Sophie had invited him, and the truth was he hated spending even one night away from her.

He'd marry her tomorrow if she'd say so, but they had decided to wait. However, something had been running through his mind the past few days.

"I was thinking, Sophie."

She made a soft, satisfied sound, her fingers playing with his chest hair. She was probably almost asleep. He'd need to leave soon to avoid being seen by her landlady, who was blessedly less meddlesome than Rose Palmer had been.

"What if we did it at the same time?"

She pushed to an elbow to meet his gaze. "Do what?"

"Get married in Jerome at Christmas, alongside Lucas and Olivia."

Sophie had confided that Olivia was with child, hence the urgency. Considering how inconsistent he and Sophie had been with their lovemaking, he was certain she'd be expecting any day now, an outcome he was perfectly fine with.

"Is there a reason for this sudden change in plans?" she asked.

He took hold of a strand of her hair and wrapped it around his finger, enjoying its silkiness. "After our meetings with Russell and listening to his ill deeds, I find myself sympathizing more and more with my mother."

His father had been sentenced to twenty years in the penitentiary, and there was a good chance he would die there, and Benton wasn't sure any compassion for the man was justified. Russell had driven away Benton's mother. He'd endangered Sophie the night he took her and Harry hostage and forced them to reveal the location of the gold.

"Since you'd expressed interest in going to Jerome for the nuptials," he continued, "I thought it would be nice if she could be at our wedding, at least in spirit, and I would like to replace her headstone with something better."

Sophie brought her face to his and kissed him. "My answer is yes," she whispered. "Do you think your aunt and uncle could attend?"

"I'll send a letter to them first thing tomorrow."

"And I'll write to Olivia and make certain she's amenable to sharing her big day. And—"

"I'll visit your father," he finished for her. "We can return to Dove Crossing with Anna next week. And I could make a stop at the Hardy homestead for questioning. Could you get a few days off from the newspaper?"

"I'll ask." She climbed atop him, soft and warm, her naked body covering his, and she tenderly kissed the scar on his left shoulder.

"More doctoring?" he teased.

"Absolutely not. From now on, I'm deferring to Anna or my mother for all things medical. I'm only interested in loving you."

She kissed him, and his body stirred.

Since that day at Nighthawk Ranch when she had agreed to give him a second chance, he hadn't taken it or her forgiveness for granted. He would spend his days proving himself worthy.

"I love you, Soph. I owe you my life."

Her lips stretched into a smile against his mouth. "One that we'll spend together."

Don't miss Anna's story in THE SWAN. Malcolm Hardy has created enough distance from his family name to find a quiet purpose to his days, but then Anna Ryan walks back into his life, and his hard-won peace is in jeopardy. (https://kmccaffrey.com/the-swan/)

Don't miss the introduction of Sophie Ryan and her cousins in the novella THE SONGBIRD. (https://kmccaffrey.com/the-songbird/)

Sign up for Kristy's newsletter for exclusive content and book news. (https://kmccaffrey.com/subscribe/)

WINGS OF THE WEST
FAMILY TREE

S ince I've been writing about the children of the main couples in Books 1-4, here's the family tree I've been working from. I don't have plans to write about each child, so I've been having "cousins" show up in the new novels. I also don't have full names for every character but will update this as stories develop. (Children are listed from oldest to youngest.) ~ Kristy xx

MATT RYAN AND MOLLY HART – THE WREN

- Elijah "Eli" Robert – ECHO OF THE PLAINS
- Katharine "Katie" Rosemary – THE SONGBIRD and THE STARLING
- Josephine "Josie" Elizabeth – THE SONGBIRD and THE FALCON (coming soon)

Logan Ryan and Claire Waters – THE DOVE

- Anna – THE SONGBIRD and THE SWAN
- Sarah – THE SONGBIRD and THE CANARY

- Sophie – THE SONGBIRD and THE NIGHTHAWK
- Eleanor "Ellie" – THE CANARY*

Nathan Blackmore and Emma Hart – THE SPARROW

- Lucas – ECHO OF THE PLAINS* and THE NIGHTHAWK*
- Jeremy – THE CANARY*
- Travis
- Jacob
- Ethan

Cale Walker and Tess Carlisle – THE BLACKBIRD

- Dolores – THE SWAN*
- Loretta
- Isabelle
- Doreen

Tom Simms and Mary Hart

- Robert – THE BLUEBIRD*
- Molly Rose – THE BLUEBIRD
- Evie

**Molly, Emma, and Mary are sisters.
Cale Walker is Molly's half-brother.
Matt and Logan are brothers.**

*Side character in that novel

The Swan
Wings of the West Book 11

Oklahoma Territory
November 1899

Dr. Anna Ryan has been spurned by the Dallas medical community for the simple reason of being a woman. Wanting more than a rural practice alongside her mother, also a doctor, Anna accepts an invitation from a mentor to join a private hospital for disabled children in Oklahoma City. But when she falls in with a band of women attempting to liberate a town of innocents, she'll need more than her medical training to survive.

Malcolm Hardy has skirted the line between lawlessness and justice since escaping the mean streak of his father and his no-good half-siblings a decade ago. In Oklahoma Territory he created enough distance from his family name to find a quiet purpose to his days. But then Anna Ryan walks back into his life, and his hard-won peace is in jeopardy.

The last time Malcolm saw Anna, she had been a determined girl he couldn't help but admire. Now she was a compelling woman who needed his help to find The Swan, a mysterious figure with a questionable reputation. But one thing was clear—Anna's life path was on a trajectory for the remarkable while Malcolm's was not. Surrendering to temptation would only end in heartbreak.

Anna is the eldest daughter of Logan and Claire from THE DOVE.

Read Now
https://kmccaffrey.comthe-swan/

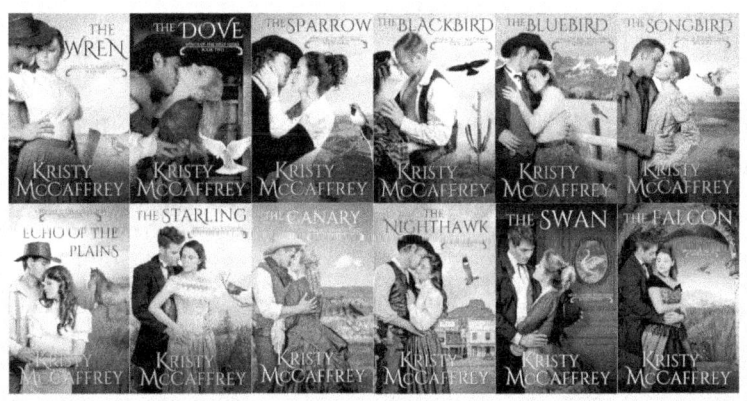

Don't miss the Wings of the West series

Honorable men and courageous women. Experience the grit, the hope, and the romance of the Old West.

"Ms. McCaffrey writes from the heart..." ~ The Romance Studio

THE WREN – Captured by Comanche as a child, Molly Hart was assumed dead. Ten years later, Texas Ranger Matt Ryan finds a woman with the same blue eyes.

THE DOVE – Reunited with Logan Ryan on the steps of the White Dove Saloon, Claire Waters hides under the guise of a fancy girl...and lets the ex-deputy believe the worst.

THE SPARROW – Within Grand Canyon, raging rapids and ancient spirits sweep Texas Ranger Nathan Blackmore and Emma Hart into a wild adventure.

THE BLACKBIRD – Haunted by a deadly attack, Tess Carlisle

turns to bounty hunter Cale Walker to find her missing *padre*. But in the land of the Apache, can he free her heart?

THE BLUEBIRD – Molly Rose Simms arrives in Colorado to meet her brother, but instead finds herself searching for the mythical Bluebird mining claim with a man known as The Jackal.

THE SONGBIRD – In this novella set fifteen years after THE WREN, Matt and Molly are attending a fair in Denton, Texas, when they uncover a connection to Molly's past with the Kwahadi Comanche. You'll also meet their daughters—Katie and Josie Ryan.

ECHO OF THE PLAINS (a short story) – Seventeen-year-old Eli Ryan, Matt and Molly's son, plans to capture the renegade stallion known as Echo but Cassie Callahan stands in his way.

THE STARLING – Pinkerton Henry Maguire is about to gain an unwanted "wife" in the form of new agent Kate Ryan (Matt and Molly's daughter).

THE CANARY – Sarah Ryan (Logan and Claire's daughter) and paleontologist Jack Brenner search for an elusive dinosaur fossil in the Painted Desert.

THE NIGHTHAWK – U.S. Deputy Marshal Benton McKay is undercover tracking the notorious train robbing Weaver gang when he's forced to work with reporter Sophie Ryan (Logan and Claire's daughter).

THE SWAN – Malcolm Hardy has created enough distance from his family name to find a quiet purpose to his days, but then Anna Ryan (Logan and Claire's eldest daughter) walks back into his life, and his hard-won peace is in jeopardy.

THE FALCON (Coming Soon) – Mateo Almirón, known as The Falconer, has come to Mexico for a horse exchange with Matt Ryan when he is entrusted with protecting the man's daughter, Josie (Matt and Molly's youngest child).

Learn more about each book at Kristy's website
https://kmccaffrey.com/books/

Into The Land Of Shadows

A Stand-Alone Novel

This book was previously published in 2013 under the same title. While the text and cover have been updated, the story remains the same.

It's been five years since a woman came between Ethan Barstow and his brother, Charley, and it's high time they buried the hatchet. When Ethan travels to Arizona Territory to make amends, he learns that Charley has abruptly disappeared after breaking more than one heart in town. And an indignant fiancée is hot on his trail.

When Charley Barstow abandons a local girl after getting her pregnant, Kate Kinsella pursues him without a second thought.

She's determined he set things right, and even more determined to end her own engagement to him, a sham from the beginning. But an ill-timed encounter with a group of ruffians lands her in the company of Charley's brother, Ethan, who suggests they search together.

As Ethan and Kate move deeper INTO THE LAND OF SHADOWS, family tensions and past tragedies threaten to destroy a love neither of them expected.

https://kmccaffrey.com/into-the-land-of-shadows/

Don't miss this collection of short stories filled with chills and romance.

It's Hallowtide in the Old West. Join three bounty hunters fighting dark magic and the women destined to love them.

The Crow and The Coyote

Among the red-rock canyons of the Navajo, bounty hunter Jack Boggs—known as The Crow—aids Hannah Dobbin in a quest to save her pa's soul during Hallowtide.

The Crow and The Bear

When no one will help Jennie Livingstone enter a haunted ravine to find her papa, she must accept the aid of enigmatic bounty hunter Callum Boggs, sometimes called The Crow.

A Murder of Crows

Eliza McCulloch is determined to reclaim her family book of spells and her only hope is Kester Boggs, a manhunter named The Crow.

These stories were previously published separately.

"A suspenseful ride into the supernatural with a western twist." ∼ Devon McKay, author of *Lead Me Into Temptation*, Gold Dust Bride Series

"With just the right amount of mystic and adventure…" ∼ Michelle Reed, Sunshine Lake Reviews

https://kmccaffrey.com/the-crow-and-the-coyote/

ABOUT THE AUTHOR

Kristy McCaffrey has been writing since she was very young, but it wasn't until she was a stay-at-home mom that she considered becoming published. A fascination with science led her to earn two mechanical engineering degrees—she did her undergraduate work at Arizona State University and her graduate studies at the University of Pittsburgh—but storytelling has always been her passion. She writes both contemporary tales and award-winning historical western romances.

An Arizona native, Kristy and her husband reside in the desert where they frequently remove (rescue) rattlesnakes from their property and try to coax their American bulldog, Jeb, to go for walks (he's moody and lazy). She also spends her time reading and researching her next book and playing with her three grandchildren.

Connect with Kristy
    Website: kmccaffrey.com
    Newsletter: kmccaffrey.com/subscribe
    Facebook: facebook.com/AuthorKristyMcCaffrey
    Instagram: instagram.com/kristymccaffreybooks
    BookBub: bookbub.com/authors/kristy-mccaffrey
    TikTok: tiktok.com/@kristymccaffrey

www.ingramcontent.com/pod-product-compliance
Lightning Source LLC
Chambersburg PA
CBHW061131200626
46817CB00016B/732